teach me

teach me

a novel by

R. A. NELSON

razor
bill

Teach Me

RAZORBILL

Published by the Penguin Group
Penguin Young Readers Group
345 Hudson Street, New York, New York 10014, U.S.A.
Penguin Group (USA) Inc., 375 Hudson Street, New York, New York 10014, U.S.A.
Penguin Group (Canada), 90 Eglinton Avenue, Suite 700, Toronto, Ontario,
Canada M4P 2Y3 (a division of Pearson Penguin Canada Inc.)
Penguin Books Ltd, 80 Strand, London WC2R 0RL, England
Penguin Ireland, 25 St Stephen's Green, Dublin 2, Ireland
(a division of Penguin Books Ltd)
Penguin Group (Australia), 250 Camberwell Road, Camberwell,
Victoria 3124, Australia (a division of Pearson Australia Group Pty Ltd)
Penguin Books India Pvt Ltd, 11 Community Centre, Panchsheel Park,
New Delhi - 110 017, India
Penguin Group (NZ), Cnr Airborne and Rosedale Roads, Albany,
Auckland 1310, New Zealand (a division of Pearson New Zealand Ltd)
Penguin Books (South Africa) (Pty) Ltd, 24 Sturdee Avenue, Rosebank,
Johannesburg 2196, South Africa

Penguin Books Ltd, Registered Offices: 80 Strand, London WC2R 0RL, England

10 9 8 7 6 5 4 3 2 1

Interior design by Christopher Grassi

Library of Congress Cataloging-in-Publication Data

Nelson, R. A.
  Teach me : a novel / by R.A. Nelson.
    p. cm.
  Summary: A high school student enters into an affair with one of her teachers.
  ISBN 1-59514-084-0
  [1. High schools—Fiction. 2. Schools—Fiction. 3. Teachers—Fiction.] I. Title.
  PZ7.N43586Tea 2005
  [Fic]—dc22
                                                    2005008148

Printed in the United States of America

To my family: Deborah, Zachary, Alexander,
Christopher, and Joseph.

But were it told to me, to-day,
That I might have the sky
For mine, I tell you that my heart
Would split, for size of me.
—EMILY DICKINSON

In memory of Dona Vaughn. Thanks to Sue Corbett, Diane Davis, and the generosity of the YAWRITERS list for establishing the Dona Vaughn Work in Progress Grant to honor this wonderfully giving writer. Thanks also to Stephen Mooser, Lin Oliver, and the Society of Children's Book Writers & Illustrators. This grant helped make this book possible.

Thanks to my matchless editor and friend at Razorbill, Liesa Abrams, whose amazing mind and indispensable talents have made me a better writer. Thanks also for the invaluable contributions of Eloise Flood, Margaret Wright, Karen Taschek, Christopher Grassi, Polly Watson, Andy Ball, and Archie Ferguson.

Thanks to my extraordinary agent, Rosemary Stimola. Rosemary is simply perfect. I couldn't ask for a better champion and friend to chart my career.

Thanks to my writerly compatriots, Kathleen O'Dell, Linda Zinnen, and Charis Kelly. Their priceless support helped my career become a reality.

In memory of Linda Smith and thanks to Linda Sue Park and the dazzling denizens of write4kids.com. I'm grateful to Jon Bard for putting it together.

To Brian Nelson, Craig Nelson, Randy Nelson, Ronnie Nelson, Rikki Nelson, and Doris Nelson, thanks for believing through all those years of typing and dreaming.

Hey, Ms. Gonzalez, I did it!

the physics of falling

Welcome to my head.

Let's hit the ground running. I will get you up to speed. We need a short learning curve here. Those are things my dad likes to say. He works for NASA. He spends his days figuring out problems like this:

If an object weighing 8.75 ounces traveling ten thousand miles per hour strikes the earth, how big a hole does it create?

Answer: One exactly the size of my heart.

Call me Nine.

Everybody does. When I was three, I couldn't pronounce Carolina; it came out Caro*nina*. My math-crazy father thought that was cute and shortened it to Nine. I've been a number ever since.

Right now I'm sitting with my parents in Mom's Victorian room, surrounded by drapes with tassels, photographs of long-decomposed relatives, muscle-bound furniture. The sofa is covered with pictures of golden English villages I am desperate to live in that don't exist. And on today's menu:

The are-you-a-lesbian conversation.

Not that Mom would ever use that word.

I've broken her heart. She's drowning in hay fever tears. All because at this penultimate moment in my eighteen-year-old life, two weeks before the senior prom, I'm just not interested.

Mom sobs explosively into a Kleenex. She's allergic to her own head. She just got a new perm. If she sneezes one more time, her sixty-year-old mucous membranes will flop out on the Cavendish rug.

That's right. My parents are old. Older than satellites, rock 'n' roll, or color TV. They married late; I'm the only fruit of their looms.

"But you're so smart, Nine," Mom sputters.

Exactement, I want to say. Don't you know that boys don't like smart girls? But men . . .

I look out the window so they can't see my eyes.

My teacher, Mr. Mann, said the same thing the day the craziness started that knocked my heart out of its orbit. He was standing under a tree with an angel halo of moonlight around his face. Then he asked me this:

"Did you know Emily Dickinson wrote a poem with your name in it? *Awake ye muses Nine, sing me a strain divine.* Not one of her best, I'm afraid."

Two hours later, behind the Wal-Mart Rule the World Super Center, he kissed me.

"Why doesn't Schuyler come around anymore?" Dad says, bringing me back to Earth for a fiery reentry.

Schuyler's my best friend. We've known each other since the supercontinent Pangaea split apart. Well, second grade. He and Dad have always liked each other. Schuyler is family in this house, the brother I never got to have.

I'm hiding from him.

I don't want him to know what I've done. The trouble I'm in. How far, how fast I'm falling.

"He's busy," I say.

"But what about any of the other boys?" Mom says. "What about that one in your—"

"I'm invisible," I say to keep from saying anything else.

Dad laughs. "Invisible?"

Dad's an engineer. He thinks in spaces, measurements, volumes.

A six-foot chunk of girl-woman with a thirty-five-inch inseam and brown chair-stuffing hair can't be invisible. Not the Kevin Bacon/Claude Rains movie kind, where you take off the bandages and poof, disappear.

I'm this kind of invisible to boys: I see you, but I don't care. I'm not going to look a second time as long as we both shall live. But to men . . .

"It's not just the prom, darling." Mom goes down the list.

I'm not sleeping. I talk too little. Lose my college paperwork. Push away my favorite Spamburger Helper. Disappear to God knows where doing God knows what. Is it dangerous? Illegal?

What am I supposed to tell them?

That my heat shield has failed? That I've fallen to Earth and disintegrated? That no one can reassemble the pieces of my life and tell the story of my death?

"It's nothing," I say.

in the crackling forest

Sunday morning.

I used to hate Sundays, first cousin to black-and-blue Mondays. But instead of jittery and crazed, today I wake up strangely peaceful.

Today the birds are chirping like lunatics and pooping the patio purple and white. The sun is a gigantic nectarine. Black holes, beware. There is no suction today.

Today my insanity has curved so far back in on itself, I've clambered out of my emotional gravity well.

I have a plan.

Today is the day of my teacher's wedding.

Today Mr. Mann and Alicia Sprunk, his darling little Bride to Be—the White Dwarf I saw in the wedding announcement in the newspaper—will be joined in Holy Bondage. I used to hate weddings too. Loathed, despised, abominated. Now I'm going to one and I can't wait.

I tell Mom I'm going to the mall. She trusts me so much; they both do. I could tell them anything—they would believe it. I have so many Good Girl Points built up. But I'm burning through them dangerously fast.

She follows me outside, eyes desperately hopeful, hair like half-boiled spaghetti.

"Are you going with someone, darling?"

"Wilkie Collins," I say.

"Oh, good!" she says a little hysterically. "Have I met him, sweetheart? Is he in one of your classes?"

"No."

"Why don't I come with you? I've got your prom dress all picked out at Dillard's. Wilkie might like to see it too. Does he have a date for the dance?"

Wilkie Collins is my car.

He farts teal smoke. His doors stick. His heat doesn't work unless you jiggle two wires together in a precise, calibrated, impossible-to-duplicate way. But he has never let me down.

Swoosh.

May used to be my favorite month.

School is dying, flowers are blooming, windows are open. I drive very fast and safely to the Crackling Forest. It's an L-shaped strip of woods just off the interstate. It used to be part of a forest, but now it's a patch of surrounded, abandoned, wasted Alabama wildness behind the Firestone Holy Tire Palace.

I grab the gym bag I've packed for this special occasion from Wilkie's spongy trunk and step into the trees. This piece of woods smells of oil, not bark. Things crackle here. Leaves, gum wrappers, burger boxes. Used condominiums.

That's what Schuyler calls them.

My heart bangs. I miss him so much. There are so many things I need to tell him. But what would he think of me now?

I yank my clothes off and stuff them in the bag. The moment I'm down to my underwear, the grinding roar of a diesel truck rushes at me. It whines higher and higher as the sound waves crash against my body. Then the sound gets low and drawn out as the sound waves stretch away again. This is called the Doppler Effect. It happens with stars and galaxies too. Only then it's called the Red Shift, meaning light waves moving away from you shift to the red end of the visible spectrum.

It's thrilling standing here utterly exposed in this unexposed space. My own skin turns me on. I remember Mr. Mann's weight on my legs. I remember his warm breath on my shoulder.

Stop it.

I have a theory: Life is a Doppler Effect.

In the beginning, the Life Waves rush up on you, all high-pitched and energetic, then stretch away, moaning lower and lower. You were supposed to be a hero, a movie star, Bill Gates.

In love forever.

But the Life Waves passed you by.

I pull on a dead woman's long froofy dress I bought at the Goodwill store. It's covered with huge purple flowers. I raise my arms in the I-give-up position; the dress settles over my shoulders. The collar looks like a lace doily. No slip, and the material is so sheer, I'm sure you can see my tiny black bra in the sunlight. The one Mr. Mann bought for me when he got tired of looking at white.

I ball up my bunchy hair with some of Dad's mongo NASA paper clips. Next, a wide garden hat that has an industrially manufactured feather the color of lilacs attached to its brim. The shade is perfectly wrong against the flowers on my dress. I am a Woman Utterly Without Taste.

This begins my real transformation.

The minute the hat touches my head, it's like that old egg-cracking gag Dad likes to pull. He knocks two fists gently against the top of my skull, then opens his fingers and draws an imaginary yolk down my hair. Just like that, I feel my new personality slipping over me, a soft, invisible, eggy rain.

I use Mom's compact to apply the makeup. I pause when I touch my neck just below the line of my jaw. This is exactly the place Mr. Mann kissed me the first time we knew—what did we know? This is how Emily Dickinson said it:

> *THAT I did always love,*
> *I bring thee proof*

I close my eyes, remembering Mr. Mann's lips touching me there, his whispered promises. Both as soft as a boy's. I nearly break the lipstick off in my fury.

The shoes are Mom's worst pumps from the bottom of her cedar closet. Ghastly lavender. Brutally tight on my size-ten feet. Good. They make me feel pinched and prickly, tightly wound, all a piece. Last are the gloves. They come to my elbows. It takes every ounce of upper-body strength I have to drag them on. The munchkin fingertips are pointed enough to poke out eyes.

I come out from the Crackling Forest, ankles turning painfully. I've never worn heels before. I slide into Wilkie Collins and consult the handmade map on the seat beside me: Latham Methodist Church on Lilly Flagg Road.

I pull out on the highway and turn southeast.

eating paul

I did it.

It's over. I survived.

But I can't stop shaking.

Driving back from the wedding, I clench the steering wheel tightly and stare straight ahead. I might burst into flame. I might explode. I need to scream loudly. I don't.

What does Mr. Mann think of me now? After what I just did? How can he possibly explain it to his new wife? Is he furious? Amazed? Horrified? Ashamed?

I wonder if he will come to me now.

And what about me? As Dad would say, do a Systems Check:

Am I happy? Miserable? Terrified? Triumphant? About to projectile vomit the Corn Pops I ate this morning?

Yes.

Cold cream is the worst.

I feel like a baked potato. Back in the Crackling Forest, standing under the flapping leaves, I furiously scrub my face. But this is good: it not only cleans my skin, it helps reboot my emotions. My clothes are warm from being in the trunk. As I change back into my real self, I watch the Firestone Holy Tire Palace through a gap in the branches. A man in a blue uniform turns a tire lovingly in his hands, brushes it over with water from a hose, impales it on a pinnacle of red steel.

Men make the world for themselves, I think. And then they go away.

I don't know where these words come from.

Back at the house, we make Paul Newman spaghetti. I tell Mom Wilkie is fine.

It's a beginning.

ecstatic time machine

Scream.

"Look who's here, darling!" Mom yells.

The last bite of Paul catches in my throat. Someone is standing with her in the Victorian Room. Mr. Mann? My hands curl into fists. Kill him. Run into his arms.

It's only Schuyler.

Schuyler!

Please. Not tonight of all nights. What do I do? What do I say?

But the pang in my chest instantly tells me how much I've missed him. His mind, his laugh, his eyes.

I miss his hair.

Tonight it's bent all in one direction. So thick, it holds whatever shape it's been pressed into. Our eighth-grade English teacher, Ms. Gonzalez, once said, "With hair that beautiful, you should've been a girl." We were in the middle of a test on Robert Frost, the room quiet as Ganymede. Schuyler wanted to put laxative gum in her candy jar.

Schuyler wants to do a lot of things. That's how we're different, I guess.

Wanting and doing.

He's slouching uncertainly next to the sofa as if he doesn't know what to say, what to ask me.

I was a head taller than Schuyler back in seventh grade. One of our teachers called us Eek and Meek. Thanks a lot, Mr. Rombokas. But Schuyler's finally caught up with me these last few months. It's made him a little more fumbly-stumbly. I have a theory: Tall = shy. But I can also see the imprint of the future man.

"Hey."

"Hi."

The moment feels like the naked part of a dream. Or the first bite of a weird new casserole. My face is still throbbing. Can he tell? Mom thankfully comes in and blows up the silence:

"Put on some pj's, Schuyler, we'll have a pajama party!"

I stare. I just now realize Mom's got on her old-lady-can't-hang-past-seven nightgown and fuzzy pink Kmart slippers. She's a Dr. Seuss character. She touches Schuyler's arm—"Let me fix you something to eat, honey"—and shuffle duffle muzzle muffs off to the kitchen.

Schuyler frowns.

It's the way his face is shaped. People always think he's mad at them.

Is he mad at me?

"I know you saw me coming out of calculus," he says.

"Yeah."

"This has got to stop, Nine. You don't call me back, you duck out at lunch, you ignore—"

"Okay."

He brightens. I'm the only one besides his mom who could tell: his ears go up.

"Just like that?" he says. "You're not going to tell me what's been going on?"

"Nope."

He looks me over for clues. "Okay. You're dying. You're hooked on Ecstasy. You're *Mariette in Ecstasy*."

"I'm tired."

The ears droop. When one of us throws out an obscure reference, the other is supposed to immediately regurgitate the source.

"Come on," he says. "*Mariette in Ecstasy*. Book about a gonzo nun."

I turn away and slump on the sofa. My cat, Kitty Nation, knows when I'm feeling lost, hurt. He jumps in my lap and starts kneading my stomach with his paws. "Don't make me think tonight," I say. "I can't."

"Not possible," he says.

As usual, he's right.

I'm hot-wired for thought. And right now I'm thinking just how badly I need him to go. He's too important to me. I'm too used to telling him things. I can't hold it in much longer without him finding out.

Say something. Anything but that.

"Wait a minute," I say.

Schuyler despises cars. His parents refuse to drive him any-where except work until he gets his license. He's tried three times. I even lent him Wilkie Collins. Now he's spooked about it, cursed.

"So how'd you get here?" I say.

"Whaddya know, there's this thing called a cab service. You pay them, they haul you anywhere you want to go. No extra charge for the hip-hop ambiance. So where's your dad?"

I nod wearily at the hall. "Dreaming of xenon injectors."

He plunks down beside me. I'm excruciatingly aware of the pleasant man-boy scent on his T-shirt. I scrunch away as far as I can, pulling Kitty Nation to me like an orange pillow.

"What's wrong, you contagious or something?"

"I'm just—just." I refuse to explain myself. How can he know he's the last person I need to see tonight? After the wedding, after seeing Mr. Mann again, I'm tired. I'm sad. Worse.

I'm explosively frustrated. Yeah, that kind.

Schuyler tries to get in through a different window.

"Hey! They fixed the streaming audio at the Kansas City

Ghost Club last night. We heard a million bumps in the abandoned morgue. *Mirabile dictu!* You've got to check it out."

Schuyler's invented a prissy psychic who chats with True Believers on the net. Name: Darkwillow Nightseer. No joke. He drives the ghost hunters rabid pretending to spot all sorts of phony ecto crap on their ghost cams. They've banned his URL twice.

Now that I've passed over to the Other Side, his virginal enthusiasm creeps me.

"I don't feel like anything," I say. "Not tonight."

"But why, what's—"

Chuffing footsteps send us back into Mom mode.

"It's ready, Schuyler dear."

The Lorax escorts us into the kitchen, knees creaking like saddles. We watch Schuyler lap up a plate of spaghetti and talk about nothing much. Until:

"Are you going to the prom, Schuyler?" Mom says.

My foot twitches uncontrollably. If I didn't love her so much, I'd kick her dear little shins in two.

Schuyler frowns and glances sideways at me.

"Not really, Miz Livingston. Nobody psychotic enough to say yes."

Mom smiles. After all her worries about me lately, I realize she loves having Schuyler here. This is a rare moment of security, a return to a simpler time when I was practically perfect in her eyes. A time she could better understand. "Well, I know of a certain darling girl—" she says.

"Mom!"

"All right." She sighs and gets up from the table. "It's past my bedtime. See you night owls in the morning."

We watch her go until the bathroom door shuts and we hear water sandblasting the sink.

"Anybody ask you?" Schuyler says, looking at me probingly again.

"They better not. Hey, I'm beat. Can I run you home?"

I grab my keys before he can answer.

We're quiet on the way to his house. I refuse to tell him anything about Mr. Mann or the wedding. In retaliation, Schuyler finds a program on public radio he knows I hate. Now we're submerged in blubbery moans posing as Space Music.

"Please turn that off," I say.

He cranks up the volume threateningly.

"Nope. Not until you swear things are going to be regular again."

"If that whale gets enough fiber, sure."

"Come on, Nine."

I shrug helplessly. "What's regular, Schuyler? I don't know anymore." This couldn't be more true. Everything I thought, believed, trusted—

"You can start by at least not pretending like I don't exist," Schuyler says when we get to his house.

I do my best to manufacture a smile. "That's a double negative. I will do as you say. Pretend like you exist."

"Come on, Nine."

His eyes are melting.

I pull into the driveway and touch his arm, heart stinging.

"Look, Schuyler. I'm sorry. It's not you; it's me. Okay? It's my problem. I'll let you know when I can tell you everything. Just . . . not yet. Soon, really. Please don't give up on me." I waggle my fingers through his crazy hair. His forehead is hot. "But thanks for coming over."

I hope he believes me.

He hangs in my window and makes me promise to call:

"I've got ideas!"

Unless it's a time machine all gassed up and set for six months ago, forget it.

swimming to mars

Insomnia.

Sleep is a soft, cushy place somewhere below me, but I'm stuck on a shelf that won't let me sink any lower. It's exhausting up here. By some satanic miracle I'm also forced to hold the shelf up.

Mr. Mann's not coming.

He would have been here by now.

The terrible high from what I did at the wedding is gone, but the scaffold of the high is still there. It jangles my legs like an electrical field. I lie on my back to spot an orange star out the window. Mars. In another couple of months it will be the closest it has come to the Earth in sixty thousand years. It's already flooding our planet with War Vibes.

I've grown three inches in one hour. I'm being made ready for battle.

I grind my teeth. I'm flopping around so much, Kitty Nation leaps off the bed and pads disappointedly up the hall. I shift to a diagonal position on the mattress so my Amazonian feet won't hang over. You can only do this if nobody is sharing your bed with you.

Bed.

I can't stop thinking about Mr. Mann and Alicia, the newly joined couple.

What they are doing right now. Newly joining.

I wiggle my toes together, desperately pretending some of them are his. This is what marriage must feel like: a nest of ecstatic phalanges.

Sharing.

A sickening possibility washes over me:

What if the joining is not so new? What if Mr. Mann was *schtupping* both of us at the same time? I jerk up to a sitting position, hands in fists. Kill her. Kill them both.

Is he saying the same things to her that he said to me?

> *WILD Nights! Wild nights!*
> *Were I with thee,*
> *Wild nights should be*
> *Our luxury!*

Is it really that easy?

A little poetry, and we flop on our backs in the open-for-business position? Or does Emily Dickinson only work on stupid smart girls like me?

> *Were I with thee*

For the first time I realize Emily is all about words like these: *were, if, might*. Yearning, longing, pining. So Mr. Mann was giving me hints even back then, and I was too love-blind to see it.

God.

Another thought sends me springing up like a galvanized frog: Alicia is falling asleep in his arms tonight. I never could.

I smother a banana spider scream with my pillow. My lips

blubber across the pillowcase, but I'm too electromagnetic to bawl. The house is rattling in rhythm to Dad's vast asthmatic snores.

I have to do something to keep from tearing at my flesh.

Go.

I kick off the covers and haul my telescope, a four-inch refractor, out to the backyard. I'm wearing nothing but a nightshirt, but the hour feels good on my skin. I'm a Japanese carp, a koi, swimming in darkness.

Dew wets my long toes. I plant the scope's wooden legs in a grassy spot away from my parents' window. The light is okay here; Schuyler shot out the streetlamp with a CO_2 pistol the day I got my scholarship letter: *Professor Emeritus of Astronomy Stephen N. Bracewell is pleased to announce*—squat. I didn't get the paperwork in on time. So now I'm not going. I don't particularly care. Not anymore.

Mars is crossing Aquarius.

Refractors are old school but better than reflectors for resolving surface details. I take out my best eyepiece, a 25-mm orthoscopic, drop it in. For once I don't wait for the optics to cool. The altizimuth controls turn smoothly in my fingers. There it is: Mars, a tiny orange ball. I have to constantly adjust the scope to keep it in view. I used to be saving up for a clock drive that tracks the object automatically as it crosses the sky.

Used to be. What's the use anymore in dreaming, wanting, planning? What good have those things ever done me? In the end?

I look at Mars. A dust storm covering two billion square acres looks like mold on a peach. Light sweeps over the lawn as a car floats by.

A Honda.

My heart expands.

Mr. Mann drives a '99 Civic. Green with tan interior. It smells like vanilla and vinyl. The glove box is crammed with misfolded maps. If you tilt the seats all the way back, you can—he's here! He's here!

The Honda rolls away. I watch until it reaches the end of the block and turns, disappears behind a fence.

Hopeless.

When I look again, Mars has skidded out of view and the moon is rising. I put the eyepiece back in its Tupperware box and swim back inside, starting to cry.

Fact:

Koi are domestic mutations of the common freshwater carp, *Cyprinus carpio*. They are sexually mature at twelve inches in length.

What am I a mutation of?

cat splitter

_____

Monday.

The sky gray as this dissecting table where I'm sitting. There is massive suction today.

Human phys class. I'm certainly human and physical today. I've got my period this morning. I feel like Veruca Salt in the Blueberry-Squeezing Room.

So I'm not pregnant.

This makes me want to flip over tables and throw chairs through the windows we don't have.

Still, it's my turn.

Exactly five minutes past eight I march into the stinking Closet of Death and fetch Pussy Pancreatic from the blue plastic body bin. Pussy Pancreatic is the calico kitty cat we have been hacking to pieces all semester.

This is the largest dead life I've ever held. At this point Pussy Pancreatic is about as organic as Mom's Victorian hassock, but not as soft. I open the bag on the table and a smell comes into my mouth—not of something dead, but maybe a strange new type of metal.

"Phew, daddy," Hub Christy says across from me, blowing out his lips. "Gonna have some fun with you today, aren't we, sweetie baby?"

He's talking to the cat again.

Hub Christy is an offensive Offensive Tackle from the football team. He has a fifty-four-inch chest and likes to put his size-fourteen clodhoppers between my legs under the table. Ms. Larimore likes to employ the Friction Method of pairing lab partners: she believes my academic mojo will rub off on him. I wonder what will rub off on me.

Obsessive Thought for the Morning:

Mr. Mann.

But I know he won't come rescue me today, either.

By now he's on his honeymoon down in ole Mexico. Exploring Olmec ruins. Dancing around hats. Drinking bottles of stuff with worms on the bottom. Watching skeletons haul statues of the Virgin Mary through town.

Sleeping in.

Stop it.

Focus on something else, anything. That's what you're good at. I look around.

Here nobody has a face yet.

A few are attempting to speak: Saturday night, bad makeup, cars, hair. Worst of all, TV. I have a theory: Small talk and television are killing Western civilization. I refuse to take part in the slaughter.

Not that they would ask me to.

The first day we took our cats out, Susan Carter said: "Just like *CSI!*" All I could say was, "Um, yeah." I had no idea what she was talking about. Now she figures I'm a complete freak. She doesn't try to talk to me anymore.

I looked it up on the net. *CSI* is a show about criminal forensics. I don't watch much TV except for old movies with Mom, the Discovery Channel, History Channel, TLC with Dad. The other stuff is a huge waste of time. Now all the kids are hot to investigate homicides.

Except me.

They know to leave me alone.

But back to business.

Hub Christy's eyes are wet. Today he gets to use the big steel bone pliers. He already has them hooked on thumb and forefinger in rednecked anticipation. I clench my teeth and scalpel an entryway into Pussy's small head. Hub goes to work quickly, opening the skull with a chicken-crunching sound.

"Want some?"

He waves a gobbet of cat-head meat around. Only the pretty girls laugh.

"Mr. Christy," Ms. Larimore says.

But now he's attacking the membranes, the kitty cat corpus callosum. Splitting poor Pussy Pancreatic into creative side and math side. We take out the bisected brain, weigh it, slice it, seal it like a tiny stack of wrinkly baloney in a kitty cat canopic jar.

We're done way ahead of everybody else. Hub Christy is restless; there's not much left on this cat to violate. The mouth? He pries his way in and explores this tight little cavity with the pliers.

Pay dirt.

"Here we go, baby."

My stomach lurches. It's inhuman how far a kitty cat tongue will stretch.

Exactement, Schuyler would say.

"Stop it," I say. "Please."

Hub Christy doesn't notice my horror—that I'm about to spew. His eyes glisten as he strains.

"Come on, baby! Give!"

There it is again, the chicken-tearing sound.

Run.

I grab a pass from Ms. Larimore, push my way out to a chorus of snickers, stumble down the hall past closed classroom doors.

My head is full of blood. The empty hallway tips over on its side. My face is sweaty cold.

Nobody uses the bathroom beside the principal's office. I stagger in, find a stall, fold over, and hug my knees. It's possible to sleep sitting on a toilet. My consciousness wanders and finally blackens. I dream about Mr. Mann, his wedding picture in the newspaper. Only now he isn't smiling. His beautiful eyes are black, hollowed out. He's dead.

Serves him right.

When I wake up, my legs have gone numb.

How did I get here?

in the beginning

Time.

That's the only way to explain finding yourself behind the Wal-Mart Rule the World Super Center kissing your teacher. Rewind to January.

Picture this:

In the beginning I'm sitting in language arts waiting on Mr. Mann. He's coming over from a school in Huntsville. Nobody's ever seen him before. He's late.

New block, new year, new teacher. I picked poetry for my last semester as a senior thinking maybe, just maybe, I'm a little top-heavy in the sciences. Really I just wanted to mix up a new batch of kids.

It doesn't work.

Prime example:

"Hey, Nine, you got a pen I can borrow?"

Harold Waters is sitting in front of me. He's been asking me for pens for years. Never once has he given any of them back. I close my eyes and focus.

What do I know about him? Start with the birthmark on the back of his neck.

Color: wine. Size: penny. Shape: Large Magellanic Cloud.

Harold's head has no crown. His hair divides in a clumsy line, one rank climbing over the top of his skull, the rest spilling down in a long, silky, asymmetrical point I ache to snip.

More? He loves reruns of *Star Trek: Voyager*. Robotics. Backgammon. But most of all, HO-scale model railroads. That's right, choo-choo trains. The kind with cardboard towns and green sandpaper posing as grass.

The kind you hide in the basement.

How do I know all this? I focus. That's what I do best. I observe. I learn.

Whether I want to or not. It's a gift. Sometimes it's also a little bit of a curse.

I know these kids too well. Their voices, their minds, their eyes, the ways their bodies move, their sounds.

Which are slow, which are brainy, which probably had sex at fourteen.

I know their favorite subjects, their clothes. What they think of Asians. How their parents treat them.

Who's horny.

Okay, that's easy. Anybody can figure that last one out.

But I'm sick of them all.

I don't hate them. I don't hate. It's counterproductive. Besides, I actually find people really fascinating. It's just that, after four years—seven, if you count middle school—twelve, going back all the way with a lot of them—there's not much left to observe.

Worse, the older they get, the more crystallized they become. Harold was pretty cool in the fifth grade. This guy was a genius with Legos. Now he's becoming calcified as we speak.

That's why I'm something of a loner. It's impossible to find more friends like Schuyler. Kids who are fluid, changeable, on fire. Kids with some range.

"Oh my God, he's hot."

That's Britton Keller. Her place on the Evolutionary Scale? She has a henna bar code tattooed at the top of her butt.

Boys?

Don't even mention it.

Not one boy in this class interests me. Or any of my classes, for that matter. Too lazy. Too mean. Too cool. Too immature. Too dull. Too Harold.

He just made a grunting noise deep in his throat. You can time them. He often smells faintly of chlorine.

It's no better with the teachers.

Last semester was Mr. Fields. I know what brand of coffee he drinks. How many cups a day. What caused his divorce: credit cards and quite possibly the length of the fur in his ears.

So now, today, right this minute, I'm really looking forward to something different.

We're startled when he comes through the door. Our new teacher.

He doesn't say hello, good morning, nothing.

I don't even get more than a peek at his face. He just blows through the door and immediately starts jabbing the blackboard with a piece of chalk.

First observations:

No gut, very trim, younger than most. Black Dockers, white, long-sleeved shirt. Mr. Mann is tall, broad back, arms long. Something about the way he slouches as he writes makes him approachable, friendly. Even vulnerable. I still haven't seen his face.

There's something beautiful and wild in the sound of his slashing strokes. He's writing so fast, the clicking of the chalk sounds aggressive:

EMILY DICKINSON IS GOD

"Hey," Kenny Atkinson says when Mr. Mann stops writing. "You forgot an *O*. I did her last week."

Kenny once pushed me off the monkey bars a couple of

geologic epochs ago. He has a snarling mouth and hair the color of morning pee.

There's a sprinkling of embarrassed laughter. I wince, already worried for my new teacher.

"Mr. Atkinson," Mr. Mann says without turning around.

Wow. His voice is strong and deep. Just the slightest trace of an accent. New England? He turns to face us, bringing audible gasps from the girls. His eyes are frostbite blue, his dark hair hangs partly across his face like Johnny Depp's. How old is he? Twenty-five? Twenty-eight?

"Would you tell us, please, Mr. Atkinson, what does a poem mean?"

Kenny sits up straighter and glances from side to side as if searching for a brother or a cousin.

"Huh? What poem?"

"Any."

Kenny grins at nothing, puts his hands up helplessly.

"I don't know what you want me to say."

Mr. Mann pulls down the white screen in front of the blackboard and slaps a slide on the overhead projector. It's a poem. We read:

> *MY life closed twice before its close;*
> *It yet remains to see*
> *If Immortality unveil*
> *A third event to me,*
>
> *So huge, so hopeless to conceive,*
> *As these that twice befell.*
> *Parting is all we know of heaven,*
> *And all we need of hell.*

He claps chalk dust from his long hands and touches the poem with the tip of a finger. "How about this one? Tell the class what this poem means, Mr. Atkinson."

Kenny opens his mouth. Closes it. Opens it again. The flies are getting confused.

"I hate poetry," he says finally.

"I hate poetry," Mr. Mann says. "Why?"

"Because it's freaking boring, you know."

"Why."

Kenny smirks and looks around for the affirmation he knows is there. "Because it doesn't make any sense. It has nothing to do with nothing. It's a great big waste of time."

"Mr. Atkinson," Mr. Mann says, staring hard, "I fully agree."

"Huh?"

Mr. Mann leans toward his desk, takes the back of his chair in his big hands. His hair is floating. "Poetry is boring," he says. "A huge waste of time. Meaningless. Hardly relevant to today's world. In fact, it sucks ass."

Whoosh.

All the air rushes out of the room. Even the comatose are jolted into rousing. Mr. Mann sweeps his beautiful eyes over us, huge, blazing.

"We're doomed, you and I, to a semester of boring, ridiculous torture. An entire chunk of your lives will be lost forever. By May you'll hate my guts. You'll talk about me behind my back. Tell your friends Emily Dickinson is a brand of upscale furniture. Unless."

We wait, his luminescent gaze rapidly becoming unbearable.

"Unless what?" a girl finally says.

The girl is me.

I can't believe it. I generally never speak in class; I absorb. Mr. Mann swivels his head, eyes pumping blue fire into my face.

"Unless you help me kill it," he says.

"What? Kill it?"

"Yes. One poem at a time. It's the only way." He takes a couple of steps toward me. I squirm. My personal space is big— at least a couple of meters, and most people can quickly tell. But Mr. Mann doesn't seem to notice he is penetrating it. "But poems are tough to kill," he says. "I can't do it alone. Are you with me?"

Sandra Williams leaks a string of compressed giggles behind me—I can tell who it is even without twisting my neck. Has any teacher ever talked like this?

"But how do you kill a poem?" I say, unable to keep my own laugh from squeaking out around the edges.

He cuts his eyes to the door and back, hard, conspiratorial. "The bad ones are easy. You just leave 'em alone; they eventually fall over and die. The good ones are tough. The harder you try, the stronger they get."

"Okay, but how?"

"You start by deciding if the author is insane." He straightens up and steps away from me, looks at the whole class. I can start breathing again. "Well?"

Silence.

"She's definitely messed up," Kenny says, sneering.

Other boys join in, emboldened.

"A whack job."

"What the hell is that supposed to mean, her life closed twice?"

Snickers over the language.

"You may be right," Mr. Mann says. "Emily lived with her sick father in Amherst, Massachusetts. After the late 1860s, she never again traveled beyond the boundaries of her little town. But she managed to fall in love at least once, so bitterly she wore a bridal gown the rest of her life."

"Miss Havisham!" a plump girl named Kelly Wunderlich almost shouts, startling herself. "Like in *Great Expectations*. I mean, the wedding dress, she was nuts."

"Yes," Mr. Mann says. "Like Miss Havisham, Emily never married. In fact, some believe the love of her life was a woman."

A communal "ooh" rises from the class. "Lesbo," Kenny says.

"That makes you crazy?" Havisham-Kelly says.

"Crazy like you."

Mr. Mann is enjoying this. He jerks the first slide away, slaps down another:

> *Her breast is fit for pearls,*
> *But I was not a "Diver"*

"Muff diver," Kenny says.

The class erupts.

Havisham is waving her arm when the place finally settles down. "But that means she wasn't a lesbian. She wasn't a diver."

Mr. Mann puts down another slide.

"Different poem."

> *TO see her is a picture,*
> *To hear her is a tune,*
> *To know her an intemperance*
> *As innocent as June*

"To know her," a voice says from the back.

We're shocked. It's Matt. His hair is Rust-Oleum black. He wears a button every day that says JESUS PHREAK and prays by the flagpole every morning with his friends. I've rarely heard him speak. "That's from the Bible," Matt says. "To know somebody means—it's physical."

Mr. Mann smiles. "Interesting. Damned interesting. So, was she insane?" He pauses, glaring, puts both hands on his desk with a seismic thump. "Emily Dickinson wrote over eighteen hundred poems. Only eight were published during her lifetime. Now that's what I call insane."

An appreciative "ah."

He slams the first poem back up on the screen, points at it. The shadow of his finger looks like a gun.

"Okay. Who's ready to help me murder this one?"

I adore him already.

golden ticket

Black coat.

It comes past his knees. Not Regulation Issue for Alabama, even in January.

Mr. Mann's standing in just about the last place I would expect a teacher to stand: outside the gym, where two intimidatingly huge chunks of school wall come together. Kids smoke here. The concrete is a painter's palette of gum. His presence is a force field driving leering boys away.

The wind is weaving pieces of his hair. He's waiting for someone.

"Thank you," he says when I come out.

I don't know if he's talking to me or Schuyler.

"You, Carolina." Mr. Mann comes closer, pulling his coat around his legs. We're exactly the same height. He's inside my sphere again, making me feel electrically charged.

"Hi."

"Hi. I wanted to thank you for rescuing me."

I'm not sure what I should say. "What?"

"The first class is always the most dangerous. Thanks for helping me out like that. I was afraid nobody would answer and I might be thrown to the wolves."

I smile, embarrassed. Glance nervously at Schuyler, who is frowning, confused.

Mr. Mann sticks his hand out. "And you are?" Schuyler pushes at thick hair self-consciously—today it looks like a thatched Elizabethan roof—but shakes anyway.

My thinking apparatus is temporarily short-circuited.

"I'm sorry," I say. "This is my friend, Schuyler Green."

Mom would bust her buttons: Textbook Introduction. But why did I feel it necessary to throw in the playground qualifier? Mr. Mann turns to me again and glares beatifically.

"You spoke up when nobody else would," he says.

"Except for Kenny."

"Mr. Atkinson?"

"How did you know who he was?"

"Teachers talk. They always tell you about the worst kids first. I wish they would start with the best."

The crooked way he smiles somehow communicates that by *best* he means students just like me. His voice is soothing, his eyes hypnotic. It would be so easy to fall into them. In fact, that's just what I'm doing.

"You were amazing in there," I say, instantly horrified at my own words. I scramble to recover. "How you got everybody thinking, I mean. I've always been heavy into science. I've never read much poetry."

"People in fear for their lives do desperate things," he says. I wonder, is this supposed to have a double meaning?

"Desperate?"

"It's a goddamn trick," Mr. Mann says. "Pardon my French."

"Actually, it's Middle English," I say automatically, immediately wishing I would shut up. It's a habit from hanging around with Schuyler. Sometimes his only entry into a conversation is a chance to quietly show off.

"But originally from the Old French," Schuyler says. See what I mean? *Dampner. To condemn, inflict loss upon.*

Mr. Mann laughs. "I'll remember you two the next time I'm on *Who Wants to Be a Millionaire?*" I like his laugh. It's genuine, trusting. Schuyler doesn't. His ears sink.

"You said something about a trick?" I say.

"Yeah." Mr. Mann cups a hand to his mouth in an exaggerated, stagy gesture. "Can you keep a secret? He's made up."

"Who?"

"The person you saw in class today. It's funny—even when you've been doing this for years, it never gets any easier. That's how I survive it. I become Him. So mostly it's all an act. I'm an INFP—"

"Sure," I say. "Myers-Briggs. The personality sorter."

"Right. So you know about it?"

"Yeah. We took the test a couple of years ago. INFP is one of

the rarest personalities of all. It means you're introverted, intu-
itive. You don't mind things being open ended."

"Right. We're supposed to be loners. Writers. Actors. Artists."

"Saints. Idealists. Dreamers."

He grimaces. "Ha. I wouldn't go that far."

I can't believe I'm having a conversation with this man. Normally
his looks alone would send me into overload so bad, I'd be unintelli-
gible. "So why do you do it if it bothers you so much?" I say.

"You mean, teach? Because I love it. It's my second-greatest
passion."

"Second greatest?"

Mr. Mann doesn't say anything. I'm not sure he heard me. In
fact, I'm not even sure I actually said the words. For the first time
I notice Schuyler is gone. Force field got him.

"Well, I guess I'd better be going—"

"Wait," Mr. Mann says.

He reaches into his coat, pulls out a golden envelope, and
hands it to me. I blink. My mind is still trying to unhitch itself
from the word *passion*.

"I wanted to give this to you," he says.

"What is it?"

"Your reward for rescuing me. Someone had to."

I open the envelope and pull out a piece of stiff, formal-look-
ing paper. A gift certificate for twenty-five dollars to Books-A-
Million. It's made out to *Carolina Livingston* in black Sharpie.

"Oh! Thanks. But I don't know if—"

Mr. Mann shrugs with his forehead. "I know. Probably against
sixteen different school policies. Please accept it anyway. It's kind
of a tradition. I do it every time I start a new class. Besides, I can't
be fired until I see how things turn out."

I tuck the certificate under my arm, a little afraid somebody else might see. "Turn out?"

"At the risk of triggering your gag reflex, I like to think each class is a book. Full of characters. Twists, surprises, heroes, villains. Growth. That's the best part. I want to see how they turn out, Carolina. How they grow. Or not, as the case may be."

"Nine. Everybody calls me Nine."

"Oh. Where'd you get that?"

"From my dad. He's an engineer out at NASA. Insane about numbers."

He smiles. His bottom teeth are slightly crooked too.

"Integer chic," Mr. Mann says. "It fits you." I can feel him watching me, thinking. "Also the auditory suggestion of a Teutonic refusal. Who knows, might start a trend."

I'm afraid I'm actually blushing. I decide to risk it.

"How'd you know where to find me?"

He puts a finger to his lips. "Shhh. Trade secret. I looked up your schedule on the school LAN. So which do you prefer? Carolina or Nine?"

I think about it, feeling a ridiculous warmth rising through my chest. "I don't know. Either is fine. Anything but Amazon Woman. Hair Girl. Basketball Chick."

"Do you play basketball?"

"Nope."

"Teachers really call you those things?"

"Some. The ones who think they're funny."

"No shit. What about the other ones?"

"Other who?" Did Mr. Mann just say *shit*?

"Teachers."

I think about it. "They don't notice me."

He puts his thumb to his chin, fingers resting on his full lips.
"Which is worse."

I'm not sure it's a question. "You mean being noticed or not being noticed?"

He doesn't say anything, just looks at me.

I think about my answer for a week.

sound crazy

Masterful.

Each minute in his class is a sanctuary.

There is no suction today. There may never be again.

Even Harold's neck is suddenly more interesting. As if I could look at anything else but Him.

Mr. Mann.

As the days go by, I'm opening like a bud. Just in time for spring.

In spite of ourselves, we cram Emily's new science into our heads complete with a foreign vocabulary: *variable feet, assonant rhyme, negative capability.*

This morning he pounds his fist so hard, the transparency on the projector jumps, throwing the image out of square.

He straightens the slide and we read:

> *BECAUSE I could not stop for Death,*
> *He kindly stopped for me;*

The carriage held but just ourselves
And Immortality.

We slowly drove, he knew no haste,
And I had put away
My labor, and my leisure too,
For his civility.

We passed the school where children played,
Their lessons scarcely done;
We passed the fields of gazing grain,
We passed the setting sun.

We paused before a house that seemed
A swelling of the ground;
The roof was scarcely visible,
The cornice but a mound.

Since then 't is centuries; but each
Feels shorter than the day
I first surmised the horses' heads
Were toward eternity.

"Listen," Mr. Mann says.

But everything is quiet.

Britton shifts in her seat. The henna bar code has given way to a metal crack ring. Ouch. "What are we supposed to hear?" she says.

"Read it again. Do you hear the hooves galloping to the beat of her words?"

Mr. Mann slaps his hands rhythmically on his desk, making a drumming sound: *Tuddlelump, tuddlelump.* He attacks the blackboard:

Because / I | could / not | stop / | for Death / He kind/ly | stopped / | for me/

"Yeah," Britton says. "I hear it. Damn."

Havisham is waving her arm.

"Kelly?"

"Mr. Mann! My book is different." She holds up a white paper-back with a subluxated spine. "It doesn't say lessons; it's talking about wrestling."

Fiendish smile.

"There are different versions of many of Emily's poems, depending on how old your book is, who did the editing, even the punctuation. Some of the multiple versions came from Emily her-self. She was complex, changeable, amazingly ahead of her time." He glances at me. I'm sure of it.

"So." He moves fluidly across the room, hands clasped behind him. I'm stone drunk on his every gesture. Watching him walk does something supernatural to me. "What does the speaker fig-ure out by the time she gets to the end of the poem?"

"That her ass is dead, man." Kenny laughs.

"Bingo. And doesn't that just make you want to scream?"

"Huh?"

"When you think about it. All the things out there in the world that piss you off. The injustice. The stupidity. Sometimes in the middle of the night, it makes me need to scream. So that's what I want everybody in the room to do right now. Scream."

"No shit?" Britton says.

"Sure."

"How loud?" Kenny says.

"Jetliner crash. Make my ears bleed. Think about something that really drives you crazy and let it all out."

You, I say to myself. What is happening to me? You really drive me crazy. Wackers. Bonko. Gone.

You make me need to scream.

"Ready?"

Yes.

"Okay, I'll give you a countdown." He ticks off numbers with his fingers. "Five, four, three, two, one—"

Blastoff.

We scream, all twenty-two of us.

I pour my everlasting soul into the scream. I haven't yelled this loud since grade school. I had forgotten how good it feels. It's almost like a twisted kind of singing.

The yowling in the closed space is cleansing and horrifying. How thick are these walls? I notice Mr. Mann doesn't scream. Maybe it would be too much. Something important might break inside us.

He cuts us off with a throat-slashing gesture. It takes a few heartbeats for things to completely stop. A few people are coughing from the effort. We're waiting for him to say something, make the room okay again. He stares.

"So?" Matt the Jesus Phreak says.

"So now we wait," Mr. Mann says. "Quietly."

Thirty seconds pass. A whole minute. I'm watching him as much as the clock. Two. Are we listening for something? Whether we are or not, something comes.

The door swings open. It's our principal, Zeb Greasy.

That's not his real name, just what everybody calls him. He's
large, has dark, allergic eyes, a big head, thinning hair. A good old
Alabama boy. He should be coaching a football team somewhere;
in fact, he has. That's the quickest way to zoom up the ranks in the
Heart of Dixie.

"Is everything okay in here, Mr. Mann?" Zeb Greasy says,
scowling.

"Fine," Mr. Mann says. "We're fine. Just working on a little
drama."

"Well," Zeb says without smiling, "maybe next time don't
make it quite so . . . dramatic." And he's gone.

I look at Mr. Mann. We're fine. I'm fine. I've never been so—
Fine.

aboriginal eyes

Water.

The days sail through winter into March.

I'm driving in Wilkie Collins with Schuyler.

The road ahead is partly flooded with spring rain. The ground
is low here, but the water isn't deep. Wilkie cleaves through with
barely a twinkle.

Mr. Mann's apartment complex is next to a swamp clotted
with cypress trees. It's an orange-brick place called Sunlake.
Architectural style: Pretend It's a House.

Today there is no sun and the only sign of the lake is a

disemboweled beaver, intestines red as a can of Dad's Old
Spice deodorant.

His apartment is on the second floor. Building 9. What a perfect number. As we circle the complex a third time, I'm totaling up
what I know.

"We talk nearly every day. He's from Massachusetts. I think
his parents might be dead. He never mentions them. He taught
somewhere in Huntsville before he came here. Likes to wear
three-button pullover shirts and Dockers. No jewelry. Wallet in
his left rear pocket—"

"Cologne?"

"Ivory soap."

Schuyler makes a face as if he's about to puke and scratches at
mustard on Wilkie's dash. "I can't believe you're hung up on this
cretin. I thought you were the Girl With the X-ray Eyes?"

Schuyler has called me that since at least the sixth grade, says I
can see through anybody. What's inside their hearts, their minds.

"Don't worry. I am," I say. "I've had crushes on teachers
before. Ninth grade, remember? Something about the way Mr.
Jennings said the word *Precambrian*—"

"Horny Howard. Yeah, I remember. Something about the way
he slobbered all over Lacey Carver, too."

"Shut up! But this isn't a crush. This is Napoleon and
Josephine."

"So which one are you?"

I poke him in the ribs and Wilkie Collins swerves, nearly clip-
ping a newspaper rack. My first official act as Incorrigible Teen.
We pass Mr. Mann's building a fifth time and circle again.
Schuyler emits an Empire State Building top-of-the-stairs groan.

"Come on, Nine, I'm starving."

"Here."

I bump open Wilkie's glove box, pull out a pulverized packet from Wendy's. Schuyler tears it open, dumps cracker dust down his throat.

"Blech!"

Now he's spitting out the window.

"Hey!" I yell. "At least wait till you get out of the car, you— you Aborigine!"

"Blug! Crap—how long has that been in there? It's a plot! You're trying to poison me! Just so you can spend all your time stalking that organ-grinder."

"Sorry." I laugh.

He spits again. "And I'll have you know the Pintudjara are a dang fastidious people."

"Crocodile Dundee. The first one."

"Man. You're too good. Bleh. Come on, let's get out of here. Now I'm thirsty too."

"But he might be coming back soon."

"So? What're you going to do, knock him on the head and drag him off in the bushes?"

"I just want to look."

Atomic sigh. "I won't say he's ugly, but—"

"But you can't 'cause you know he's gorgeous. Nose just the right shape. Amazing eyes. Broad shoulders. Perfect butt."

"Swollen prostate."

"He's not that old!"

"You're making me sick, Nine."

I giggle maliciously. "Sorry. But it's too much fun."

"But is he smart? In the right way, I mean."

"Snob. Elitist. You need to take his class."

Schuyler closes his eyes wearily and lays his head back. "I'm already two language arts ahead of you."

"At the expense of your scientific education."

"So call me well rounded."

I touch his shoulder; Wilkie swerves again. "Kind of bony, actually."

"See? You want me to get any bonier?"

"Don't worry. You're not going to blow away anytime soon."

He starts tickling me in the side until I have to pull over.

"Cut it out!"

I'm laughing, trying not to squeal or pee my pants. Schuyler never used to do this. These days he's constantly touching. Tickling the back of my neck, grabbing my head.

"Stop it! Come on, Schuyler, please!"

He lets up. "You ready to leave?"

"Okay. Okay!" I'm wiping at tears. "But at least let me call. Give me Mom's cell."

"What for?"

I find the number on the torn-out phone book page and dial. On the fourth ring Mr. Mann's beautiful recorded baritone picks up. His message is loud; I have to hold it away from my ear:

"Man is the only animal that blushes. Or needs to. *Mark Twain*."

Beep.

Schuyler burps just as I'm hanging up.

"Cut it out! He probably heard you!"

"I hope he did. What a pretentious weenie roaster—"

"He's sweet."

"Uh-oh. Call Nostradoofus. The Last Days are upon us. You just used the word *sweet*." Schuyler moans and turns on the radio. The Radio Guy immediately mentions the time.

"I knew it!"

We're late for work at the Ground-Up Cow Face Burgers.

"Keep your war girdle on, Hippolyte," I say. "We'll get there."

"Mythological Amazonian queen who battled Hercules," Schuyler says. "Go!"

But I have to look one more time.

His building. Number 9.

His door. Number 220.

This number is destiny, too. It's the same number of the abrasive used to polish telescope mirrors:

Number 220 Grit.

It makes me think of a word:

Rub.

empress of grease

I'm doing it again.

Obsessing at the drink dispenser.

Brown soda flows over my fingers; makes for sticky change. "Sorry."

Schuyler's stuffing his face with cheese from the condiment shelf. I'm not hungry.

"Any sign of Beezle Bob yet?" I say.

Beezle Bob is the Pimple-Faced Shift Manager with a Little College. He drives a vintage VW Bug. The only cars I see in the lot belong to the other kids working with us, Mary Katie, Country, and Threatt.

"Y'all going to the prom?" Country says.

He fills up my space with his chest. Country is big and doughy. You can tell his mother cuts his hair. Everybody calls him Country because he speaks fluent Mobile Home.

"Yes," I lie.

"Who with?"

"Me," Threatt says. I push him as he goes by.

Threatt is a foot shorter than Country. He has the largest, most expressive eyes of any human being I've ever seen. His name rhymes with *feet*. His Cow Face Burger hat is perched at a sassy angle on his perfect hair.

"What about you?" Country asks Schuyler.

"He ain't got his license yet," Threatt says. "He's scared."

Schuyler frowns.

"It's true!" Threatt says. "But that's cool. Just get your father to hire you a limousine. It's not that much for one night. Buy your baby a big corsage. Just don't accidentally-on-purpose pin it through her nipple."

"Ooh. That's what I'm talking about," Mary Katie says from the drive-thru. The back of her corn silk hair is bobbed pink. If her pants were any lower on her Mini Cooper butt, the drive-thru would be R-rated. "Except a corsage is supposed to be pinned on the arm, not the boob, Threatt."

"But then you might stick her in her jugglers vein," Country says.

"God," Schuyler says under his breath. "This place destroys brain cells. If my mind were Antarctica, I would have just lost the Ross Shelf."

He plunges a load of fries into the spattering grease, thumbs the red timer button.

I fiddle with the cups so I can get closer to him. "Why don't you get your license just to shut them up?"

"Because I don't want to."

"Why?"

"I hate cars. They hate me."

"Hey," Beezle Bob says, coming around the corner. "I'm not feeling so warm and fuzzy about you myself right at the moment."

We take our stations. The supper crowd is arriving.

"I can't believe it," Schuyler says from behind the grill. "He's here again."

His voice is a chain pulling me back to earth. I was daydreaming of living at Sunlake.

"Beezle Bob?"

"No. Piltdown Mann."

"Really!"

It's true. Mr. Mann's coming through the door in a short-sleeved shirt, arms casually muscular. His steps are long. I feel every footfall inside my body. Molten images flare and ricochet: Mr. Mann, his shirt off, lifting me onto the counter.

"You don't have to get all jacked about it," Schuyler says. "Doesn't that cradle-robber eat anywhere else?"

Mr. Mann has been coming here off and on for weeks. *"Writers don't cook; they compose,"* he likes to say.

He's memorized my schedule. Emily by day, *E. coli* by night. He usually orders the same thing. I'm convinced he's saving all his decision-making synapses for me.

He's holding a book under his arm. I read the title upside down as he puts it next to the register: *The Annals of Tacitus.*

"Beach book?"

He shows his lopsided smile, goosing my heart. "Hi, Carolina. It starts slowly, but when you get to the murderous bisexual Nero, it's hotter than Grisham."

Sometimes I can't believe we've come this far. That we're talking this way. There's a silence. For once in my life, I'm not uncomfortable.

"You check out that Amherst web site?" he says.

I nod. "Emily's house is a lot nicer than I pictured. Two-story brick Italianate. It says they're fixing to restore it to its original color, baby-poop yellow."

"*Fixing.* A serviceable word. Can I have a mint julep with my order, Miss Scarlett?"

"Quiet! You should talk, Mr. Boston Baked Beans. Besides, you know what I mean. From her poems I was expecting Little House on the Prairie or Walden Pond."

"Things were a lot more goddamn pastoral back then."

I rap his knuckles with a coffee straw. "Control yourself, Captain Trashmouth. You're in the Bible Belt now, son."

"Saints preserve us." The dazzling eyes cut left and right. "And while we're on the subject of turning human beings into jams and jellies, I think I would make a kick-ass Seville marmalade. You I would peg as raspberry jam."

"Huh?"

"An inside joke for Trappist monks. They make their own preserves at Saint Joseph's Abbey in Spencer, Mass. Only twenty-eight miles from Emily's front steps. Tastes like heaven."

While I'm thinking about this, the places he used to live, what he looked like walking around there, he asks a question.

"Do you ever think you were born a century too late?"

I nod. "All the time. Except for the Hubble."

"Space Telescope?"

"Yep. Have you ever seen the picture of the gas pillars in M16, the Eagle Nebula?"

"I don't know."

"It's a place where stars are being born. You've got to see it. It's looks like the fingers of God; it's—"

"Nine," Beezle Bob snaps from his cubbyhole office. His face is a glowering dot-to-dot.

More customers arrive. I speed pour five drinks and return with Mr. Mann's cholesterol.

"I hope you enjoy your meal." Our fingers touch.

"Hope is the thing with feathers," Mr. Mann says. I don't know if he's quoting Emily or just being delectably weird.

"Ooh," Mary Katie says from the drive-thru, flipping her bubble gum hair.

I've got to be careful. I can't let other people besides Schuyler notice I have a thing for my teacher.

Does he have a thing for me?

Please.

It's so easy to get carried away when you know there is no chance. But if there is—if there really is? If it's not all just my imagination— what does that mean? To a man? That he likes me? Wants to be around me? Teach me poetry? Or does he want to undress me, touch me, kiss me, hold me? Be with me for the rest of my life? Love me?

Or just recommend a few killer books?

"Disgusting," Schuyler says when Mr. Mann sits down. "Worse. Antediluvian."

I giggle stupidly—he's tickling me again. Finally I can't stand it anymore and thump his paper hat in the french fry grease to get away. "Go burn something, Spartacus."

Like always, Mr. Mann takes a long time to eat. He reads one-handed. When the crowd has thinned, I drift out to the dining room to wipe things down. I polish the Formica off the table next to his. When Beezle Bob leaves early, I actually sit down and we talk until closing.

Back home I check the web and find this:

http://www.spencerabbey.org/preserves/

Then something even better:

> HOPE *is the thing with feathers*
> *That perches in the soul,*
> *And sings the tune without the words,*
> *And never stops at all*

kissing africa

Spring.

As goofy as it sounds, there's something inside my blood that's gathering steam.

But I approach the problem scientifically.

I'm methodical in my love.

I pursue without pursuing, watch without watching. Wait without waiting.

Our days become a kind of Brownian Motion: emotional molecules herding the two of us toward a particular desired outcome.

The way I hang around, the questions I ask, the not-so-accidental meetings—he has to know.

Does he know?

Confession of the Day:

I've swiped Mr. Mann's picture from the school web site.

Back home I turn it into a j-peg, blow it up 400 percent. His eyes become lakes in the Ngorongoro basin. Lips, rills of sand. Neck, a salt plain in Tanzania.

Experiment 1:

Kiss the picture. No good. Try again.

This time I study the picture a long, long time.

Experiment 2:

I put Kitty Nation out, lock my bedroom door, and bury my face in my pillow, bunching the warm, bulgy fabric against my mouth. I move my head slowly from side to side, eyes closed, lips making the cloth wet, crushing the pillow until it wraps around either side of my head, pushing hard into the softness, his face shining in my inner eye.

Better.

Experiment 3:

Now he's tilting his head, eyes gone smoky, eyelids at half-mast. He's feeling this kiss so much, he needs to close his eyes but can't—he has to watch me even though I can't watch him. It's too much to see his face this close, too intensely beautiful—I clutch at the pillow, squeezing with all my strength, pushing my body into his, mixing our particles. Forever. Forever.

Best.

The telephone rings.

I try to pick it up, drop it on the floor.

"What!" I yell miserably through the sheet.

"You got a cold?" Schuyler says. "Or were you asleep?"

"No." I'm trying to rub the pixel burn out of my eyes, actually.

"You know," he says, "it's theorized primitive man got as much as twelve hours a—"

"Please, Schuyler. Give it a rest." And give me one too, while you're at it.

"Okay. Mom wanted me to remind you, the work-a-thon is tomorrow."

No.

It all comes back to me.

Painting, cleaning, hauling away trash at the elementary school where his mother teaches. Worse, Schuyler can't go—he has a chess tournament in Nashville. Where can I hide? Bosnia? The Marianas Trench?

"Aw, man. I don't feel up to it."

"Come on. You promised. Besides, you owe me. Remember that lab animal you stuck me with for a work partner last year?"

"Hey, that wasn't my fault. Pinkeye is extremely contagious. Just call the CDC."

"Nine."

"Okay, okay. I'll be there."

Oh, well, such is life. When I settle the phone back in its cradle, I spy Mr. Mann's blown-up photo. I study it again, snuggle back into the covers.

He's there, holding a jar of Seville marmalade and a spoon.

deeper

April in Alabama:

The air is full of sunlight. There's a warm, blustery breeze. The clouds are hanging like planets.

And all I've got to look forward to on this gorgeous Saturday is eight hours of paintbrushes, cleansers, hammers. Maybe day-old Tater Tots for lunch, if I'm lucky. I'm stuck at the elementary school, Schuyler's work-a-thon.

Sigh.

The sign-in man is boldly asexual, thick around the middle and balding to boot. I bet his tan Dockers won't see a single smudge all day. He glances at his watch when I come up, makes a brisk architectural notation.

"Name?"

"Carolina Livingston."

"Work partner?"

"Pinky Lee."

"What?"

"I'm sorry. Schuyler Green. But he had to go to Nashville for a chess tournament. Allegedly. So I guess I don't have anybody."

Dockers lines through Schuyler's name with a ruler and looks around. A pudgy boy jumps up from a box, citrus cleaner in one hand, booping Game Boy in the other.

"Well, Robbie, looks like we found you a—"

Please, no.

"I'm her partner," a voice says behind me.

Degreaser Boy sags. My mouth hangs open; I force myself to clop it shut.

Mr. Mann.

He's coming up the walk behind me wearing jeans and a UMass T-shirt. Scruffy white sneaks. His hair is tangling and untangling in the wind.

He extends his hand to shake with Dockers, bare arm almost touching mine.

"Richard Mann at your service. Of the Boothbay Harbor Manns."

"Says here your name is Green," Dockers says.

"That was before the operation."

"Huh?"

"Just kidding. It's Mann; it'll be on the next page."

Dockers finds his name, makes another time notation. "All right, let's see what we've got for you here."

A rush of cold horror floods my chest.

Shorts!

I'm wearing shorts.

My legs are so winter pale, you could use them to signal the cavalry. What does he think of me? My blow-away hair? And who showers when they know crushed milk cartons are on their horizon?

A quick, terrifying Systems Check: Tic Tacs, no; blackheads, yes; bra that fits like a busted slingshot. Stunning.

Mr. Mann doesn't seem to notice my wobbling knees. Dockers consults his paperwork, makes a couple of neat engineering marks on his list. "All right. Let's see what we've got left here—baseboards or trees?"

"Huh?"

"Which do you want? Scrubbing baseboards or planting trees?"

Mr. Mann and I glance at each other sideways, partners in

crime. Dockers taps his pen impatiently. "Hmmm," Mr. Mann says. "There's dirt and then there's . . . dirt. What do you think, Carolina? Knees or trees?"

"I—um—I'm—"

"No doubt struck dumb to be teamed with such an experienced work-a-thon . . . er. All right, trees," he says to Dockers. "I spend too much goddamn time in places like this as it is."

Dockers touches a pen to his flabby lips and nods at the Booper. "Big pitchers have little ears."

Huh?

Two minutes later we're escaping down the hillside with a shovel, a posthole digger, and a croker sack full of pine saplings. The school grounds loom before us, empty of people, not even a car in sight.

Is this possible?

A whole day alone with Mr. Mann.

I suddenly realize I've forgotten how to walk.

As we descend the gentle slope, each step becomes a conscious act, a series of jerky mechanical movements preceded by careful thought. I'm a stumbling idiot, a giraffe. Is he watching my legs? My butt? Say something, anything!

"My prince."

Except that.

Mr. Mann grins. "Glad to oblige, my queen."

I somehow manage to feign a pout. "So you're my son?"

"No, *milady*. Knight at arms. Together we have just vanquished the Tan Lord and the bleeping Duke of Orange."

I giggle like an idiot, clap my hand to my mouth to stifle it.

Thirty seconds down.

Only 28,770 to go.

What's wrong? Why am I so nervous? I've talked to this man

practically every weekday for months. What's so different about this place? Being alone together for the first time? Am I afraid something's going to happen?

Or terrified something isn't.

We're there.

"Along here?" I say.

"That's what the man said. You want me to do that?" Mr. Mann touches the wooden handles.

"We can take turns. I kind of like it." It's also keeping me standing.

"I kind of like that you kind of like it."

I raise the posthole digger—"I claim thee in the name of Sir Guy of Gismond!"—and stab it violently in the trampled sod.

Stop being stupid. Calm down.

I lever the metal jaws shut, lift, pull away a bite of turf, pile.

"Hey, you're pretty good at that."

I feel myself flushing pleasurably and stab the hole again. "My dad taught me. We used to build stuff. So what are you doing here?"

"Hey, can't a new guy join the community? Actually, I promised Britton and Kelly—they pledge, I work."

I feel myself bristling.

"So how much did they give?"

"Completely confidential! Dollar an hour."

"Cheapskates."

"You get what you pay for."

"So they say."

Is this turning into small talk?

Quiet.

I dig steadily, trying not to grunt. Praying my deodorant is a shining example of Truth in Advertising. I need something to

occupy my hands, my flaming attention. I watch my feet to keep
from glancing at his back, his shoulders, his arms. The ground is
reasonably soft; the hole grows in satisfying pinches.

For a while we don't speak. I appreciate the lack of mindless
chatter. We set the first tree, shovel in the fill, pat the cool earth.
When our fingers briefly touch, an electrical impulse riots up and
down my spine. When I get up again, my hands and legs are shaking. I grip the digger harder. We move along the edge of the field,
slowly emptying the sack. I refuse to trade for the shovel.

After an hour or so of this, things are feeling a little more comfortable.

Now:

Start with the easiest question.

"There's something I've always wanted to ask you."

Mr. Mann leans on the shovel, top lip beaded gold. I love the
fact that he hasn't shaved today; his stubble is dark and bronzed at
the tips.

"Sure."

"Why Emily? You could have picked so many poets. Whitman,
Eliot, Dylan Thomas, Frost, Langston Hughes, Edna St. Vincent
Millay. Wouldn't longer poems have been easier to dig into?"

"And you said you didn't know poetry."

"I don't. But when I learn something, I learn it. What's the
internet for, anyhow?"

"EBay. I'm looking to score a set of Clackers."

"Huh?"

"Never mind." He stretches, making me nearly gasp in wonder, arms reaching over his head, broad chest pulling at the material of his shirt. "Whew. Haven't done anything like this in a
while. Okay. Why Emily."

He brushes his eyes with a shining arm. I'm glad I've got something to hold on to.

"Because she's the Queen of *Almosts*," he says.

"Almosts?"

"Almost beautiful. Almost married. Almost published to fame and fortune. Almost, almost, almost. That's even the title of one of her poems, 'Almost.' The closer she would get to a thing, the more she would cut herself off from it."

"That sounds so quantum," I say without thinking.

"Yeah, you know, you're right. It is."

I don't know what to say next. I'm too busy thinking. We move on to the next hole.

Bang.

I'm suddenly paralyzed by a terrifying thought:

Is that what this is, this thing with Mr. Mann? Quantum theory?

Am I trying to discover what's really real there?

A quantum physicist chops hunks of matter into smaller and smaller bits, atoms, neutrons, electrons, quarks, hadrons, leptons, gluons, etc. Looking for what they call the *God particle*—it has been so hard to find, some physicists call it the God*damn* particle—that final piece of matter that really, truly, concretely exists.

That final piece of something you can actually, physically Touch.

But it's never really there. You can slice away forever and not find a single piece of solid ground to hang on to.

A burning starts behind my eyes, the sudden need to bawl.

No.

I drive the posthole digger viciously.

I'm a Deep Sky astronomer. Deep Sky astronomers are used to dealing with stuff that seems impossible: quasars, black holes, event horizons, bubble universes.

I set my jaw. My voice is a little trembly; I can't help it.

"But what if some of those *Almost* things were beyond Emily's control? Forced on her by life?"

Mr. Mann blows air between his lips. "You mean, did she have a choice? Do we get to choose? On the really important things? I don't know."

I do. I'm rolling now. "Maybe she wanted to take things all the way but couldn't. That doesn't mean she didn't want to. Maybe she needed somebody else to help her. That's the answer."

Mr. Mann considers this. "Maybe we're not supposed to know the answer. It's a mystery. Life. Maybe it's supposed to be. With Emily, I believe the answers are in her poetry. I can relate."

"How?"

"Because I'm the king."

"Prince."

"Nope. The King of *Almosts*. Almost had friends. Almost a poet. Almost married."

I silently beg him to keep going, but he stops.

A blue Wal-Mart bag tumbles by, snags on one of the trees we've just planted. I pull it off and crumple it in my pocket. The moment feels inexpressibly sad.

Good. There will never be a better time. Ask him.

"But why didn't—?"

"Look at you." He suddenly touches my cheek with his warm hand, brushing at something there. I feel the blood moving to my face. "You really throw yourself into it, don't you?"

I will his hand to stay there—please, please, just keep touching me—but it goes away. "I'm focused," I manage to say. "I've always been focused."

"I like that. Teach me, huh?"

I start to say something, but he's already moving on to mark the next spot.

The rest of the day the conversation somehow expands in every direction away from him, like a gamma-ray burst from a star. No matter how I try to steer it. What is he thinking? Why does he come so close, then pull away? Is he holding something back? Why? What is he afraid of?

By the end of the day we have planted sixty trees.

I have dug every hole.

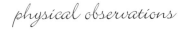

physical observations

I'm cunning.

He's not going to get away that easily.

I'm too focused. I'm gathering too much data.

I know the speed of his walk, the corners he likes to round at certain positions of the clock. His lunch table. The way he shakes his salt, crosses his legs. Like a good engineer studying heat tiles on the Shuttle, I even know the pronation of his feet by the wear on the bottom of his shoes.

It's not enough.

I'm thinking about the work-a-thon. What it felt like when he touched my cheek.

His scent, the way his sweat collected in the middle of his shirt, a dark, liquid heart shape stretching down his stomach. The distance between our skin, the way the world tasted—dirt, sun, sky, leaf—

I flop back in bed and stare at the ceiling, trying to ignore the bubbly tickle in my throat. The phone starts to buzz because I haven't dialed the last digit of his number. I let it slip through my fingers to *thonk* on the carpet. This is unbearable. I have to know, does all of this stay right here? I can't live with that. I can't. But I have to know:

Does it go on?

I'm ready to make something happen.

Please.

closer

Lunch.

He's missing from his table today.

I put my tray away, hurry up the hall, rap on the door to his office.

It opens a crack and Mr. Mann pokes his lovely head out. The spiral staircase of paperwork on his desk behind him tells me he's busy. He remains standing, doesn't invite me in. But he smiles.

"Carolina!"

In the split second before I speak, I study his face.

Worry? Joy? Fear?

How can I be getting all these signals at once?

My visit is so soon after planting all those trees—he has to see I'm climbing up to the next plateau. Will he take my hand, haul me higher, up to where he is?

Or let me fall.

"Hi! Mr. Mann, I was wondering—could I talk to you for a second?"

"Sure, what do you need?"

What do I need.

The question interrupts important chemical reactions in my brain. Fires up others. What do I need? Whatever you have. Whatever you want to give. Whatever you can share.

"I was just wondering."

He grins. "You said that." His hand is still on the knob.

A boy with a book bag banging his butt slouches by, smirking. I can't help but notice, Mr. Mann glances at the tiles until he's gone.

"Could I come inside?" I say.

"Well." His voice drops several decibels. His eyes move left and right. "I'm not so sure."

I don't know if he's serious. "What?"

"Maybe it wouldn't be a good idea."

Is this good? Bad?

Is he afraid of being seen with me?

Because he likes me? Because he's afraid of where this is going? Or only of what people might think.

My fingers are slipping—the route I'm climbing is suddenly crumbling beneath me.

It's not real, it's a waking fantasy, the product of an over-heated mind and quantum theory.

"Why?" I say.

"Well."

There's another noise behind me. Mr. Johnson from agri-science. He's carrying a wooden toolbox that looks exactly like a birdhouse with no roof. For a very long bird. He waves a silent *hi.*

"I've been thinking," Mr. Mann says. He watches Mr. Johnson pass with a solemn smile.

"About?"

Touching my face? Telling me you're lonely? That you dream about me in building 9, room 220?

"Okay?" I say.

"Maybe that's my problem. I think too much."

This sounds more promising. I've found a fingerhold; I'm pulling myself back up.

"I've been accused of that myself," I say. "What about?" I like this feeling. We're dancing up a new trail, and I'm getting to lead.

"Things. Anyhow, what did you need?"

Dead end.

I glance at my shoes. There's a spot of dirt on the toe of my left sneaker. Instantly, I can see the ground between us, the sky, pushing the earth around a new tree, our fingers meeting. Don't lose that day.

"I just felt like talking. Mars! That's it! Did you know it's coming up on its closest approach in sixty thousand years?"

"I didn't know that."

"It won't be this close again until 2287."

Smile. "That's not sixty thousand years away."

"I know. It doesn't work like that. It's variable."

"Which pretty much means—"

"We'll both be dead the next time." Dead. Get it? So let's do the important things now. I can't stop it; the words come pouring out. "So this is our only chance, if you think about it. I've got a refractor. It's only a four-inch Meade, but would you like to come over and look sometime? Or we could go farther out where the light is better."

"Nine." The door opens wider. He's wearing a forest green T-shirt—it must have been underneath the sweater I saw in class. "I'd love to. It's just—"

He stops. His eyes are suddenly sad. Has something happened? Is it something I've done?

No. It's something he wants to do. I can see it. Something he wants to do so badly, it's eating him up inside. But he's holding back. He's a good man. He's such a good man.

This is my part. This is where I have to make him know it's okay. That I want him to help me climb. He has to see that, feel it. Understand it. Has to see that I'm old enough, strong enough, smart enough. That he can take it one step more. I have to give him a sign.

"It's all right," I say, smiling. "Whatever you want, it's okay."

"Yeah. Sure. I'm just—I don't know. Maybe we could do that sometime. Was there anything else?"

"No. Nothing else."

"Thanks," he says. "Thanks for asking me."

"You're welcome."

The door slips shut.

I stand there.

Falling.

Why?

"Why are we doing this?" I say to Schuyler.

We're sitting in my room, lights turned out, on this dead and dying day, watching a computer screen. As if I haven't already fallen far enough.

The Kansas City Ghost Club.

Schuyler scrolls down the black chat board—the same sad screen names: Mandymoo, clARkaSHton, spookielee36, coldSPOT, TorqueMonkey. A dozen more. Endlessly chatting, flaming, flirting, fighting.

We're all watching the same long, grungy, empty, dimly lit, paint-peeling hallways in an abandoned hospital morgue.

Home page music: "Fear," by Disturbed. The streaming audio cranked to Maximum Crackle, listening for every little spectral knock. The club boasts EMF arrays, night vision, heat vision, thermal captures, all that energy, night after night, thrown out into the Void—

And nothing ever happens.

People from all over the country have capped hundreds of images from the ghost cams. Check the archives. An indistinct smudge—it's somebody's head. A fuzzy ball of light—a tormented soul trapped on the astral plane. But if you come here often enough, you finally begin to realize—

Nothing ever happens.

Maybe that's why I'm here.

I need this dreary dead-end place of the dead to teach me not to get my hopes up. That no matter how excited I get about things, how focused, how obsessed, ultimately—

Nothing ever happens.

"Look at the piano," Schuyler says.

He points at a battered upright squatting in the corner on one of the ghost cams.

"What about it?"

"It's moved since yesterday. I swear. I think Darkwillow Nightseer needs to let his Spirit Brothers know." His fingers fly across the keyboard.

I slump wearily across his shoulders, put my chin on his collarbone. I can feel his chest muscles move as he types. "That's easy for you to say. It'll be my IP address that gets deep fried this time."

"Aw, I promise to play nice."

I sigh. "Oh, go ahead. Who cares."

"What's bugging you?"

Mr. Mann.

Like the ghost hunters, I'm a believer in something nobody else can see.

"Nothing," I say. "Maybe I'm just too old for this."

What's happening here?

This isn't like me. I was happy. I was focused.

Kitty Nation follows me as I walk over and flop on my bed, watching Mars hurtling toward my window, getting closer and closer. I'm trying to remember the last time I did something crazy.

Two years ago.

We were having a snowball fight in front of Schuyler's house. We don't get snow here very often; the battle lasted for hours, it was so much fun. Finally the streetlamps came on, making the road sparkle. It was freezing cold, both of us so tired we could barely stand. We met under a light. I touched his cheek. It was frozen.

I can't explain what happened next.

If I could, I would say something like this: When I touched his face, a new kind of language came up inside me. A language made of ordinary words hooked together like molecules to make new ones: *smokecozyfire, whitehappyfrost.*

I kissed him.

Just leaned over and did it. I was just so happy at that moment, I guess I had to do something with it or burst. Why can't every single piece of your life work that way?

It was my first and only kiss. We didn't talk about it. Didn't say anything at all. We never kissed again.

The truth? I'm scared. He's too important for that. Boyfriends are people you break up with. Friends like Schuyler you keep forever.

So where does that leave Mr. Mann?

"Hey! Look at this!" Schuyler's shaking with laughter.

Mandymoo reports she has just seen Kurt Cobain on a lightbulb. Kill me.

angle of his light

Career Day.

No poets.

Even astronomers and astrophysicists are scarce. So, what else, I hang out with the engineers. I can't help but notice the mortician draws the largest crowd. *CSI* must be the hottest show on TV.

Drone, drone, blech. Is this what we have to look forward to? The world of adults feels like a universe that has reached the end of its expansion and is inexorably collapsing back in on itself.

Where is he?

Have I scared him into hiding? Pushed him too fast? Too far? Am I nuts? Imagining a connection that was never there?

After school I cruise by Sunlake, but his windows are dark. Somewhere galaxies are colliding, stars are bursting into thermonuclear flame. But there's all that space in between. Ultimately everything that exists is somehow alone.

At the Ground-Up Cow Face Burgers his table is bereft. I'm worse. I pull all the sesame seeds off a bun one at a time and mope like a sick kitten. Schuyler threatens to brand me with the chicken tongs.

Don't go crazy.

It'll be okay. But I can't stop. Can't stop thinking about the way he stands. How he twists his mouth when he's listening to something interesting. The dimple on his cheek. How he walks in long, deliberate strides.

His legs.

What do they look like inside his pants?

We've spent so much time together, talked so much. But there are still so many things I don't know. His parents? Alive or dead? Childhood. Painful or happy? Chest. Hairy or smooth?

What does he look like when he sleeps?

I touch my face, examine the imperfect reflection on the metal door where we keep the burger boxes.

Am I pretty enough?

It's hot in here. I could spontaneously combust. I run my fingers along the line of my jaw, pretending it's his. His arms would be warm around my shoulders. What's it like to look into those impossible eyes when our lips are touching?

"Carolina."

I jump a little bit. Mr. Mann is standing next to Wilkie Collins when I clock out. His clothes are black. His hands are inside his pockets as if he doesn't trust them. I'm astonished and overjoyed.

I'm not sure I know what to say. I'm just so happy he's here. "You're here," I say without thinking. "Why didn't you come inside?"

He doesn't answer. I tell myself I know why. Schuyler's gone home early. Mr. Mann has been waiting for just this time when we could be alone. Alone together.

"I'm sorry about the other day," he says. "I was worried about something, preoccupied."

"I thought so."

I watch him, wondering what do we do next. Stand here? Talk? Don't talk? Go somewhere in his car? It's happening, I realize. Oh my God. He's helping me climb.

I have to ask it:

"Are you still worried?"

"Yeah. No. Well, of course I am. I don't know."

All our familiarity counts for nothing now. This is a new country we are building between ourselves. After this, after waiting for me here like this, nothing can be seen as accidental, unintended. What does he want? Is it the same thing I want?

The night is cool, perfect for talking, but at first we don't talk. We lean side by side in the shadows, touching Wilkie's trim. Across the way Threatt and Country scoot by with the french fry grease. We hunch into the darkness as they empty the mess into a plank door padlocked in the asphalt. When they're gone, we walk over. The door is painted with a message:

$500 REWARD FOR INFORMATION
LEADING TO ARREST AND CONVICTION

"Arrest and conviction for what?" Mr. Mann says.

"Anybody stealing the grease."

"Why?"

I'm so thankful for something to talk about that is not connected to us, my relief almost makes me light-headed. "They sell it to cosmetics companies. They use it to make lipstick, junk like that."

The incandescent eyes widen. "Are you serious? Damn. Makes you think twice, doesn't it?"

"Good thing I don't wear any." What am I saying! In case—in case—just maybe. You want to—no, stop. Slow down. "Schuyler would dock you a quarter, by the way."

"Why?"

"We have an agreement to pay each other if we cuss. Schuyler says cussing is lazy. It's for people with lightweight vocabularies and fewer options."

"He doesn't much like me, does he?"

I'm saying too much, speaking too fast, but I can't help it. "Schuyler doesn't much like anybody. He can be pretty grandiose sometimes. I got him this job. He won't even try to get his license. His parents have to drive him if I don't. But he's amazing if you give him a chance."

He reaches over, touches the top of my hand.

"So are you."

my personal planet

Drive.

I follow.

We're moving slower than I would like. Maybe he's afraid of losing me.

We haven't said where we're going, but it's in the opposite direction of Sunlake. Everything around me is alive, bursting with feeling, meaning. But I'm a little sad for the other cars, their destinations.

I can't believe this is happening. But somehow I can.

We turn off the parkway, enter a service road. It's easy to see where we are going now. A massive wall of gray-and-crimson buildings pushes itself in front of us: the Wal-Mart Rule the World Super Center. I'm surprised. Not as many shoppers this late, but it still feels a little too public.

Ah.

Now I see where he's going. We circle around back to auto repair and park away from the lights next to a line of stunted trees. I'm on the left, he's on the right. We sit.

First Act of Societal Defiance: getting into his car.

This is not as simple as it sounds.

Stepping out, touching the silver handle of his door, hauling it open, heavy in my hands—each action shimmers in my brain like an aurora borealis. His car could be touched with St. Elmo's fire. It's not a car, but a ship at sea in some far northern place. Taking me somewhere.

Sit down.

"Hello," he says, as if we haven't been talking for the last couple of hours.

"Hi."

But everything is new. The interior makes me dizzy for a moment, the exciting scent of his concentrated presence. There's a stack of papers on the floor; he reaches down self-consciously while I hold my feet up and tosses the stuff in the back. I look, making the moment last. There's some kind of case on the backseat. I don't know what it is; he never brings anything but slides and printouts to class.

Seeing the teacher sticker on the windshield in reverse, the way he sees it every morning, makes me feel a little weird; this place is amazingly forbidden. I've broken and entered.

"Does this make you feel uncomfortable?" he says.

I don't want to answer the question. I turn to look at him.

"It's okay. I like it."

"Really?"

"It's okay. Really."

I'm not sure what to do. I'm waiting for him. He seems to be waiting too. Maybe I should say something.

"Are you an atheist?" Too much. Way, way too much.

"No. No, I don't think so. No."

"So you believe in an afterlife?"

"Sure."

I like that he doesn't hesitate on that one. Bonus points: he doesn't question my question. I talk quickly, suddenly afraid of thinking.

"Nothing against atheists. But, I mean, look at the world."

He smiles. "But an atheist might say the world is evidence there is no God."

"I'm talking about nature." I point my fingers at the strip of woods straddling a culvert where a stream used to run. "The real world. You have to believe in God to believe in trees."

"Oh."

Be quiet. I settle back in the seat. I'm talking too much.

"So, your family, do you go to church?" he says.

"No. We used to when I was little. We're Methodists. I think my parents finally just got tired. All that extra stuff you have to do when you belong to a church. Fund-raising for stuff that doesn't really matter, plus all the social junk. So I kind of have my own thing."

"Church? Or religion."

"I don't know what you'd call it. It's really important to me. Being spiritual. It's just that—it's just I feel closer to it in a forest, under the stars, than I do in a building."

"Yeah. I understand that. Me too."

If I gulp air any faster, I'll be hiccoughing. But I can't stop; stopping might let in too much.

"See, I have this theory. In the afterlife we're all gods. So after I die, I'll come back to Earth and stitch together all the overlooked, abandoned pieces of city forest into an Undiscovered Country. Then I can be its king." He's supposed to laugh at this last little part, but when it comes out, it doesn't sound like something funny.

"King Carolina. I like that." He touches my hand—it's the first time he's touched me since I got in his car. It sends a delicious shiver up my back. "I don't like to think about you dying."

God.

For the millionth time I secretly guess his age. I would ask, but asking would bring the difference into it. Let's say twenty-seven. I'll be eighteen soon, so when he's seventy-nine, I'll be seventy. Practically no difference at all.

"Boys?" he says.

I suddenly realize he's asking a question.

"A few should be allowed to live."

He laughs. "No, I mean, you don't have a boyfriend, do you?"

"I know what you meant. Maybe I just don't know how to answer the question. I have a friend who's a boy; you've met him. That's about it."

"Do you date much?"

What should I tell him? That I haven't been on a date my whole senior year? That I haven't wanted to? That the sum total of my experience with the opposite sex consists of a few fumbled moments with Schuyler in the snow?

I study the Wal-Mart wall. "I'm afraid of stopping," I say.

"Stopping?"

"I don't know if I can explain."

"Try."

Now I am getting light-headed, drunk on contact with his skin. "Stopping my life," I say. "Stopping my dreams. I think maybe—I think I'm afraid sex will strand me with some stupid guy who won't understand me, won't let me do the things I've come here to do. I—"

"It's okay," Mr. Mann says.

As desperately as I want him to hold me, it helps that we are just sitting here first. That he has this perfect chance, but he's showing control. The door can still be opened. I can still get out, walk away.

"I'm sorry," I say. "I've never done anything like this before. Ever. I don't want you to think—"

"I know. I know." He looks at me. "It's okay. I'm not like this, either. I mean, I've never done this before. Well, not with a—not with someone from school. I'm not like that. I want you to know that. You're just so . . . different."

Gulp. "I hope that's good."

"Different? Sure. Different is good. Different is—goddamn amazing."

It's too much. I pause to take a breath.

"It's not that—that I didn't have chances with guys. It's just so important, you know? Who it is, why you do what you do. I think everybody's here for a reason. We're not supposed to waste our lives just messing around. There are too many fantastic, amazing things to do. You can't screw it up."

He smiles with his eyes. "How'd you get so intense?"

I think about it. I remember the message on his answering machine. "I'm like Mark Twain."

"Twain?"

"He said he was *born excited*. I understand that. That's me. I don't waste time on people who aren't. I can't. I have this Master Plan."

"What? Tell me about it."

"You'll think it's crazy."

"No, I won't." He holds up three fingers like a Boy Scout, making me smile. Making me safe. "I promise," he says. "Tell me."

"I'm going to——" Should I really say it? Make it real? Take another breath. "I'm going to discover things people have never seen. Unbelievable things. Beautiful things that will change everything we know about the universe. Where it came from, where it's going. What it is. Who we are. Someday they'll all want me, and then——"

He leans over, puts a finger to my mouth.

"It's all right. I believe you."

Is that what I'm trying to do? Make him believe?

What if I'm messing it all up?

What if I'm too strange, too stupid, too smart? What if I've let too much of myself out? What if the inner, secret Me is a brick in a wall I'm building between us? Maybe he wants someone else. Someone more, someone less, someone braver, stronger, weaker, wilder, crazy, pretty, sane——

Suddenly he circles my shoulders with his arm, pulls me to

him. It's happening. It's happening. I close my eyes, letting go, letting go, letting go.

We stop. Still holding.

"Bucket seats suck," he says.

Yes.

We move to Wilkie Collins.

The reverberating screech of the passenger door momentarily keeps us apart. Now the moment is new all over again. I'm embarrassed. The dusty seats, the french fry smell. Still, we slide our hips together. His arm settles around my shoulders again. I feel the heat of his torso. I'm instantly overloaded. My non-corporeal body blows out to the edges of the galaxy, swallowing a billion billion stars.

I open my eyes and look into his.

I am here.

This is what I've wanted. Everything is breaking open. Everything I've revolved about, my core. Everything is crumbling, opening. It's going to happen, it is. His arms are pulling me up to the last, sweet place. Cracking my imagination like a mold that was wrong and small.

Yes.

Our faces come together. Like people meeting in a hallway, we can't figure out which way to lean. His eyes are shiny. What does he see in mine? What does he see in me?

I feel a choking coming in my throat. "You could have anyone. Anyone."

"Your mind," he whispers, eyes moving as if to intercept my thoughts.

"I'm yours?"

"Mind-*duh*. With a *d*. It's luminous. It dazzles me. I wish I could describe how you make me feel. I'm supposed to be good with words. But I'm speechless. Lost."

But how could he be? How could he be all of those things that I am?

"God," I say. "You—it's everything. I'm coming apart, I'm coming to pieces—"

He kisses me.

Until this moment, this time, until my mouth opens against his opening mouth, until his tongue touches mine, gentle, alive—it has always been something that might only be a thought, a wisp of fantasy, a dream. Something that might never happen.

Now it's very real and I can't stop feeling that it's real. The sensations I didn't know to expect are there, magnified, huge. I didn't know I would hear the blood moving through my ears. I didn't know a blue light would turn on in my head, beginning with a tiny dot and growing to become a circle. I didn't know everything would happen slow and fast.

I didn't know he would taste this sweet.

My hand moves up, discovering his face. His jaw is lightly bristled with evening whiskers. My hand touches both our faces, feeling the joining of our lips as it is happening.

"I can't believe it," I say when our faces move apart.

"I'm sorry."

"No, I can't believe it."

I can't stop shaking, either.

I'm on completely alien ground. Levitation is a possibility. Before I can absorb the consequence of the first one, he kisses me again.

"Maybe you'd better run," Mr. Mann says when we surface for air.

I open my eyes, try to sound as if my head is still attached. "Where?"

Because there is no other place.

His laugh sounds bitter. "Damn it."

We kiss again. My head is totally gone; there is nothing left but my heart. Suddenly I'm not afraid anymore.

"I love you," I whisper.

I hope he can't see my tears in this light. I burrow my face into his chest and smell the day on his shirt. He clenches his fist against my back and speaks into my neck. His voice is warm.

"I didn't mean to take it this far."

I lift my blurry eyes. "That still means you meant to take it."

magnification of breath

Joy.

Holy sweet goodness.

It's with me every waking moment.

But it's a terrified, shivering, fragile joy. The next morning I wake up silently shrieking, the sheets in knots around my legs. Did it happen?

Has he forgotten? Changed his mind? Lost it?

The world is a whole new place.

I touch my fingers to my lips. Feel him there. I would know for sure if I could see him.

But—no!—I've got a dentist appointment today. I miss his class.

The dentist says my wisdom tooth, the one that's lying on its side, the slacker, should come out as soon as I can schedule it. I'm not listening; I'm staring deep into the oval-shaped light above my head. There are thousands of little golden diamonds glistening there. They help me focus. I don't want to think about anything that takes me away from thinking about Him.

God, it happened. It did.

I'm sugar-shock frantic by the time I get to school.

Mr. Mann is sitting with the other teachers in the lunchroom.

He's swinging his fork, legs thrown out casually, ankles crossed. I'm desperate to talk to him, hear his voice, confirm by some semaphore or sign the connection between us. But approaching the teacher tables today would feel like running naked through the mall with my hair on fire.

I hope he can see me.

I watch his mouth move as he talks, eats, smiles—how beautiful. Now it's my mouth too, in its own way. I have laid claim to it. My lips, my teeth, my tongue. How can he be using all of them without touching some part of me?

But today, in this new light, I'm not sure of anything. The space between us, the emptiness, the distance, could be a guarantee last night was a dream—no, a fever. Maybe if I—

"Where've you been?" Schuyler says, plunking down on the plastic seat next to me, making it go *schooch* on the floor, pinching my arm. "Listen."

He's gushing about something that happened five hundred million years after the Big Bang, the beginning of the universe, perfectly certain that I care. His hair is shaped like a bell with only one side, a living entity separate from the rest of his body. But he's so cute in a Schuyler way. Red barbecue chicken gore stuck to his teeth, Vlad the Astrophysicist.

"So before stars, galaxies, quasars could form, the temperature drops in all that empty space and it starts snowing!" he says. "All over the universe! Hydrogen snow!"

I sit in my own empty space, the one-half meter of nothingness around my chair, let his voice flurry over me.

The gabble of voices around us makes me feel like I'm in a nuthouse. Excuse me, an asylum. My mouth paradoxically hurts from too much attention and too little. I can't stand this lack of control, this ache that can't be instantly addressed, only magnified by all the other aches around me.

Each moment away from him feels like a slippage, a backsliding into the miserable kiddieland where I lived before. I have to be active about this or I will lose him forever. I don't care how crazy this feels. I only care that I—

He stands up.

"I've got to go," I say.

I grab my tray and rush after him.

I catch him beside the garbage cans. He smiles, but not too hugely. "Carolina." This is the only name in the world for me anymore. We scrape our trays with ultra-deliberateness.

"Hi," I say.

"Hi. You don't have to whisper."

"Hi."

"I'm happy to see you too."

"I still can't believe it. I'm trying to make myself believe. Intellectually I know. I know that it happened. It's just—it's just so good."

"Yes. It happened. It did. I thought about it all—"

Somebody comes by. Mr. Mann says hello, glances around nervously, hunching over his empty tray as if deciding on a last secret bite of something that is already gone. It isn't safe here; I can tell that's what he's thinking.

"Of course. Of course it happened," he says. "You were there."

"I was there!" I'm sounding so stupid, but right now I don't care.

"But where were you this morning? I missed you in class."

He missed me! He was thinking about me at the very same time. We have to talk about this. I have to remember it so we can. And try to get the time just right. The exact moment. Crazy. This is crazy.

"The dentist," I say. "I'm sorry! I couldn't help it! He says I need to get my wisdom tooth out. Great."

"Don't be sorry; it's okay. Really." He lowers his voice. "The lucky bastard. That means he gets to see you again. Maybe I'll be sick that day."

This makes me smile as though I might never stop smiling.

"Any cavities?" he says.

"Nope," I say. "Well, one."

"Where?"

I start to touch my chest right where my shirt is buttoned. "Here," I want to say. "Right here." At the very last second, I realize how idiotic that would look. What am I turning into?

"Nope, not really."

He grins. "How can you *not really* have a cavity?"

"I'll tell you about it later."

"Don't," he says.

"What?"

Somebody else has got his attention again.

We shove our trays together through the slot in the wall, meaty steam bathing our faces. He heads out the door into the empty hall.

"We probably shouldn't be doing this," he says when I catch up.

I'm wounded infinitely. It's as if a rogue star has raced across my path, ripped my sun away. I apparently can't keep the pain out of my face.

"Damn. I'm sorry, no, I didn't mean to scare you. I didn't mean last night. No! I meant talking about it at school. It's—you can't believe how bad it would be. We have to be really careful. You know that."

I'm back, out-of-body experience over. "Oh. Oh. You're right. I'm sorry, that was stupid. I'm sorry. Sometimes it's just—you know that feeling you get when you're not sure anything is—"

He reaches over, squeezes my hand. Just as quickly, he lets go, is looking straight ahead, speaking to me sideways. "Don't be sorry. Don't ever be sorry at all. Meet me after school. Wait for me in your car. It'll be about thirty minutes after everybody else is gone. Can you?"

Can I?

My heart flies away.

It's real.

His shoulder brushes my hair as he turns to go. Now I'm an exploding star, a supernova, throwing out all my energy in a single titanic burst radiated directly at his departing back:

Love.

I love him so much.

For a long time I close my eyes walking up the hall after he's gone. Knowing there is no possible way I can hit anything. Not now, not ever.

dawn of creation

Wait.

I'm in a frenzy of anticipation the rest of the day.

His car is still there when I come out of the gym. Kids are streaming past me. For once in my life, I can't study them. I'm not even a part of their species anymore.

I sit in Wilkie Collins, head down, as if interested in something in my lap. I wish I had a book to read, but the only thing in the glove box is a cheapie Easy Eye paperback from Mom's seventies collection. I can't concentrate enough to read anyway, especially *Return of the Native*. I'm parked a few rows from his Honda, every muscle tense, body quivering with questions: What now? Where to from here?

It's the ultimate exercise in self-control.

There.

I laser beam him with my eyes as he slowly makes his way from the gym to the little green car in the teachers' lot. How I worship his walk. Why isn't the ground cracking open in his wake? Why aren't the clouds above his sweet head moving in a weird new way?

Why do I love him so much? What is it? I think it might be this:

He's not showing me a new world; he's showing me an old one. One I've kept buried deep inside under layers of science, grades, math, my parents' expectations, my hyper-developed sense of responsibility, my achiever's overdrive—

It's a world without boundaries. One that I remember from being a kid. A world beyond measure, beyond physical stuff. A world that's more like the universe than science will ever be.

That's what he's promising me, whether he knows it or not. He said it himself: *It's a mystery*.

I roll down the window; he puts his hands in.

"Follow me."

I follow slowly out of the lot and we drive forever across town to an overgrown research park waiting for future soft industry. I've seen this place before with Dad. Because of NASA, Huntsville is a high-tech boom town, gobbling up land as fast as it can be annexed and zoned.

Right now this place is nothing but monster roads cutting through a lot of meadows and cotton fields gone fallow. We find a dead cul-de-sac and come to a stop at the broken end of the asphalt under the shade of a sycamore tree. We're surrounded by acres of waving broom sage the color of straw, a massive sedge pond across the way. A long bird with its legs hanging down flaps by and settles in the water. Everything, the world, is so large today.

He slides in next to me. I'm so hungry for him, I can barely breathe.

"It'll be safe here," he says, taking my hands. I can't speak. "This is the worst and the best thing I could ever do," he says. "I got home last night, told myself, *You're crazy. What the hell are you doing?* But seeing you here, now—I missed you so much. It nearly drove me insane."

His arms.

We kiss for hours or minutes, I'm not sure which. I'm completely smothered by my need for him. Have I ever been anywhere else but here in his arms? Is this our place? Our new home? In between kisses we watch lines on the pond, the bird, the sun pushing the sky around. But mostly we just look at each other. He's framing my face with his big hands. I love the smell of his hair.

I've never seen anyone more beautiful in my life.

It's real.

He hasn't gone, vanished, become something that only exists in this universe part of the time. For a very long time we don't talk as much.

We're too busy creating joy.

More time.

What happens to it?

The hours and weeks run together into May like watercolors.

I'm so hungry for his touch, I could hold him for days or years. We see the unseen side of every shopping mall, the backs of dozens of stores. His car has working air; mine has couches. The state park. Abandoned playgrounds. A particular church. But the place by the pond is best.

Today we're sitting there in tall grass on the edge of a sheltered meadow.

Mr. Mann is sitting behind me, massaging my neck and shoulders with both hands, his legs beneath my legs. No one has ever done this for me before. Ever. It's hard to keep still; I feel selfish. But he's also making me feel so impossibly good, so loved.

Let him.

In the distance a coyote tracks its way through a deadfall on the edge of the wood. The falling sun is painting the new leaves gold. There is no place on earth but this, a sheltered meadow exactly equidistant between two industrial complexes. But only on Sunday afternoons. The rest of the time it's a concrete plant.

"The trucks and buildings are just the other side of those trees," Mr. Mann says. "Oops, there goes one."

"A truck?"

"Nope. I sometimes see tiny spots in front of my eyes. They call them vitreous floaters."

"Weird. Do they bother you?"

"It's no big deal." He moves his hands down my back, around my sides, making me squirm. I am one gigantic nerve ending, raw, but not raw with pain, only pleasure. He goes on.

"I remember the first day I ever saw them, the floaters—I was fourteen and terrified. We were camping, getting ready to go to Six Flags. Nobody would believe me that I was seeing spots. I thought I was dying. Or that maybe there was something in the pool water."

"What do they look like?"

He thinks about it, squinting. "Tiny corkscrews and geometric patterns. But very indistinct. Diaphanous. I can see right through them most of the time."

"My, what a big vocabulary you have, Grandma."

"The better to eat—"

"Uh uh uh." I wag a finger over my head; he closes his teeth over it.

"My ears ring all the time," I say, touching his lips behind me when he lets my finger go. "It's called tinnitus. It's not bad. I only notice it when it's super-quiet. A kid threw a bunch of cherry bombs in a campfire when I was lying beside it."

He's nuzzling my neck now, moving along the hairline, lightly nibbling. "Lying?"

"Okay, gutter mind." I laugh. "It was a church picnic. There were a bunch of kids around. I was thirteen. The big drama of the evening was a girl who tried to run away from home with a Barbie suitcase full of five hundred pennies."

His hands move down and he hugs me around my middle, face against my cheek, his legs thrown out on either side of me now.

"Why? Why did she want to run away?"

"She thought she was pregnant."

"God. At thirteen!"

"From French kissing."

He laughs and kisses my right ear, takes the lobe gently in his teeth. "I'm sorry. I'm sure it was sad. Did she make it?"

"Nope."

"We never do, do we?"

I turn in his arms, straddling his legs so I can look at his face. His eyes are the color of newborn stars. "Did you try to run away?"

"I tried a lot of things. Almost."

"There you go again. No Emily talk today. So you were a messed-up kid?"

He doesn't talk much about his childhood. I have to wonder how happy he was.

"Yep, pretty much. But I can touch my elbows behind my back," he says. "If I stand holding a door frame and push. At least I think I still can. Tell me something about you."

I think. "I have to spit in every river I cross. It's almost a compulsion."

"Ha. I like that. What if you're in a car?"

"Then you get to experience what engineers call a little blowback."

"Hee. Okay. My turn. Let's see. I won a national poetry award back when I was dumb enough to think it was easy."

"Really? Why didn't you keep going?"

"Health benefits sucked."

"No, really." I run my fingers over his eyebrows, smoothing them.

"There's not much to tell. It just wasn't going anywhere. Poets get paid worse than hamburger flippers. No offense."

"None taken. Can I read it sometime?"

"Sure."

"Okay. Here's something. I cried the first time I saw a Hubble picture of Supernova 1987A."

He touches the tip of my nose with the point of his tongue. "With a name like that, sounds like a tax form. I'd cry too."

"You wouldn't say that if you saw it. I'll show you on the net. It looks just like the symbol for infinity with a ring of fire super-imposed over it."

"No shit, really?"

"Exactly."

He suddenly kisses me deeply; we don't speak for a while. All thoughts are pushed out, replaced by sensation.

"Apples?" he says when we pull apart.

"Gala," I say.

"Fuji."

"I can live with that. Sure."

We move ever closer to a center.

Eighteen.

Twice Nine.

It's my birthday today.

What does this number mean to me now?

It used to mean graduation, freshman year at college, one more candle on my cake.

Now it's something waited for, yearned for, desperate, dying, living, hungry, howling—

Fearing.

Am I scared? I am.

Am I brave? I hope.

But.

Somehow I don't feel one bit different.

Somehow everything feels different.

Has he touched me?

Yes. A thousand times.

But.

Has he touched me?

A mountain of fire rushes at my head.

I'm back to Earth.

Oh—I'm here. It's my birthday dinner.

My folks, the Greens, Schuyler. We're all sitting in my favorite Japanese restaurant. The hostess is beating a gong; the chef is juggling eggs with a spatula. Skewers are whirling in front of my nose around one knuckle of a single finger. Now he's threatening to singe off my eyebrows with fountains of flammable saki. Anything to snare my attention.

I'm barely noticing. Schuyler pokes me with a chopstick, missing my right boob by the width of a bra strap.

"Hey!" he says. "Snap out of it. What are you thinking about? You've been on Planet Nine all day."

"What?"

"Earth to birthday girl. They're about to sing."

"Oh no, you didn't."

"Don't look at me."

I endure it. I have to.

I know I've been neglecting Schuyler, and he knows it too. But what can I do? What can I tell him? This thing I have going on, this love, is so huge, so real—Schuyler would never understand. It would freak him out completely. I don't know if I could ever get him back. As much as I would hope he of all people would get it—he wouldn't. I don't know if anybody on the outside can.

Worst-case scenario:

He might even turn Mr. Mann in.

Shit.

Middle English, Schuyler would say, and dock me a quarter. But this is the first time I've thought of that possibility. Now I'm eighteen, sure. But for the moment, Mr. Mann is still my teacher.

And the longer the deception goes on, the worse it gets. I hate lying. Like the way I've been lying to Schuyler about the watercolor lessons I'm supposedly taking on the nights when I don't work. Luckily, he hates art, so there haven't been many questions. Which of course would just lead to more lying.

The chef has made a volcano out of an onion. He's slipped it next to my plate.

Time to go.

"I've got to run some errands before the places close," I tell Mom and Dad when we're done.

"I'll help," Schuyler says.

"Nope. It's not anything big. Just some things I need for my art lessons."

"Oh." No way he's coming now. Great.

I thank everybody and pull out from the curb before he gets a chance to climb in.

I hate lying to Schuyler—I hate lying in general. But I have to get rid of him somehow. If he finds out what I'm up to, what's going to happen tonight—he would call me insane. He just might try to stop me.

But.

I have the inertia of worlds on my side. He might as well try to stop a spinning planet. Try to stop the seasons from the tilt of the earth's polar axis. Try to stop the tides from the pull of the moon.

I'm going.

the house of tomorrow

Now.

My last chance.

This is it. I have arrived at every parent's nightmare:

His apartment.

I'm not as terrified as I should be. Everything is golden. The sun is falling into the lake—you can see it from here. Mr. Mann goes up first, unlocks the door, slips inside. I wait a few beats down in Wilkie Collins, realizing I could wait much longer, even forever. This is not something he is making me do. I'm choosing this, to be here, now, with him. He's giving me the best way out.

I don't take it.

I climb the wooden stairs, hands not even touching the railings. There's a moment on the landing when I'm looking at the lake, still have the choice before me. I rap the knocker, feeling elated and electrified.

The door to number 220 opens.

Mr. Mann appears, pulling his fingers through his hair, a well-fancy-meeting-you-here look on his face. The door clicks shut behind us; the moment is over. Mr. Mann throws his keys on the table, eyes apologetic.

"Welcome to Casa Mañana," he says.

"The House of Tomorrow?"

"It's small, but I like the location. Close to school."

I hear myself in the single word: *school.*

Quiet.

I look around. His apartment is a pepperoni pizza: Papa John's, thin crust. Wal-Mart bookshelves. Particleboard furniture. White plastic chairs. Not enough light. A cretaceous-era Macintosh squats in the corner. The sink is a ziggurat of dishes.

"I meant to get to those," he says, as if I would care.

There's a gift sitting in the center of the small table, silver foil tied with a green ribbon curled at the ends with scissors.

"Happy birthday," he says.

My eyes fill. "Really? I can't believe you got me something too."

I tear at the foil; it's a heavy glass jar with something golden inside. I hold it up to the light. The label says TRAPPIST, below that, SEVILLE MARMALADE.

"The monks! You didn't."

He doesn't answer, instead unscrews the cap, dips his index finger in. The scent of oranges floods the room.

"Taste."

I take his finger in my mouth.

We move together in the center of the room. Circling each other, almost a dance. He's constantly touching. My cheek, my back, my neck. His fingers are as long as mine. Through a narrow door I see his bed waiting in sallow dimness. He catches me looking.

"What are you thinking?" he says.

"You once told me teaching is your second-greatest passion. I was wondering about your first."

"Ah. Here we go."

But instead of leading me to the bedroom, he's rummaging on a shelf. He pulls out a square brown case. What's he doing? I make a grab at it. He holds it away.

"But what is it?"

"Nope. I'm master of this box."

"Let me see, please."

He fends me off, laughing. "Nope. You're in here."

"I am?" I can't describe how good this makes me feel. "How can I be in there? Is it a journal?"

Instead of answering, he swings to face the shelf and unsnaps the box, extracts a CD. He drops it into a Bose Wave Radio, the one nice thing he owns. I pick up the CD cover, puzzled: *Split Enz*, *Soft Cell*, *Gary Numan*, *Wall of Voodoo*. Who are these people?

"New Wave," Mr. Mann says. "Circa 1982. I was just hitting

puberty. Huge vinyl albums were still the rage. Music videos were brand-new. MTV wasn't even a year old."

I don't hear any of the rest. I'm frantically doing the math:

Just hitting puberty = 1982.

He's in his thirties. Maybe as old as thirty-five.

God.

Nearly twice my age. This is a body blow. I realize my mouth is gaping; I snap it shut and do my best to recover. Does this make a difference? Is he changed because he's older?

Am I?

"You—you said I'm in there."

"You are. All that longing. All those crushing feelings. New Wave helped me get through it. We didn't know it at the time, but New Wave was just an extension of disco. The anti-disco disco. A lot of it was atonal as shit but still danceable as hell."

He turns up the sound. A driving guitar begins thumping the walls.

"Billy Idol, 'Dancing with Myself,'" Mr. Mann says.

He lets go of my fingers and does a goofy Molly Ringwald *Breakfast Club* kick step. First one foot, then the other, dipping his head to the beat. He looks ridiculous and surreal. I adore him.

He's saying something.

"What?"

He stops dancing and turns down the volume. "I knew you would like Billy."

"I do," I lie. "But if you're talking old, my taste runs more to the Cranberries."

He laughs bitterly. "Ancient!"

"Or Johnny Cash."

"Good God, prehistoric." He means it this time.

"Watch his video, *Hurt*," I say quickly. I'm not used to defending my love for a man born around the time Pluto was discovered. "A million years old and he's covering a Nine Inch Nails song."

Mr. Mann grins. "Tell me something else you like. Something I don't know."

It's hard.

Wildflowers. Goofy old musicals like *Meet Me in St. Louis* or *Seven Brides for Seven Brothers*. Thanks, Mom. Carpentry. Thanks, Dad. Colonial archaeology. Historical trees. These I blame on myself.

"Historical trees?" he says.

"They collect the seeds from famous trees around the country and sell them. You can buy acorns from George Washington's Mount Vernon tulip poplar."

His eyes are sadly joyful. To be looked at this way feels . . . spiritual.

"How did I find you in Alabama?" he says.

"And on a Shoe Day, too."

"What?"

"Y'all godless Yankees think we're all barefoot racist rednecks."

"And your point is?"

I shove him. He responds by taking me in his arms and kissing me hard.

His tongue moves inside my mouth, lightly brushing my tongue and finding the edges of my teeth. My legs go boneless. It overwhelms me that I overwhelm him.

"You're so damn . . . tall," he says. "I've never kissed anyone tall before."

I want to tell him the things I've never done before.

The couch is fake leather and cold.

My hand moves under his shirt. His chest is unfashionably hairy. I like it. What is he thinking? Touching me. What am I thinking? I'm blown away by competing sensory inputs. The words I need are too big.

There is a shocking pinpoint of decision, then his hand cups my breast. I respond with an involuntary, liquid sigh. It's strange to be adored, understood, hungered for. Most of the time I'm still not used to it.

He frowns and pulls away. His voice is almost inaudible. "This is where I'm supposed to be strong."

I twist a piece of his hair around my ring finger. "Why."

"I'm sorry, Carolina. It shouldn't be like this. Not your first— I'm not thinking straight." He sits up and massages his forehead. "All of this, you, it's making me do crazy—"

"I'm not crazy."

"But—"

It's my turn to stop him with a kiss. We linger, lips barely touching, breathing each other's air. His resistance without resisting is— irresistible.

Move.

We go in.

The bedroom brightens and darkens. The only illumination is a couple of fat yellow candles on a nightstand in the corner. They smell nothing at all like vanilla. He had to take the plastic off them. For all I know, he bought them for just this occasion.

The walls are bare except for a large framed poster of Emily. She floats like a ghost above the bed, neck long, face pale, hair tight as Lycra pants. She's not smiling but looks as if she could.

The reality of the first kiss was nearly beyond my comprehension. What can prepare you for a time like this?

Nothing.

As we get on the bed, I'm numb, standing somewhere outside myself. Processing oceans of thought right to the very end. Assembling impressions, observations, moments, touches, exhalations. It's impossible to keep up with this kind of flow. I'm a satellite passing through a powerful magnetic storm, all my sensors pinging at the limits of their range.

Mr. Mann presses his lips together determinedly, pulls my shirt slowly over my head. I cover myself instinctively with my arms. My skin prickles with goose bumps. He kisses them, moves his mouth up under my arm. The feeling as he kisses me there is indescribable. He helps me to straighten my arms.

My turn. I unbutton his shirt, throw it on the floor. I spend an uncertain amount of time nuzzling his newly exposed skin. Every part of my body is suddenly connected to my toes.

I feel myself changing, shifting. Now I'm tugging at his pants and then at mine. He's kissing me everywhere, squeezing me, running his fingers over places no one else has touched.

It's too much; it's frying my wiring. I close my eyes. The same thin blue light starts up again, just like when he kissed me. It starts as a line behind my eyelids. The blue line grows, becomes an arc, then a circle. I'm suddenly aware of the miracle of my bare skin against his bare skin. Just as the blue circle behind my eyes is completing itself, he—

Now there is no thought. It's not possible anymore. Everything is scattered. All control and focus are gone.

I break an unspoken promise to myself not to cry.

Not from the pain. It hurts, just as he said it would. But it hurts in more ways than he even knows. It hurts the way dying must hurt, if you truly see a new world rushing at you.

"Richard."

It's the first time I've ever said his name out loud. I try it again and again.

electromagnetic love

Sweet.

Indescribably sweet.

It's Saturday morning.

My heart tells me first—the world is still here. I'm letting it settle around me. I would have spent all morning in bed if I could. Reliving it all. Everything, him. Us. The outlines on the wall. But maybe I would never get up ever again.

But I have to. I'm helping Mom make my cake. There wasn't time yesterday since I was gone. Gone. Is that what I was? I have never been more Here. We're using my favorite green ceramic bowl. I inhale the scent of vanilla extract, touching my fingers to my lips, my tongue, remembering.

The candlelight, his bed. Emily watching over us, a pearly, schoolmarmish god. The end of it all, when I opened my eyes just in time to see him open his. The paradoxical feeling of safety and release in his arms. I didn't wash his scent off. He's still there.

It happened.

"No," Mom says. "Oh no."

She has to run to the store for lemon juice. While she's gone, I sit at the table stirring languidly, letting my eyes go in and out of focus, staring a thousand yards out the window at nothing.

This seeing without seeing is comfortable, reassuring. I don't want to lose it. Then it hits me: this is the single happiest moment of my life. It's funny Mr. Mann is not here to share it. He's the engine of its existence.

"You want to talk about it?" Dad suddenly says from behind me.

He approaches life the way he pores over an electrical schematic. Missing the wiring necessary to intuit, he has methodically, patiently learned to observe.

I know I've heard his voice, but I keep staring out the window. You can always talk to people. A moment like this might not come again.

"What?" I say finally.

He gives my shoulder a paternal Vulcan pinch.

"Nine."

"Yeah?"

"What are you thinking about? College? Moving out?"

"Nothing."

How could I even begin? I can't. I turn on my toes and stretch to kiss him on the cheek. His big gray eyes are watery and golden at the center. He sighs.

"You remember, I'm sure, there are several different types of Nothing," he says. "There's the Nothing that is pure zero and the Nothing that is a negation. One is just before the birth of everything, the Nothing of not having been born. The other is the Nothing after the death of everything, the Nothing that is beyond all existence."

"Charles S. Pierce, *Logic of Events*."

"Good girl."

"I never thought about it before, but he's talking about the Big Bang, isn't he? Before the creation of the universe and after its death."

"In 1898?"

"Well."

"So which Nothing are you thinking about?"

I rock my chair back with my sock feet. "Neither."

"Then, by process of elimination, you must be thinking about a Something."

I sure am. The biggest Something ever. The Something that has cracked open my life and set me free. "I don't think I can put it into words."

"Like to try?"

"No. I'm happy, that's all."

His shoulders relax. "I'm glad. I'm going to miss you something terrible. Where do the years go?" It's his turn to stare out the window. "Do you remember when I carried you over the Haunted Bridge at Moore's Mill? That tree fort we built that almost killed the sweet gum? Do you—?" He stops, eyes misting, unable to continue. "Come here."

I put down the spoon and he hugs me into his Old Spice. It's been a long time since we've done this. His gray hair needs a trim; the way it floats above his collar in the back makes me need to cry.

Love must be an electromagnetic field that attracts like particles. Then I think of it—just as there is more than one kind of Nothing, there's more than one kind of Love, too. I've always had the kind that was there before there was anything.

Now I have the kind that is there after everything else is gone.

throbbing star

NASA.

The Marshall Space Flight Center.

This is my birthday treat.

Well, second best.

I can't stop thinking about the first. To be apart from Mr. Mann tonight is exquisitely painful. But there's a deliciousness to my agony that wasn't there before—I know he's not going away. I know it's real. It's real inside my skin. It's real throughout my bones.

Tonight I'm sitting with Dad in the Morris Auditorium. The same place where Werner von Braun used to speak to the troops. We're waiting on a film.

"Hi, Dan, Pete."

Dad knows just about everybody here, some of them going back to his Apollo days. I know a lot of them too. There are two hundred people in the audience, almost all engineers and aerospace types. Chrome domes, black eyeglasses, and mismatched clothing are inordinately well represented.

I desperately wish Mr. Mann could be here. I wish everyone else couldn't. We're watching a blank screen on a stage surrounded by walls built of local limestone. The head of the Chandra X-Ray Observatory comes out and speaks.

This is a movie of a pulsar in the Crab Nebula. A pulsar is a rotating neutron star that spews radiation out from its poles. The movie was made by stringing together photographs taken by the Chandra over a period of months.

The lights go down; the film begins.

Gasps.

The nebula is rippling, pulsing, enormous, alive. A gigantic red heart twenty trillion miles wide.

I miss him with that kind of ache.

woman exponential

Come closer.

I'll let you in.

There's a halo around the moon tonight. This happens when ice crystals refract the light in high cirrus clouds. Right now I could hug the world.

We're standing in a field behind the Sunlake tennis courts. The johnson grass makes my legs itch. Somewhere a bird thinks it's morning.

"When the Chinese look at the moon, they don't see a man, they see a rabbit," I say. "What do you see?"

"John Lennon."

I jab him in the ribs. "Pay attention."

Mr. Mann hovers clumsily over the eyepiece. Finally I see the full moon painted in miniature on his eyeball. "Well, I'll be switched," he says in his best faux hillbilly. "It's shot plumb full of holes!"

I push him out of the way and put my eye in his place. "Stop teasing me about my accent. You come from a state with toll roads."

"And better schools."

"Kids on crack."

"Crystal meth."

"Pond-fed catfish."

"Swordfish. With almondine sauce."

"Pork barbecue. With white sauce."

"Got me there. Truce."

"Truce." We shake hands.

I feel him behind me now, his breath on my neck. His arms encircle my waist.

"Besides," he says, "that's not teasing; this is."

Slowly he brings his hands up my stomach and then my chest until they surround my breasts. His touch spreads heat throughout my body like a fast-acting drug. We rush to pack the scope away.

He's right.

Sex is more intimate than stratospheric.

This is what I'm thinking about as he's lying in my arms after it's finished. I watch a square of reflected light above the bed. The feeling is this: not being able to get close enough.

I'm desperate to occupy his exact same space-time coordinates. The largest expanse of his skin must touch the largest expanse of mine. Dad could calculate the total area in square centimeters. I do it in kisses.

"How many?" I say.

"How many what?"

"You know."

"Women?" He scratches his hair. "I can count them on one hand."

Somewhere inside I'm infinitely glad he said *women* and not *girls*. I guess I should have known there were some. There had to be. Now I know I can finally ask it.

"Why didn't you ever get married?"

"Ah." He stretches out to his full magnificent length. I marvel at my access to his body, how I can study every part of it; he doesn't mind a bit.

"Now that's the great mystery, isn't it?" he says.

"Not another one of those conversations. Let's keep this one a little more anchored, Little Cloud."

"Ouch." He smiles. "Well, I did almost get married once."

I look at the wall teasingly. "Like Emily?"

"A really sweet girl from New Orleans. She had black hair, liked to eat rocky road ice cream. Her name was—"

"I don't have to know that."

"Okay. I'm sorry. She tried to get me interested in Cajun music by taking me to see a bunch of awful zydeco bands. We were living in this dinky rental house close to Lake Pontchartrain—"

"I don't want to hear about it." The more he talks about this girl, this *woman*, the more real she becomes and the less real I become. Living together. That's not an arithmetic leap from where I am. It's exponential.

Should I push it? How much do I want to know? What is it like for him, on that side, the decision?

"How old would I have to be?" I say.

"What?"

"Never mind."

"No, really. What are you thinking?"

"I don't know. I'm eighteen now. When I'm out of school— would it be okay?"

He sits up on his elbow. "Okay to live together?"

"My parents would kill me."

"Your parents wouldn't kill a flea. Carrying bubonic plague."

"I know. But it would be worse. Worse than if they were just mad at me."

"They would be so disappointed?"

"I guess. Yeah. I don't know. Horrified. Shocked. But."

"But?"

"Would it be okay then?"

"Well. Depends on your definition of *okay*. If you mean legal, sure—"

I'm up on my elbows now, talking fast to get it all out. "Like you did with her. Going places out in public, not caring what anybody thinks, who knows. Waking up together. Going to sleep together." I make a sour face, letting my thoughts swirl. It seems impossible.

"I'm sorry," he says. "I wasn't thinking. I shouldn't have said anything about it."

"Goofy." I tickle him, brightening, clouds gone. "No more talking, not right now."

We hold for a long time.

Then we work on the stratospheric part. He promises to be my teacher. An uncomfortable moment:

He is.

river suicide

Time.

I take a bowl of Corn Pops to my computer.

Eating is changed for me. It is one of the most beautiful things on Earth. I could stop tomorrow. I don't care. Either way, I'm filled.

My home page is a push cam with a shot of Niagara Falls. Like God, I watch from above as a white bus smaller than a grain of wedding rice parks in front of the Niagara Fallsview Sheraton. The refresh is fast. Cars on the highway lurch forward like snap beetles. The falls in the background form a smoking horseshoe. I stare hard to see if I can see any tourists at this distance.

There.

They are getting out of the bus now. They crawl like microbes toward the roiling water. What thoughts are they thinking? Are they married? Do they love each other the way I love Mr. Mann?

How do I love him?

Our love is spiritual, slow, rushed, hidden. It's punctuated by vows, tears, narrow escapes, plans. It changes so beautifully from day to day, like the weather. Today it is fall, today it is storms. And it sounds like this:

"I don't really deserve you; you know that, don't you?" he says, voice muffled. We are kneeling in bed; I take his head against my shoulder.

"I love you," I say. "So you deserve me."

"I love you too, but it's all so crazy."

"That's one of the things that makes it so good. It's crazy, but without the crazy, it never would've happened."

"But it's—I just wanted you so much."

"Is that bad?"

"But maybe you should have gone to college first, Nine. Seen what things are like out there. I'm taking all of that away from you."

"You're not taking anything away; I'm giving it. And who says I'm not going to college? I've got the papers to prove it. Come here."

I hold him close, smother him with my need to absorb his love.

"We'll need a bigger apartment," he says.

I love how he can blow from one emotion to the next, effortlessly. Without all the thinking, the processing, the steps.

"Marry at the end of your sophomore year." I feel the rumbling timber of his voice in my collarbone.

We're both laughing now. "Why sophomore?" I say. "What's this prejudice against freshmen?"

"Who knows. You might get rushed. Some big asshole from the football team, a tight end—"

That does it. We collapse in a heap, shaking with teary-eyed laughter.

Then quiet.

"I know where the honeymoon will be," he says after a while. "I've got it all figured out. That's the easiest part."

"You do? Where?"

"The archaeological complex of Cacaxtla."

"Really? God, I love you. Do you love me?"

"Yes."

"Cacaxtla? Is that in Mexico?"

"Yes. Descendants of the Olmecs. It's amazing."

"How long did they last?"

"I can't remember."

"How long?"

"Forever. I promise."

Time.

Storm over.

Now I'm back in my room, looking at the computer screen, Niagara Falls.

More honeymooners get off the rice bus.

The hurt of his love is there every time. I'll never be rid of it.

Finals.

After I ace his test, I won't have to take a single one.

Mr. Mann is quiet. I keep track of his eyes as my hands jitter over the paper. He's sweet, trying so hard to look at anyone else. All the other heads are bowed. I cross my eyes, point my tongue at him; he pretends not to notice.

I scratch away at the paper, answering questions about Emily. Is there something I can put between the words, hieroglyphics only he will understand? A chemical signature of the elements that make up my heart? *I love you* in Assyrian cuneiform?

There's a shape to happiness that can't be described, only experienced. I've been inside his arms so much I'm taking it on.

I'm not making sense. I can't.

The world doesn't make sense. My thoughts jump to the evidence of our love. His eyes in the night, his smell in my clothes hamper, the squeak of our combined body weight on his bed— nothing is linear anymore. This is what is real: the times we spend together and nothing else.

By the end of the period my hand is cramping. I can't remember writing anything. Last night he kissed the shiny bump on my middle finger. It's almost over now.

I wait until I'm last out of class. So he can do this:

Touch my arm.

"We have to talk," he says.

For the first time he sounds like a Teacher.

I had been planning to pinch him. Now I can only say, "What is it?"

"Not now. It's something I never thought—no, not now."

"What!"

But his next class is already trickling in.

Something inside my chest breaks loose and falls. It never stops falling.

Something final has occurred. He's not at lunch or his office. The rest of the day is an agony of sickened anticipation. I don't remember my other classes or how I get through them.

There is one moment of ringing clarity: I see Schuyler coming out of calculus. His face tells me he's watching a train wreck but doesn't know how to pull my body out. We are carried away on a sea of heads in opposite directions.

I wait for Mr. Mann thirty minutes after the school has emptied. He motions as he crosses to the teachers' parking lot. I try not to run to his car but fail.

"What! What is it?"

His voice is barely working. "I'm so goddamn sorry, Carolina. I won't ask you to forgive me. There is no forgiveness for this."

My head is mashed into single syllables. "Oh, oh, what."

"It should never have happened. It's my fault. I take responsibility. But everything has to stop. Everything. From this moment on. We can only talk in class. Don't meet me anywhere. Don't come to my apartment. Ever again. Everything has to stop."

My mouth opens, but I'm choking on pieces of words.

His hands are shaking. He won't let me touch them, make them still. His eyes are the color of mountain lakes in winter.

We are pupil and teacher talking. I can't leap into his arms and beg him to fix me. I suddenly know with a crystal certainty I'm going to be broken forever. The landscape is freezing around me.

"Why? I don't understand. Why!"

"I can't talk about it. I can't. It has to be this way, that's all."

"But you have to talk about it! You can't just say that and go! You have to tell me, give me a chance to make it right!"

"This is not anything that is your fault. You can't change things, Carolina. It's just the way it has to be."

"Please, Richard, please. Richard."

Saying his name closes his eyes. I stand there unable to do anything but beg.

"Let's go somewhere, somewhere we can talk!" I say.

"No. I told you I can't. I won't."

"You have to! You can't just do this!"

"Please, Nine. You're killing me."

"What do you think you're doing to me!"

I scrabble at his shirt. I want to hit him, knock him down. I want to hold him until we both take root and grow together into a laurel tree.

He pushes against me, trying to pull away, then suddenly takes me ferociously in his arms, smothering me in his strength, my arms bent and pinned against his chest. He looks at me helplessly, inhaling the intensity of my need. I look into his eyes, bring my voice down to a growling whisper, speaking through my teeth.

"Richard, you've been inside me. Do you hear me? Inside me. You've been inside and told me that you loved me."

"I do. I always will."

"I know you do! Why—"

"I'm so sorry. I shouldn't have let it happen. It's my fault. We shouldn't have done anything. If I had known—"

"What? Something happened, I know it! Please tell me—we can get past it! I can help! I know we've been saying crazy things about the future, marriage, our own place. That's just how much I love you! I'm not trying to force anything on you. It can stay just like it is! Really! This is not—please—"

He turns my head into his neck, shutting off my words. For a few moments we're shuddering silently against each other. My cheek is wet with furious tears. He kisses the hair against my temple.

Now he's letting me go.

I try to take his arms, but he's sliding away from me. He has his hand on the car door, is pulling it open, sliding into the seat. He's moving so quickly, I'm in shock. All I can do is cling pathetically to the door. We struggle with it for a long moment, pulling in opposite directions. He wrenches it free and slams himself in. Just before he pulls away, he lip-synchs through the glass:

"I'm sorry."

I don't want to rap on the window; I want to smash it out. I get my nails on the curve of the Honda, almost daring to slip them in the crack along the roof line. Let him rip them out. But he's already rolling away. I stand helplessly, arms hanging, the smell of his sweet exhaust hanging in my nose. As his car turns out of the parking lot, the sun on the trunk knocks my eyes back in my head.

A glacier has rolled over my life.

What is after this? What is after this?

Emily. Emily.

> *Parting is all we know of heaven,*
> *And all we need of hell.*

heat death of the universe

The wedding announcement.

lessons learned

Lost.

A dying spacecraft falling at ten thousand miles per hour loses bits of itself on the way. Some parts are built to endure almost anything. Others are big-time fragile. If the fire of reentry, five thousand degrees, gets to the fragile parts, they warp, melt, vaporize. Sometimes instantly. Soon there's no recognizable center to the craft; it's all flying apart on various trajectories.

NASA calls the aftermath of a catastrophic event *Lessons Learned*.

Here's mine:

It takes time to set up a wedding. So Mr. Mann has known about this for a while. Yet he was with me right up to the very last minute.

He has a substitute teacher for his classes. I haunt his apartment. He's never home. Speed dial his number. The message has been changed:

"I have discovered that all human evil comes from this, man's being unable to sit still in a room. *Blaise Pascal.*"

Beep.

I put the phone down.

Scream and beat my fists against things that can't beat back.

Spend hundreds of miles in aimless driving.

Walk through an empty house, a fragment of living death.

After they take my wisdom tooth out, I fall into bed for three days, waiting to die.

Dad calls this the Trophy Room.

From here all I can see is a sickening, dusty, useless collection of testaments to my mental perfection. Willpower, obsessions. My framed National Merit Finalist letter, perfect attendance certificates, science fair trophies, Scholar Bowl cups. Egghead awards and citations of every stupid description imaginable.

Mom and Dad blame it all on my tooth. My crash. Thank God.

My tooth was killing me, that's what it was. Driving me insane. But now that it's gone, I know what they want, what they expect, even if they can't say it. They want me to find the girl I used to be.

But as I sink lower and lower, I realize, what does this room add up to? This person? What risks did she take?

When did she die?

I can't go back there. Ever.

One night I feel myself plunging literally through my mattress, too weak to stop my fall. I'm falling into a darkness larger and colder than deep space. This is it. The Last Days. I'm going, lost, gone.

There is nothing beneath me anymore, holding me up. I'm in midair flying apart. I have no center. I have several potential trajectories, up to and including:

Trajectory 17:

Kill myself.

But.

Something touches my hand.

How does my cat still know me? He rubs against my hanging arm just the same, no different. No different at all. Doesn't he find me strange?

This is a start.

This is where I begin to find my way back. Realizing that if Kitty Nation senses something there, something worth touching, something real, then something must be there. And finally, after a time—

After a long, gruesome, ridiculous struggle deep inside a black, desperate, featureless, void—

Absolute zero with a bullet—

I choose Trajectory 1:

Remake myself into something that doesn't burn.

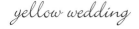

yellow wedding

I hope I'm late.

I'm wearing the long, froofy dead woman dress with the purple flowers. On the way to Mr. Mann's wedding.

In this disguise, I'm as disconnected from the world as an astronaut.

I pull into the half-full parking lot and cut the engine. Wilkie Collins ticks and farts as I rummage the floorboards for my wedding gift. It fits in the palm of my hand.

The church looks like a hundred other churches. Architectural style: Big Doghouse.

Even before I enter, I sense that awful captured feeling of a place where only a limited range of human activities is allowed. Even scratching an ear must be done a certain way. Never with the end of a pencil or the point of a key. I hurry-hobble up the steps and tumble through the air lock.

Whoa.

Here's the bride herself, Alicia Sprunk.

A butter bar of spring sunshine slaps her across the temple as I open the door, causing her to look up. Expression: Petrified Belle. I could strangle her with my bare hands.

I could. But instead I kill with my eyes. My smile.

Alicia is younger and prettier than her picture in the paper. Her veil perches on her billowy curls like a bucket rider about to plunge over Niagara Falls. Dress: phosphor bomb white. She appears to be legless.

A man I take to be Alicia's father is holding her arm. Mr. Sprunk is large. He glares at me with the cold intensity of a Komodo dragon. I'm an intruder, a purple monstrosity. Something to be masticated to death. I smile again and brush past them to grab a seat in the back.

The sanctuary is suffocating under huge sprays of golden daffodils and tulips. In the center of all this gush, there he is, at long last, my teacher. Mr. Mann.

So beautiful, dark hair hanging just so. I hate how even now he takes my breath away. The groomsmen are ganged around him like linemen protecting a quarterback. Six horrifying bridesmaids stand on the left. I will never wear yellow again.

I won't talk about the ceremony, that near-death experience.

I will talk about the end.

Alicia and Mr. Mann are kneeling before the minister, heads tipped forward reverently. My heart pounds, gathering steam to cross this mountain. I'm The Little Engine That Could. The minister intones the famous demand:

"If any man can show just cause why this couple may not be lawfully joined together, let him speak now or forever hold his peace."

My Lullaby League gloves slip on the pew in front of me as I begin to stand.

I see faces turn toward me. The weight of the personalities is terrifying and intoxicating.

No. I can't do it.

I'm not going to smash them. Not now.

I pull at my dress, smooth the pleats, sit down again.

On with the show.

I look at Mr. Mann and Alicia and cock my head empathetically. My eyes flood with unexpected tears. I'm projecting myself in Alicia's place. How ecstatic I would be, how complete.

At the end of the ceremony, the congregation applauds when the couple is presented. I let go of the pew and clap with all my might. The sound of my gloves beating in the puckered space is the fluttering of a large, frightened bird.

Truce over.

We move into another building.

This is a gymnasium, I realize. There is the basketball goal. Time to score.

Help me, Emily.

I HEARD a fly buzz when I died

I surge aggressively through the crowd as the band excretes sixties tunes. Along the way, an elderly man grabs my fingers and tries to whirl me around. I resist with shocking strength and he nearly falls.

At last I stand beaming before the happy couple. My gift is clutched in my gloves. The video camera can't help it. It's drawn to me. The lens rotates to zoom in. I will be on Mr. Mann's wedding video a hundred years from now.

He suddenly turns pale as the icing on the cake.

"Carolina, what—"

"For you," I say.

I press the gift into Alicia's small hands. She holds the package the way you would hold a smallpox-infected pudding. Without her Raging Cataract Hairdo, she's nearly a foot shorter than me.

I don't hang around to watch her open it.

Inside is my wisdom tooth the dentist broke from my jawbone. And a violently scented note that says:

> *MINE by the right of the white election!*
> *Mine by the royal seal!*
> *Mine by the sign in the scarlet prison*
> *Bars cannot conceal!*
>
> *Mine, here in vision and in veto!*
> *Mine, by the grave's repeal*
> *Titled, confirmed, - delirious charter!*
> *Mine, while the ages steal!*

So it begins.

moon wife

Climb.

I'm the last person on earth who would do this. Or maybe the first.

The giddy couple is still honeymooning down in Mexico. They'll be home any day now. This might be my last chance. The wooden stairs are warped by sun and rain. From his door you can see the lake. Just in case, I abuse the knocker. Silence.

Security is lax, but I have no idea how to pop even a simple lock. Credit card? I bend Mom's *Home & Garden* Visa trying to fit it in the slot. There are two windows I can reach. One has a small tear in the bottom of the screen. I make it larger with my finger and lift; the window miraculously gives. Hallelujah.

Somehow a daylight break-in feels completely safe. I can already hear the police officer: *A girl?* I make a show of what I'm doing. *Fixing this screen, see? I live here, don't I?* All those moments, hours—his bed—it sure feels that way. I screwdriver the frame loose and I'm in.

The apartment smells disused and empty. Hot as Venus in here. I bump the air down to sixty-four and the building rumbles subserviently. Everything is just as I achingly remember it, a charming wreck. I see his little brown box of New Wave CDs on the shelf and my heart cracks open.

Slam it shut.

Okay, what first?

I rifle everything. Papers, cabinets, closets, boxes, drawers, even CD cases.

Nothing. No letters, no photos, no evidence of Alicia or the wedding or even a past. Mr. Mann dropped out of the sky one morning in January.

Tacked to his bulletin board is a printout of a receipt from JetFare.com. I don't know how this can help, but I pocket it anyway. The answering machine has seventeen calls, all mine.

I press the button, listening to myself sounding more and more desperate. Crazy. Pathetic. Halfway through, I stop the tape. I hate whoever that person was. Now she just makes me angrier.

I turn on the decrepit computer and mouse through his files: lesson plans he never uses and not much else. I check his bookmarks and history file. Everything looks familiar, including the honeymoon trip we picked one night on a lark while he fed me strawberries.

The trip they are on now.

Meander through canyons dotted with ruins of Mesoamerican civilizations! Splash in the waterfalls of El Encanto! Relax in the hot springs of Rio Antigua! Climb the spectacular pyramids at Teotihuacán! Feast on exquisite Mexican cuisine!

Contract flesh-eating streptococcus!

One can hope.

See, I've sunk to the level of schadenfreude.

Definition: *a malicious satisfaction in the misfortunes of others.*

Or at least a dangerous first cousin. Schuyler told me about this. It's bad for your karma. In this case the misfortune hasn't happened yet, but daydreaming about it doesn't let my soul off the hook.

God gives a rat's ass. I'm not sure I do.

Put that one on my tab, Schuyler.

I fall over on the white couch. What am I doing here? What do I hope to accomplish? My eye falls on Mr. Mann's beloved copy of Emily's poems, a paperback published the year Kennedy was assassinated. I jerk the book open and start to rip it in half along the spine. I can't bear to tear through the words themselves.

Wait.

Several lines jump out at me:

> *SHE rose to his requirement, dropped*
> *The playthings of her life*
> *To take the honorable work*
> *Of woman and of wife.*

Yes.

I reverently put the book back in its place. It's not Emily's fault. I should have known she would have the answer.

It's time to make ready for the newlyweds. Time to make a Wife.

I exit by the front door, leaving it unlocked.

Rush to the Wal-Mart Rules the World Super Center and come back loaded with supplies.

I scrub the dishes, splash the kitchen with pine cleaner, the bathroom with Ajax. Mom is right: what men don't see doesn't exist. I straighten everything. The trash goes on the landing. I make a great show of opening the front door each time I go in and out; I live here, don't I? I certainly deserve to.

Mom's voice nags in my ears, scolding: *What a miserable little vacuum.* And: *Well, no wonder, if you never change the bag.*

When I start to strip the bed, something breaks open again. I burrow my face into the sheets while Emily watches in white loneliness from the wall. When I'm finished, I ball up the old sheets and leave them on the landing.

Crisp new sheets are tucked in a shopping bag in the hall. Lightly lavender, dotted with honeysuckle and crocuses. Alicia

will love these Laura Ashley horrors. I snap them over his mattress, make the hospital corners neat and square.

One thing more.

In medieval times, honeymooning couples were given a one-
month supply of mead to drink. Honey = mead, moon = month.
If they drank a cup each night, within one year their union would
produce a baby.

I have no mead. This will have to do.

I tear the wrapping paper and silver bow away from the package Mr. Mann was supposed to open.

The label on the jar says TRAPPIST, below that, RED RASPBERRY
JAM. Unscrewing the top is like turning the core of the earth.
Those monks must be Bowflex junkies. I dip a finger in, dangle a
string of the stuff on my tongue; it's warm from sitting in the car.
Mr. Mann was right: I taste like heaven.

I jerk the bedspread back, use three fingers to smear jam
across the bottom sheet.

I can't stop. I scoop out economy-sized globs and finger paint
until the jar is empty.

A bloody Rorschach nightmare.

Happy birthday, Richard.

I remake the bed crisply and leave. Grab Mr. Mann's sheets on
the landing and stuff them in the car.

Wait.

Come back and set the air to ninety.

Mom.

"Darling, you're home!"

Her hair looks freeze dried; if you broke off a lock, it would feel like coral. Her eyes aren't quite so red today. Pollen count must be down. I'm barely inside before she's peppering me with questions.

"Where have you been? Is it that hot out there already? You're flushed, sweetheart!"

"Springtime in Dixie," I mutter.

Mom reaches up to touch my shoulder. "Don't do anything in the bathroom, dear. We're out of paper."

"Okay."

"I'm going to get some at Kroger's. I won't be home right away. There's a used book sale at the library. If there's an emergency, I put some tissues—"

"I said okay."

"Can I get you anything from the store?"

"Thanks, Mom, I'm fine."

I'm also exhausted. I sit at the table and find the dining room window. Trees still green, sky still blue. Our neighbor, Mr. Garner, is trying to mate with his garbage can. Life stumbles on.

"Are you sure? Your father will be home a couple of hours late. He's out at the test stands again. You might want to order a pizza. I believe Terry's is having a special—"

"Mom. I'm fine. Truly. Skedizzle. Think about yourself for a change."

"But I worry about you, darling. Is it all just too much?"

"All what?"

"The end of school, being so awfully sick, everything."

Everything.

But my cat loves me.

After Mom is gone, Kitty Nation steps into my lap to sniff my breathing. I scratch his sweet flat head. Kitty Nation is the color of grandma afghans and leaves and burning. I will kill anyone who tries to formaldehyde him.

The empty tub is coldly supportive against my back. The rug is soft. This is my favorite reading place. I wrap myself in Mr. Mann's sheets. His scent suffuses the space around my head. I spread open my copy of Emily's poems across my knees:

HEART, we will forget him!
You and I, to-night!
You may forget the warmth he gave,
I will forget the light.

When you have done, pray tell me,
That I my thoughts may dim;
Haste! lest while you're lagging,
I may remember him!

Remember him.

I'm forgetting something. Yeah.

I reach into my pocket. It's still there.

I crash out of the bathroom to my computer and slap the JetFare receipt next to the mouse.

Quick.

I slip into Mom's bedroom and get into her things.

Her Mary Kay Pink Cadillac makeup and orange jogging suit. I cinch the flabby waist and hike the short pants to my knees like knickers. Crimp my hair with colorful old lady barrettes, pull a bushy ponytail through a hole in the back of Mom's VIVE LE LIVRE baseball cap. I pull the bill of the cap low and put on her narrow sunglasses and rush outside to Wilkie Collins.

Screech.

The Huntsville International Jetplex.

I haven't been here in a while. It's smaller than its name implies. Still, I see long glass buildings, overnight parking with its lazy yellow bar, the control tower like a Junovian golf tee. I scrabble quarters out of the ashtray for the meter and sidle Wilkie against the curb.

A security guard walks toward me with the unmistakable look of the vocationally stunned. I bustle past him with authority and make my way through the automatic doors.

Somehow the sunglasses make me confident. I'm anonymous, dangerous, impermeable. A soccer mom juiced on steroids. A family of four hurries in front of me as if pressed in the back by my pathological stride.

They won't let you all the way to the terminals these days unless you're a passenger. I look for the luggage carousel. Up ahead a group of travelers is watching suitcases being pooped through flaps of carpet onto an aluminum slide. My head swivels, reconnoitering. None of these people are the Manns. I dig out Mr.

Mann's itinerary and glance at my watch. Seven minutes to spare. Surely I haven't missed him. Now what?

For the first time I realize I have no idea what I'm going to do.

This is the thing that smashes me. My whole life I have always had a plan, but I have no plan. Only a raging need. A need for what? What can I hope for? What is this wildness inside that is pulling me on like I've fallen into a flooded river? I try to keep my breathing in check and look around for stones in the current to hang on to.

A mother struggles with her monsters, hair desperately tucked behind her ears. A man sucks on an unlit pipe and prissily snaps his newspaper. Another man in a wifebeater shirt reads from a huge black Bible. His ropy biceps stand out like pods of butter beans.

Overhead the Announcement Chick booms about boarding for exotic locales like Cleveland and Baltimore. No news from Mexico.

People are talking about things I never like to talk about: shoes, cars, TV. Mom says this is why I have no friends, other than Schuyler. She doesn't know that I can't bear it, that it feels like being tattooed against my will.

Do I wish there were more people like me? Sure. Every day. I wish it and hunger for it and almost believe it could happen. But the more I see of things, the more I realize that we can't have what we want. We can only have what we can have. I had no idea life could be so lonely.

Zammo.

Here they come, the lovebirds.

My fingers curl on the plastic seat. I don't understand. I simply don't understand. I will never, ever understand. How could he? How?

I can't compare this feeling to anything I've ever experienced before.

My first instinct is to fly at them, pile drive Mr. Mann into the industrial carpet, straddle him, beat his face with the back of my knuckles. Knock her down too. And hope her head bounces.

But something else is there too. Every second I ever spent with him, touching him, kissing, longing, completing. The rushing heat of all the connections we've shared, my fingernails against his skin, the point of his tongue beneath my ear.

Alicia is laughing delightedly, hair like an oversized seashell. Mr. Mann looks tired. He's tanned; his lovely hair is clipped short. This loss makes me think briefly of suicide. I tell myself it makes him look old.

I hunch into my ponytail. I've got to be quick. Quick about what? I could rush them, force them back on the plane, make it fly to the Great North Woods and have it out there. The three of us, naked, animals on the ground, claws, dirt, teeth. I might not win, but I guarantee you, I won't be the first one down for the count.

I wait. They're not thirty feet away now. Alicia leans into him; he straightens and touches her elbow almost consolingly. She giggles and puts her arms around his waist. Alicia is burned pink and is wearing something long and blousy that splits alarmingly up the side. Ankles like fence posts. Poor Richard. I laugh bitterly in temporary satisfaction.

They're distracting each other. Suddenly I see a familiar-looking bag at the top of the chute. I focus on it. It's a no-name cheapie with a fat belt looped over the top through a scarred buckle. In my memory I can see it on a closet shelf in Mr. Mann's apartment.

I used to imagine where that bag would go with us someday.

Why not.

I edge slowly around the far side of the carousel, watching for my chance. It's his, all right; there's the dark tear near the handle. The suitcase tumbles down in noisy flops to smack on its face. Now. My fingers close over the handle and I lift it in one clumsy motion—heavy!

I glide away at medium speed, stepping purposefully. With my long legs, I'm soon in the middle of the pedestrian flow, increasing the distance away from the carousel in big, easy strides. I'm making my way down the main concourse before I dare to glance over my shoulder.

I have no sense of being chased. Mr. Mann hasn't even noticed that the suitcase has come and gone; he's tugging at an expensive-looking black leather bag, obviously Alicia's. By now I'm thirty yards away and gathering steam, a high-octane traveler in danger of missing a connection. The sunglasses help, make me expressionless, fierce.

I swoosh past a big security guard who doesn't even raise his eyebrows.

Dinky as airports go, the main building is still track-and-field capable. I look back again. Mr. Mann is almost unrecognizable from here.

I pass an opening to my left; two uniformed women suddenly rush over from a side tributary, going some place important. I'm not sure they even see me. I turn down the hall they just exited, find a seat in a secluded archipelago of anemic rubber trees. Whew, feels good to sit down. What's he got in this thing?

Wait.

Five minutes, ten. Longer.

He's not coming.

I unbuckle the suitcase, unzip the flap, and throw it back. Books, a couple of them coffee-table sized. I heft one out: *Cacaxtla: Fuentes Historicas y Pinturas*. Sorry, don't read Spanish. I pick up another, flip through it: spectacular photographs of basaltic sculptures, jade objects, richly decorated pottery vessels, colossal Olmec heads hacked from giant boulders. On the title page, there's an inscription in green ink:

> *To my darling Ricky,*
> *May our love last longer than the Star of Venus Chamber.*
>
> *Your Ali*

Die, you. Just die.

Besides, Venus is not a star. Moron.

The female guards suddenly scuttle by again, freezing my heart.

They don't seem to be particularly looking for anyone, just hurrying. My pulse rate begins to go down. Back to the bag: his shoes. I've never seen these, black leather and barely scuffed.

I drop them on the floor.

A shiny belt. A stack of slacks in varying shades. Blue shirt, white shirt, olive green. I hold a handful up to my face; these clothes don't even smell like him, they're so new. My temper surges—she bought these; I just know it.

I ransack the rest of the bag, nothing much of interest.

No clues of any kind. No journal, receipts, notes, date book.

Just boxers.

No.

Please, no. Mr. Mann wears athletic briefs that hug his lovely thighs. Always. He looks like a god in them. Standing against the window. Watching the rain. Please.

Not these. These plaid and striped and checked boxers.

She has burned me out of his life in every way imaginable.

I'm ready to die now.

I turn the case over; clothing begins to spill out. I drape the boxers, all six pairs, over the rubber tree plants. Arrange them for maximum effect. Is anybody watching? I don't care. Something small and white tinkles on the carpeting.

A bell.

I pick it up. It's a tiny replica of a mission bell, painted bluish gray with two robin's egg stripes and a pearl-colored ribbon tied at the top. A keepsake. Something to remember the trip by. Maybe they shared a kiss beneath a church bell just like this one and wanted something to take home that would perfectly symbolize their treasured union forever. Lucky it didn't break.

I put it beneath my heel and stomp.

Again.

One more time.

Now grind the pieces into a bluish powder.

As I walk away, leaving it all, the bag, everything open, exposed, the underwear spread out on the rubber trees, it's the last thing I see:

The ribbon.

killer comet

Doom.

The last week of school.

I'm standing with Schuyler, watching Matt and the other Jesus

Phreaks link hands around the flagpole. They're praying about the Last Days.

"They've got it all wrong," Schuyler says. "The world won't come to an end until 2086."

No special reason. Except that's the year he turns one hundred. Today would be fine with me.

"Good morning," Mr. Mann says. His face is wooden.

Some of the kids gape. He's never said this before. He usually attacks the blackboard without a word and we're supposed to jump right in. Is he afraid I'm going to stand up and scream? Denounce him before the world?

Gut him like a deer?

Is that what he's waiting for? The final freak-out, the break with sanity, the secret made known, scandal flung to the winds?

I watch. I tell myself I can't see a difference in his eyes, but his hands jitter nervously over the top of his desk, feeling their way. Did he prepare himself? Did he stand in front of his small bathroom mirror this morning and think, This is it. Today, everything is over. I'm dead. Crushed. Finished.

He doesn't look at me. I don't think he can.

"Why didn't you tell us?" Havisham-Kelly suddenly squeals. "We could have thrown you a party."

"So, did you get some?" another voice says. Snickers ripple horribly around the room.

Mr. Mann grimaces good-naturedly. What a guy. "Hello, Mr. Atkinson."

I don't do anything.

I don't want to. Not here. Not now. I smile as sweetly as I can through his class but never directly at him. Through the compliments and congratulations and questions and girly squeals and double entendre nasty boy jokes.

Because maybe today the world really is coming to an end.

How nice that would be.

But before a comet from the Oort Cloud slams into the Pacific Ocean, I have something I need to do.

Somehow he senses this. He takes my arm at the end of the period.

"What's your next class?"

"You know what it is, sir."

"Then skip lunch. Meet me in my office. We have to talk."

"Yes, sir."

"And please drop the *sir* bullshit, Carolina."

"Maybe you could teach me, sir. You're good at dropping things."

Before he can reply, a girl from his next class sidles through the door, a look of embarrassed curiosity on her face. Why is this teacher holding my arm? Why is he squeezing it so tightly?

"Go," he says.

Time.

The white industrial wall clock ticks expectantly. I've seen this kind of clock before. It can only measure the passage of serious things.

So now I get to see the inside of his office.

Now that the danger is over. Now that the fun and games are finished. Now that I'm safe, legal, even appropriate. Now that we're no longer *lovers*. God, I hate that word. It feels sickening, revolting, disrespectful. Is that what we were doing? *Lovering?*

The walls are painted a sectarian beige. Like me, the cloth on the brown furniture is stretched to its limits; beneath the armrests

I can feel the staples. His desk is small and short-legged, a vulnerable, neglected marsupial.

No pictures of Emily, no New Wave tapes, nothing personal from a hyper-personal man. I'm a little surprised. Only over-stuffed shelves and stacks of paper left in fanned disarray. The owner of this room is in a state of perpetual search.

What is he looking for? I thought it was me.

Where is he?

The door opens; Mr. Mann drops a stack of books on the desk with a dusty bang, shuts the door behind him. His posture says this: This meeting will be Short and Conclusive.

It pisses me off how he is using his age.

When he needs it, he uses it—it's not there when he wants somebody younger, but it's his crutch when he needs to fall back on it, become somehow superior.

"So, okay," he starts, reaching to brush back a lock of hair that doesn't exist anymore.

"Okay."

"Are you proud of what you did in my apartment?"

"Yep. Are you?"

Bull's-eye. He blows air from his cheeks and settles wearily in his chair. "You have every right to hate me, Carolina. Go ahead. Most of the time I even hate myself."

"You should. And don't call me Carolina. I don't know if that person is even alive anymore. Call me Nine. I'll always be a number to you. The only thing is, which one?"

A dark figure skulks dangerously close to the mullioned glass in the door, then moves on.

"You know it wasn't like that," he says. "You know it."

"Okay, then tell me. What was it like?"

He looks down, fingers roving over his desk, picking things up, putting them back. What is he deciding? Which hat to wear? Lover or teacher? Boy or man?

"I can't blame you for what you did. I deserved that much, at least." He tries a halfhearted grin. "One of the things I love about you is your creativity."

Even in the middle of my anger, my heart wells up. "You said love. One of the things you love about me. Present tense."

"Oh God, Nine. I—well, maybe I did. But you have got to let it go and leave me alone."

"Why?"

"What do you hope to accomplish?"

"What do you?"

He leans back. "I know you're angry. Hurt. Hell, when I was your age, I would have at least blown up your mailbox by now."

I lean forward, pulling up some of his papers between my fingers, crumpling them a little, menacing. I have to do this, do anything physical; otherwise I will be at his throat.

"No, you wouldn't have."

"What makes you say that?"

"Because you're a coward."

His eyes flinch. You sank my battleship. Good.

"We both know it's not your fault," he says.

"We both know no matter how much apologizing you do, it won't help."

"Agreed. In case you haven't noticed, I'm not defending myself. But things are different now. I'm married and you have to respect that. If not for me, then for her. She's done nothing wrong."

"Yes, she has."

"What?"

"She got you."

He thrusts himself away from the desk as if needing a break from my personal Sphere of Pain. The chair tilts too far, nearly toppling him over. He finds a point of equilibrium and hangs there ridiculously, heels off the floor. "What do you expect me to do?"

"That's my question."

"Okay. Here's your answer. I expect you to go on. Live your life. Dream. Explore. Move on. What happened to college?"

"You."

"Bullshit. Don't use me as an excuse. You've got too much going for yourself, Nine."

"You never sounded like a cliché before."

He groans. "I never had to. What I did was a huge mistake, and I take full responsibility. But it's over."

"Nothing's over. In what way have you taken responsibility? You've got your bouncy new wife; I've let you keep your job. So far. What have I got? What have you left me with?"

"Look, you've had your revenge." He puts his hand to his temple. "What do we call 'even' in a game like this?"

"Who said this is a game."

"You're making yourself sound like a goddamn nut."

Am I? A jolt of fear stabs me. Is he right? Is that what's happening to me? Is this what crazy feels like? This blind anger, this desperate need to strike out, to somehow make him understand, even if I have to hurt him to do it? I can't think. I can't think. Not about that. That's what he wants, wants to turn it around on me, make me believe I'm the problem and he's the rational one. No.

"Maybe I am," I say.

He leans forward; the chair nearly throws him out. "Look, nothing you do will ever make up for what I've done. You'll only be hurting an innocent girl."

"Hurting? Is that Alicia's idea of pain? Washing out a few sheets with OxyClean?"

"Okay. But the ball is in your court. What do you want, to get arrested next time? You do realize you've committed a crime, don't you?"

"Do you?"

"Is that a threat?"

"What do you think?"

He rocks forward out of the chair and lunges at the desk, stares hard into my eyes. It's difficult not to look away from all that blue, but I hold my gaze. So now he's going to be tough? But it doesn't fit him. There is something inside him that always feels as if it is hiding from everything else. It's always been a big part of what I love about him. Finding that center of his deep inside, the place he wants to keep hidden, dragging it out into the light.

"Do you really want to do that?" he says.

"No. But I will. Unless."

"Unless what?"

"I don't know." I swore to myself I wouldn't do it, but I start to cry.

"No."

I stand and come toward him. "If I could just hold you, if you could just tell me."

He backs away defensively. I'm close enough to touch his shirt. He glances at the door. "Tell you what?"

"That it's all a mistake. The wedding didn't really happen."

"But it did."

"But why did it did."

"What?"

"Why. You owe that to me."

"I told you, Nine, I can't tell you."

I put my fingers on his chest. He's warm. How can a piece of paper and a few minutes in a church make this any different? I know what he feels there. I know it can't have just gone away. "Then tell me that it didn't happen," I say. "Lie to me. You know how to lie."

"I never lied," he says.

"Call it what you want. It's still a lie." This gives me an idea. I brighten a little. "Maybe we could still meet? Yes. Please! That's it! She doesn't have to know; I won't tell her."

My tears are coming harder now. I'm trying to take him in my arms; he's pushing me away.

"Carolina, stop." He shoves me hard. My eyelashes are so wet, I can't make out his face.

"It's finished," he says.

"Why? Why? I love you. I know you love me."

"That's just the way it is. It's beyond love now. I've got to go. You've got to move on. Enough."

I drag my forearm across my eyes and put my hand on the doorknob. Just as I open it, I turn.

"It'll never be enough," I say. "Never."

dishes make love

Night.

It's when all the other things come out.

The scariest things, thoughts, fears.

Plans.

I'm trying to recognize myself.

Where does this massive anger come from? How deep does it go? How connected is it to my core, my center? Is it a part of me? Has it always been there? Waiting for something in my life to go insanely wrong?

Or does it come from somewhere else? Is this how I get rid of it, by bleeding it off, or will it always be there, waiting for the next time I need it?

I need it now.

Wilkie's steering column crunches as I crank his tires around. I can see piney woods on the left side of the road here. The fence in front of me is topped with razor wire. The official-looking sign in the headlights says:

U.S. ARMY INSTALLATION

NO TRESPASSING

TEST RANGES

SUBJECT TO DAY, WEEKEND, AND NIGHTTIME USE

This is where the army practices with bombs and tanks. The Space Flight Center sits in the middle of Redstone Arsenal, surrounded by thousands of empty acres used for war games. Dad says this place is full of land mines and canisters of mustard gas and chemical weapons left over from World War II.

As much fun as it would be to play here, this is not the side I want.

I park and get out.

My war is across the road.

Across the road from the test range is the swamp where the beavers live. Eventually the swamp becomes a lake.

Sunlake.

The swamp is harder to skirt than I figured. Along the edges the water is reasonably shallow, but the muddy bottom sucks at my feet, threatening to pull my sneakers off. It takes fifteen minutes to wade to the back of Mr. Mann's complex. Swamp water is amazingly cold, even this time of year. I'm terrified my toes will be eaten by snapping turtles.

I count the units until I know I have the right one. I can't see his car from this side, but I'm pretty certain they are home. The lights are on.

Good.

I come to a place where the bottom under my feet turns hard and I nearly fall; chunks of limestone have been tumbled along the bank to prevent erosion. I'm standing in the lake. I climb out of the water and come free of the trees. Edge along the strip of wasted yard behind Mr. Mann's building. This is where they hide the air-conditioning units, power transformers, curly black downspouts.

The apartment below his is dark. It won't be that hard to get to the second floor. I step on the ground-floor porch railing and haul myself up, holding one of the support columns. I stand there, toes of my sneakers on somebody's handrail, catch my breath. My legs are shaking a little—from the effort of balancing or the intense fear of what I'm doing?

Only crazy people and criminals do something like this. And me. Where do I fall on that spectrum?

Falling.

A really bad word.

This is the last possible stopping place. It would be a little weird getting caught hanging on to some guy's porch, but climbing to a second-floor balcony, that's off the scale.

But I'm going through with it, aren't I?

Yes. Yes, I am.

No one around, not too many lights. Go.

I grab the spindles on Mr. Mann's deck and start to haul myself up. It's a little tough to boost myself from here using only my arms—my strength comes from my legs—until I get a toe between the railings. At last I swing my leg over and drop as quietly as possible to the deck.

I've done it. I'm here. I'm really here.

I wait a few beats of my screaming heart to decide if anybody has heard me. My teeth are dry, breath sibilant, mouth awful. When did I eat? When did I bathe? Who am I?

Nothing. Not a sound.

I look around. No curtains on the slider, but the room is dark. I scuttle over as slowly as a spider with arthritis in every leg. Crouch behind a rusty gas grill and peer through the glass. The living room is empty and dim, but the small kitchen beyond is glaring.

I wait, trying to breathe deeply. Are they here? Then I hear movement, voices inside. I nearly jump to the railing, but instead I force myself to be still. Strain my senses to the bleeding point and wait.

I want to see how they touch.

Mr. Mann shows up first, freezing the breath in my lungs. No shirt, and he's scratching his shoulder near the armpit. I've rested my head there. We were watching *Random Harvest,* with Ronald Coleman and Greer Garson. Ronald Coleman had lost his memory. Greer Garson was desperately trying to make him remember how much he loved her—

Crap.

This is crazy.

Intellectually, I know it's not likely they will come out on the deck at this time of night.

Emotionally, I'm completely freaked, scared witless. What am I doing here?

I've been here so many times, it feels supremely weird to be on the outside, watching through the glass. Everything inside calls out to me, says I should be able to stand, call out to him.

Rush into his arms.

Alicia suddenly moves into the kitchen with her back to me, making my heart drum. She's tugging out plates and doing something at the stove. To help keep myself calm, I make observations: her hands are small, arms short, movements precise and compact; I wonder, does he kiss each finger as he kissed each one of mine? He leans across the short bar on his elbows, watching her work. I hear the rumbling vibration of his baritone but can't make out the words. Alicia laughs.

Still they haven't touched. What are they talking about? I can't stand it anymore—my miserable curiosity overcomes my terror. I extend my arm under the grill to the nearest edge of the slider. An imperceptible pull and it gives. With obscene patience, I tug it open a few inches, then take my hand away again.

"Wish it could be another way," Mr. Mann is saying. The words roll through me like medicated steam.

"But I've always had my own account," Alicia says as she

pushes things around on the stove. "I'll go first thing in the morning and set it up. You'll see. It'll be easier to organize that way."

Mr. Mann's shoulders sag. "Your mother—" he starts, but stops himself. "But I like to keep things together. It'll be so complicated to keep up with it if we divide them up that way. I have enough trouble balancing one. Won't it be too complicated?"

Alicia turns, spatula in the air. "No, silly, it'll be easier. I promise. You just have to be sure to use the right checkbook. We'll get them in different colors. Color coded! Green for you, blue for me. And maybe a third account—we'll make it red—only for yearly expenses. You know, onetime things like car tags."

I watch them eat.

My heart drops into my stomach—I've never had a real meal with him, something cooked and put on a table. Just like that, she's that far ahead of me already. It looks like stir-fry. Alicia rakes vegetables from a black pan onto a couple of plates. Mr. Mann sits. As he dips his fork to the plate and lifts it to his mouth again, I study the muscles moving in his back. I've tasted him there.

Alicia eats across from him. She stabs and eats her food with the fork turned upside down. Efficient and European. My fingernails dig into the wormy deck. I didn't expect this. The domesticity of the scene is worse than catching them in bed. Worse because it shows they have all the time in the world for making love. It has its place in their lives, can be as huge or small as they need, not the central axis on which everything turns.

"So are you sure you want to switch majors again?" Mr. Mann says.

"I'm sure," Alicia says, collecting the plates. "I've tried it for three years. I'm sick of all the math and chemistry. I'll never get through it. I've got enough credits to be a junior, but it doesn't add up to anything."

"But nursing? Won't it be like starting over?"

"A lot of what I already have can be used as electives. Plus I really think I'll like it. I'll be happier, I really will. I like people, not numbers."

Something inside me, a throbbing, insistent fear, eases a bit—so she's been to three years of college. That puts her in her twenties, at least. I feel guilt wash in with the letting go of the fear—there is something so amazingly wrong about overhearing a conversation like this. It's harmless, but it's not harmless. But I can't stop, not now.

They clean up, load the dishwasher; she pops him with a dish towel while he pretends not to notice. If they turn on his music, I will set fire to the building.

They flick off the kitchen light, head up the short hall. All is quiet, show over.

Now.

I turn my entire body into an Ear and listen for several more minutes. Nothing. Then, just when I'm about to give up and leave—as if on cue—I hear Alicia giggle horribly. A black fury rises up in me, overwhelming anything else.

I brace for sexy laughter. Nothing. I can smell the heartbreakingly familiar cheap carpeting in the exhalations of the room mixed with a hint of ginger. And Him. His scent is there too. I can never forget it. I close my eyes a moment and let the air from inside wash over my face.

Big thump.

I tense, scurry back on my heels. Was it the bedroom? My face feels as if it has been injected with novocaine. I'm not sure I can move the muscles that control my lips, my eyes. I get closer again and force myself to wait. The numb tightness travels down my shoulders to my arms and hands.

Are they? Could they?

No. Not with me here. It's too evil.

The bathroom door suddenly swings open, throwing a rhombus of yellow light across the hall. I'm frozen. I hear the oceanic sound of flushing. Mr. Mann pivots on his heel, still zipping up.

"!"

He doesn't say a word, but he's seen me through the door.

I scramble away in horror. In two steps I catch my leg over the rail and I'm spinning in space, free falling. I land on my side with a terrible *whump* on the soggy squares of unanchored sod. Then I'm up, limp-running toward the swamp.

I don't remember getting into Wilkie Collins, starting his popping engine, driving away. I remember Mr. Mann's face. The shock and hatred on it.

Why, why, why?

> MUCH madness is divinest sense
> To a discerning eye;
> Much sense the starkest madness.
> 'T is the majority
> In this, as all, prevails.
> Assent, and you are sane;
> Demur, — you're straightway dangerous,
> And handled with a chain.

Am I becoming one of those people Emily is talking about?

I'm horrified that I am. One of those people—you can see it in their eyes. You might be doing something simple, just going through the grocery store; you come to the next aisle, and there they are, not ready for you. The way they are torn up inside—they've let it show on their face, even if only for a moment; it pops out, and you just happen to accidentally be there to see it—the way they feel deep inside, completely open and exposed. How ripped apart they are, how close to death or even worse than death—close to losing their minds. It is pushing right up to their eyeballs and leaking out, so that the only way to get relief, the only way, is to let it all come screaming and tearing out sometime when you think nobody is looking, right here, right now, in the goddamn cereal aisle at the grocery, but when you do—

Am I madness? Do I need to be chained?

big black blue

Home.

In the driveway, I can't get out.

I'm shaking all over, lying on my hurt side, my face on Wilkie's dusty seat. Land of a Thousand Butts.

I realize with a plunging horror I'll never be one of those Great Souls you hear about. Like Mother Teresa. I'll always be a girl who can be just as good as the world is to her. Like Bill Clinton or Madonna or Sammy Sosa or my next-door neighbor.

For the first time I see nothing ahead, not even the chance to hurt him. As dull as it sounds, I see blackness. Not an absence of

light, but an absence of a path, a direction. The blackness is a bar-
rier. A blockage, a foulness in a pipe.

This is not the Nothing that exists before everything or the
Nothing that exists after all is gone. This is a definite Something,
but it comes from somewhere outside my experience. This is what
people must feel when they enter the hospital for the last time or
take too many sleeping pills.

A noise.

I can't let my parents find me like this; what will they think?

I pop up painfully just as a black car passes, menacing, interminable, the interior lights blinking goofily on and off. Surely no
car can be this long. It's a limousine. Some of the windows are
rolled down. Screams of laughter.

Prom night.

How could I forget?

I stumble into the house, slip into my room, and change my
wet clothes before Mom can see me like this. She's watching
Wheel of Fortune in the den. I want to lift the TV and throw it
through the window.

"I thought you were at work," she says.

"No."

"Nine, come here."

"I don't feel so good."

"What is it? What's wrong, honey?" She forgets the clacking
wheel, clacking contestants, ageless Pat Sajak.

"Nothing, Mom."

"Schuyler called."

"Great."

"Aren't you going to call him back?"

"I don't know. Maybe."

"And what's wrong with Wilkie? Doesn't that boy ever want to come meet us?"

I laugh, and it's an awful laugh. Mom looks at me and blinks.

"I made him up, Mom. I'm sorry."

"What?"

"Wilkie Collins is my car. I got tired of you asking about boys and the prom, so I made him up."

"Well."

I can't tell if she wants to laugh too or maybe just cry.

"Well," she says again. By then I'm moving to the bathroom. I haul my jeans down and check my hip in the mirror. In the morning it's going to be black and blue.

Dad meets me in the hallway when I come out:

"One week to go," he says. "Countdown. Final sequence check."

He says this as if sensing something. Only Dad can't sense. He can watch and estimate and measure, then make an educated observation.

"I guess," I say.

"Can you believe it?"

"I don't know what to believe these days, Dad."

He doesn't seem to be listening, but sometimes that is when he is listening the hardest.

"Today, at work, a single man lost the entire CRPS database," he says.

"That's nice."

"Nearly a year's worth of NASA budgetary figures."

"No backups, huh?"

"He lost the database performing the daily backup."

"Oh." My eyes can only see what's in my imagination: Mr.

Mann. Accusations. Shame. Disgrace. "I hope they fired him. I hope they threw him out on the street."

"No," Dad said. "He still has his job. He's a good man."

"And you're telling me this because?"

"Because everybody can make a mistake. Sometimes very big ones. You don't throw a good man out because of that. Then people get afraid to take risks."

I don't know what to say. Is Dad channeling my teacher? Or is he talking about me? I start to speak, close my mouth.

He smiles and touches my hair. "I'm so proud of you, honey."

"I don't deserve it. Seriously, I don't. I'm no better than anybody else."

"Modest, too. What's for supper?"

"I'm not feeling all that well. I don't know."

"Hmmm?"

"I'm tired, Dad. Just let me go."

"Okay."

I turn on my computer and watch Niagara Falls at night. Nothing but darkness flecked with a few tiny lights.

But the falls are still there, roaring.

zeb in mourning

It's Senior Skip Day.

I skip it.

Meaning, I go to school instead. The halls feel like arteries on a powerful blood thinner. Hub Christy's seat in human phys is blessedly empty. Ms. Larimore looks at me oddly. What am I doing here?

Maybe I had to say goodbye on the last day to say goodbye. I would've missed this, whatever it is. Certainly not a ceremony.

Pussy Pancreatic is tucked in her bag for the final time. What do they do with all the dead, carved-up kitties? Do they remain in the Closet of Death from one year to the next, piling up, unchanging? Is there no method for burial, no decency, no release to a better world?

Why is this hitting me so hard?

The smell of stoppage as I handle the bag sends the room spinning around my head. Maybe if I leave Pussy Pancreatic's bag unzipped, the air will take care of her, carry her away in microscopic bites where at least she can go to ground again, become something useful.

"Carolina."

My head is down, but I see Ms. Larimore's stringy shanks and sensible shoes. I wonder, Does her husband adore her? Does he smile when she comes home at night? Does he dream about holding her, kissing her, when she's away?

"Carolina."

Something is required of me. Why don't I answer? What's wrong? I'm a First-Born. I take care of my responsibilities.

Booyah.

"Huh? Um—yes?"

"I guess you didn't hear the speaker, Carolina."

"Huh?"

"The counselor's office; they just called you."

"Oh. Oh. Tell them I'm attending a funeral."

"What?"

The eight other heads who decided to come to class all turn in my direction, the morning suddenly interesting.

I'm damaged. Crashed, wrecked. I don't know how to fix myself.

I look at the Closet of Death, close to tears. "We should have done something for them. Why didn't we do something for them?"

"I don't understand," Ms. Larimore says.

"I know."

I leave. I'm halfway to somewhere when I realize I've forgotten my destination. Lunch? Too early. Home? Why would I go there?

His room.

Maybe his class is out swimming, little kois getting ready to join the big ones. Get eaten. Maybe he's sitting at his desk, no one to teach, washing the blackboards for summer. We could close the door, I could kiss him again, awaken from this dream.

"Need help?"

A big man wearing a dark suit and a tie the color of bile is blocking my way. He's bald without appearing bald—the slope of his forehead combined with a few wispy hairs creates this happy illusion. Long nose, skanky nostrils, yellow teeth. He smells of Wal-Mart musk.

"Hello, Zeb," I say.

It's Zeb Greasy. Our illustrious principal. A person who is *first, highest, or foremost in importance, rank, worth, or degree,* according to Dictionary.com. Zeb Greasy is none of those things. He's simply Large and in Charge.

"Excuse me?" Zeb says.

"There is no excuse, really."

"Carolina?"

The prime criterion for a good principal: a prodigious memory for names and faces. Of course, mine is easier than some. Unnaturally tall girl with hair shaped like a Christmas tree. Ought to be playing basketball; why isn't she? Couldn't catch a man with track shoes and night vision goggles. So serious. What's the matter with her? Thinks every other student is stupid. Well, who's the dum-dum now?

"Are you all right?" Captain Combover says.

I don't know what to tell him.

I could just say it: *Mr. Mann. He's the one; he's responsible. He made me not all right. Fire him, hang him, drag his carcass through the restrooms facedown.* Here's my opportunity.

No.

"I'm going to see the counselor," I'm shocked to remember. "They called me."

"Oh. Well. You looked kind of disoriented there for a moment. And the counselors are on the upper floor."

"Right. I needed something down here." Someone, actually.

"All right, then. I'm going that way; I'll walk with you."

Going what way? Maybe I haven't gotten what I need yet?

But I fall in step beside him, arms swinging. Our steps click in the emptiness. I notice that Zeb Greasy's hands were built for opening water mains. Or strangling livestock.

"Excited about college?" he says.

"I was."

"Excuse me?"

"Yes, yes, sir, I am."

"Good."

We climb the echoing no-slip stairs and don't speak again until we reach the counselors' door.

"Here we are."

Zeb gives me a pat and I go in.

Ms. Peggy Foster.

It says so on her desk. I've seen her around, but I've never been to this one before.

She's not the academics counselor but the one for Student Issues. The one people like Kenny Atkinson get to know. What does she want with me?

"Have a seat."

The room feels as if it's on casters, rolling about. I have to hold my arms tight to my body, or they might flutter and gesture independent of my conscious thoughts. I sense my personality dissolving, disintegrating, actually. Expanding in all directions, fusing with the concrete objects around me.

Focus, I tell myself. Focus or lose everything.

Ms. Foster's the first woman I've ever met with a well-defined Adam's apple. Her hair's undone, glasses hideously large for her small face. Her left hand perches atop a skinny paperback, *Spenser's Epithalamion and Renaissance Pastoralism*. As she speaks to me, she thumbs a corner of the pages again and again. It makes a miniature poker-playing sound, elves playing Texas Hold 'Em.

"Do you know why you're here?"—she pauses to look at a folder—"Carolina?"

"No."

"It was recommended by a member of the staff that you are having some emotional difficulties outside of school. Problems you need help sorting out."

I sit bolt upright. "Who recommended me?"

"I'm not allowed to discuss that. It was thought—"

"He did it, didn't he?" The room is no longer rolling; it's swimming. The hands on the clock tick like a wrench banged on a pipe in a prison camp. My fists tighten. "The son of a— He's trying to make you think I'm crazy."

"What did you say?"

"Nothing."

"Would you like to talk about it?"—pause—"Carolina?"

"No."

"I'm guessing it has to do with boys, am I right?" Ms. Foster smiles hyper-sympathetically, eyes huge behind her glasses. "I can remember when I was your age, I was in a similar predicament where—"

"I can't believe that bastard turned me in."

Ms. Foster's hands jiggle over the folder. She swallows; her Adam's apple plunges up and down like a scarab beetle traveling under the skin of her neck.

"No, not at all. Recommended you as a student in need of counseling. A shoulder, someone to talk to. All confidential. It's up to you. We have materials that can be"—she leans back hard enough to show every feature of her Granny-in-Training bra— "helpful. Here!"

She slides across a brochure with a forest on the cover. THREE RIVERS COUNSELING CENTER. Ms. Foster waits for me to flip it open, gives up and does it herself. Inside, the happy faces of teens on powerful antipsychotics.

"I've seen the facilities myself," she says. "It's impressive what they are able to do. Where does you father work? I'm sure the outpatient services at Three Rivers are covered by—"

Out.

Patient.

That's exactly what I do.

I race down the hall and turn at the first intersection I come to and hide in the janitor's closet. Ms. Foster's anxious steps click past me. I wait in the ammonia-scented dark, count to 140.

When I open the door, she's gone. I'm not used to coming to the bastard's class from this direction. I descend the stairs and there it is, first door on the left. The door is shut. I peer through the glass, see rows of dark heads.

Get ready.

push

Enter.

As I push through the door, Mr. Mann sees me.

This is the last microsecond before the car wreck, two drivers, two people sliding together, helpless before their own momentum. The crash is imminent, but in this last moment we can still pretend things are normal before our lives are changed forever.

Then.

I shove the door so hard, it bangs against an unused podium in the corner.

There's an air-emptying, collective inhalation. In spite of everything, the primary emotion suffusing the room is one of wrongness—I shouldn't be here, not this period. These faces are alien, removed in time from my connection to this place. I fight the urge to run back out.

"Carolina, I—"

The bell rings like a shriek, making everyone flinch. The class stands uncertainly, wondering looks on their faces. Imagine what they would do if I knocked their teacher on his ass.

"It's all right," Mr. Mann says as they begin reluctantly filing out. He shuts the door behind them. Waits, touching his hair, rubbing his hands together. Starts to say something when he feels like it is safe. I cut him off.

"I can't believe you turned me in."

"Carolina, no, I thought it would—"

"You've got them thinking I'm crazy. A head case. In need of help."

"What am I supposed to think? When you—"

"Shut up, just shut up. There's nothing you can say."

I take one long step and shove him hard against the blackboard.

The metal chalk tray shivers and falls off with a clang.

My face is numb. I'm not doing these things; I'm witnessing someone else do them. This never happens in your own town, your own school. How will it play out? Do I have a gun? Should I scream? Fall to the floor, protect myself? I'm witness to and agent of the fear at the same time.

Mr. Mann swipes at my arm, trying to get control of me, misses as I jerk it away.

"Let's go, come on," he says quietly.

But he can't get hold of me. His next class will be here soon. Schuyler once did the calculations, actually, how long our breaks last: we have exactly 7.5 minutes before the kids start coming in— less if some of them have lockers close by. If Mr. Mann doesn't want it all to blow up right here and now—

We struggle, a flurry of intense arms and noises.

Stalemate.

Mr. Mann realizes he's the center of gravity in the room and lets go first. He steps through the door without me. I have no choice but to follow. He makes his way quickly up the hall and around a corner. He's heading for his office. I'm right on his tail; I slam the door shut behind us when we get there.

He won't sit down. Is probably afraid to. "What do you want?" he says.

"You know."

"No, I don't. I don't know anything about what you want anymore. This is crazy. After last night, you're lucky I didn't call the police."

"Why didn't you?"

"You don't understand, do you? You really don't understand."

I lean in close, menacingly, spit the words out. "Then teach me."

He makes a pained face. I say it again.

"Teach me."

"For Christ's sake, Nine. Are you out to ruin me? Go ahead then, turn me in."

"Like you did me."

He chews his bottom lip. "No. I was only trying to help you. I thought it could have been some help."

"Stop pretending to be a grown-up, Richard. You suck at it."

He laughs bitterly. "Shit."

I grab his wrist and hold on. I dig my fingernails into the skin covering the bones and tendons there. I dig in harder and harder. I haven't done this since my seesaw days. I have to do it now. To keep from biting.

He lets me.

I dig harder and harder. Surely he will bleed soon. Or scream.

Neither happens. I let go. The skin is not even broken; it's marked with angry crescent moon indentations. Badges of my frustration.

"What can I do to make you stop?" he says.

"I'll stop when you stop."

"I don't understand."

"Stop being with her. Stop loving her instead of me. Stop stop stop!"

"Carolina."

"Stop calling me that! Do you love me, Richard?"

"Nine."

"Do you love me? It's an easy question. It used to have an easy answer."

In my peripheral vision I see someone hover past his door.

"Well, do you?"

"Nine, I—"

"Do you! Do you do you do you!"

Only now do I realize I'm screaming.

I've grabbed Mr. Mann by his shirt. I'm shoving him against the cinder block wall harder and harder, screaming at him. He's putting his hands on me, trying to get control of the tornado I've become.

"Nine, please, Nine!"

This is where you slap someone hysterical; I've seen it in the movies. A good stinging slap to make my feet touch the floor again. But he can't do that; it's beyond the realm of possibility. But it's possible for me. So very possible. Every time I get loose, I'm swinging at his face. His eyes become blurry comet streaks as our heads jostle, arms move, shouts echo.

I have to stop this—I'm going too far, my fury is too huge. What am I trying to do?

Hurt him. Kill him. Make him feel what I am feeling, even if only for a second.

Stop it, stop it now.

I spin away and slump against the door, scrabbling at the knob. I'm spilling into the hall now, pushing away from the door, backpedaling, now finding my feet and running. Running anywhere. The halls are emptying, but there are still a few kids here and there. I'm banging past them, trying to find my way to some kind of exit, some kind of door that will lead me out of this nightmare, show me things I can understand again.

Where is the parking lot from here? I'm disoriented. People are shouting now; I'm not listening. I run. At the intersection of a hallway I crash headlong into a solid mass of human being—it's a large person with hugely sturdy legs. I sprawl to the floor, feel my cheek kiss the cold surface. I've never seen the tiles this close, the big square tiles in the hallway. Gray, flecked with bits of black and brown in random sprinklings.

Someone helps me up. I slap and tear and pull at this someone, feeling large hands under my arms, lifting.

He's saying something to me, but I can't understand the words; I'm fighting him too hard. We're walking away fast, but it's not really my legs doing the walking; it's somebody else and my strides are matching his.

He's much stronger than me; there's only one thing, one thing I can do, swing and make it good, make it count. I get one arm free, swing as hard as I can with my fist, connect against the meat and bone of his face.

Zeb Greasy.

"Here."

Schuyler hands me a cup of water.

He didn't skip on Senior Skip Day, either. Today he's playing office aide.

I can see the reflection of my own devastation in his eyes, the way the blood has drained from his face. "Now what is—?" he starts.

"Wait," I say. "Please."

I can't bear to look him in the eye.

Instead I look into the paper cup and sip. Sip again. My hands are trembling so much, the water pulses in concentric circles. The forest fire of my anger has settled down to a few smoking embers. I'm coming back into myself, realizing the horror of what I've just done.

The clock on the wall makes a sound like a blade coming down with each tick.

I know he's aching to talk, but I appreciate that he is letting me have a moment to collect myself, survey the carnage.

Zeb Greasy and the other People Who Count are behind closed doors debating my future. His door is thick, but not so thick we can't hear the subsurface rumbling of their voices.

At the other end of this narrow space is Ms. Jackson. She's the person who checks students out for doctor appointments, field trips, attempted homicides. Her desk is surrounded by American flags, desperately misshapen bald eagles, wooden slogans:

THESE COLORS DON'T RUN

I'm supposed to be cheered by this display. Ms. Jackson never looks up. She's not a color.

I look up. Schuyler's holding a pen above some official-looking documents.

"Talk to me," he says.

"No."

He leans forward and whispers, "Don't worry about her."—Ms. Jackson—"Just talk to me."

"It's too much. I don't know what to say."

"But what did you do? What's going on?"

He knows I've never been in trouble before, not for the slightest infraction, going all the way back to seventh grade, when Ms. Collins caught me chewing gum.

I take another sip, put the cup down. "Just fill out the papers for me, please. I can't do it. I have to get out of here, Schuyler. You have to trust me. I'm losing it. I can't stand it anymore. I'll go crazy."

I can't tell him everything, not now. We have to have each other. That's all we have. Nobody else knows us at our centers. If Schuyler finds out about Mr. Mann—I'm so terrified maybe I won't even have him anymore. Not in the same way. Best friends don't do this to best friends. It will never be the same again once he knows. And I'll be all alone, stuck inside here. Stuck inside my head. No way out anymore.

He opens his mouth but is drowned out by the squawk box on the wall ordering all the graphics geeks to multimedia. As if the world hasn't just come to an end.

"Come on. Talk to me, Nine."

"Please. You know what to write; just do it."

"Okay. Name, rank, serial number."

"Stop it."

"I'm sorry."

Schuyler scratches away for a while. Have they called my folks? Does it matter? This is a dream. That's it. Just ride it out, daylight will come.

A door opens in the dream and God appears. No, it's not the Almighty, it's Zeb Greasy. Dream over. The look on his face says he's extraordinarily disappointed. The blotchy red spot on his cheekbone says to my horror that I nailed him a good one; my knuckles are still smarting. He motions me inside.

Schuyler reaches across the counter and gives my hand a squeeze just before I go in; this makes it infinitely worse. I slip through the door, let it swing shut behind me like a vault.

"I saw her just before it happened," Zeb is saying to the assistant principal, Mr. Pendergraff, as if I've gone deaf. Mr. Pendergraff is the Head Butt-beater and Discipline Guy. "I knew something was wrong."

I can't think anything but the most basic thoughts. A person who shares my name is in tremendous trouble. For some reason I'm here, watching. Part interested, part stupefied.

Now Zeb Greasy's addressing me, my hearing miraculously healed.

"You want to talk about it, Carolina?"

I don't speak, don't even shake my head. Do I ever want to talk about anything again? I don't know. Will they beat my butt? They can't do that these days.

Zeb's office is large. Lots of polished, beveled wood: his desk, his nameplate, lacquered copies of the Constitution, Declaration of Independence, Bill of Rights.

"Have a seat."

Zeb gestures and I sit. His chair makes an officious farting noise as he settles into it.

I turn my attention to Mr. Pendergraff. He remains standing. He is just the opposite of Zeb Greasy. Small featured, small boned, small voiced. If they lock us in a cage together, he's a dead man.

Mr. Pendergraff creases his flat butt against the edge of a table. He's wearing colored prescription glasses that scream Gamblers Anonymous. His wrinkly skin has no snap; surely he must be a smoker.

"I've called your parents, Carolina," Mr. Pendergraff says. "Do you understand what I'm saying to you?" He's mouthing the words as if I'm a lip-reader or buzzed on Ecstasy.

I devote just enough juice to the question to allow me to weakly nod. This is happening to someone else in a galaxy far, far away. Through some tangle in the space-time fabric of things, I'm able to witness the destruction of this strange, obsessed girl.

"You physically assaulted Mr. Deason," Mr. Pendergraff says. "Like to tell me why?"

"No. I can't."

So they think this is all about me and Zeb. They don't know what happened in Mr. Mann's office. Don't know I almost wanted to kill him.

Where is he? What is he thinking right this moment? Is he terrified, praying I won't tell? Or maybe he doesn't pray.

Maybe he needs to start.

"You realize, don't you, that we could expel you for this, Carolina," Mr. Pendergraff says. "Technically. You know what that means, right? No diploma. Repeat of your senior year."

My heart plunges into my sneakers.

"But to tell you the truth, we don't want to do that. I've pulled your file—" Mr. Pendergraff touches a manila folder on the table with the tips of four fingers. "You've never given anybody a lick of trouble. Straight A's since the eighth grade, which is as far back as our college reporting goes. Perfect attendance five years running. You don't even skip on Senior Day. So tell me about it. Why did this happen?"

"I can't—it just—happened."

"Talking is always better, Carolina. Believe me. I've been at this thirty-five years. Talking is better."

Nothing.

I won't do it. I refuse to make this easy for Mr. Mann.

"Look, I'm not here to make your life miserable," Mr. Pendergraff says. "I'm here to help. Mr. Deason says you were called into the counselor's office just before the—ah—incident. Now, what's said there is private, I know that. But a student like you—a girl!—just doesn't go off like that for no reason a few days before she graduates. Something sparked it. I need to know what that something is. You'll feel better once you get it off your chest. Trust me."

I wish I could cry, scream, anything to get him to shut up and just get it over with. But he marches on.

Thirty minutes later, it's still on my chest and I'm still not in a trusting mood. Mom is in the outer office. Dad can't be reached; he must be out at the test stands again.

All I know is, it is finished.

School. For me, at least.

I'm suspended the last three days of my senior year.

A permanent blot on my perfect, stainless record. Surely not even Hub Christy could manage this achievement.

Mr. Pendergraff assures me I can still attend graduation and the baccalaureate at the Civic Center.

"The police—"

Did he really mention the police? But why would they be interested? For the first time, the full consequences of what I've done sink in. I've assaulted a faculty member. Two, if truth be known. He promises not to call them.

Why can't I stop? Why can't I just tell them, End it all now? Do I really want to take Mr. Mann's head, push it under, hold it there until the bubbles stop rising? What am I turning into? What is he?

Where is he?

Mom.

She breaks down, collects herself, breaks down a second time. Finally is able to talk to the Head Butt-beater, then we talk together, Mom getting more and more stridently hysterical. Why do adults think teenagers will heed their words of wisdom if they repeat them three times? Four? A hundred? At top volume? Do they really believe we are that thick? We heard you. The first time. We're beating ourselves up worse than you could ever imagine.

Shame.

I'm rolled up in it. Festering, smelly, crazy with fear, nuclear embarrassment, self-loathing. I've transformed myself from the sweet, perfect daughter she knows into something lower than a hairy clog in the bottom of a bathtub drain. Worse, I'm afraid for her, afraid she will blow up some important plumbing in her head with all the weeping and pleading.

"Darling, darling, tell me something!" she begs.

"Mom. Mom. Mom." I want to shake her, hold her, crush her unnaturally curly head into my arms.

"What?"

"Please, let's just go home."

"But we have to work through this, sweetheart! Mr. Pendergraff—"

"Doesn't know what he's talking about."

"But won't you tell us why you did this thing? What's happened?"

"I can't, really I can't. But please don't worry, okay? It'll be okay, it will."

Will it?

She daubs at her eyes with a hay fever tissue. Her words come out between gulping sobs. "How can you tell me not to worry, sweetheart? It's impossible. Your principal! Impossible. I knew something was happening, I knew it! But I can help—your father and I, we can help. But you've got to talk to us, darling. Don't shut us out."

She starts to say something else; it becomes a wail of despair instead.

Is this how it happens?

All those people who do dumb, crazy, idiotic things—does it start with something like this? I'm getting stupider and stupider. By some reverse alchemical process, my forehead has been transmogrified into a substance thick enough to block gamma rays.

Thank goodness they've sent Schuyler up the hall on an errand. He's not here to see this, to watch us stumbling along like victims of an air crash as Mr. Pendergraff escorts us out.

Mom clutches my middle as we stagger up the hall, putting her head against my shoulder. She's desperate to make me ten again, the last time she could truly understand me. Or take me in her arms without my chin resting on her forehead. I'm aware of the tendons radiating out from my neck, the pressure she is putting there.

In the parking lot I'm suddenly hammered with the realization: This is it.

This bleary, insane mess is the culmination of twelve years of steadfast, unrelenting effort; over thirteen thousand hours, eight hundred thousand minutes, untold millions of separate moments, mostly forgettable, others that made all the difference.

This place I've been so familiar with, the faces, walls, doors, smells, sounds, angles of light—I haven't been in the library in a week—now I'll never see it again. Not once. Everything is over. It's my turn to wail.

Mr. Pendergraff waves at us from the double doors.

"Goodbye, young lady," he says. "I hope you'll think about what we've said here today."

Young?

Goodbye, indeed.

critical mass

It's bad.

But I can't help it. Mom is so trusting.

But I've got to escape. This is killing me.

She's in front of me in her daisy-yellow Bug, driving ten miles an hour below the speed limit, left blinker stuck in the on position. Three times I've nearly rear ended her.

At the next intersection, I turn right without signaling and let her go.

With any luck, it'll be blocks before she notices. This is mean, even monstrously cruel, but I don't care. I can't face them both. Right now I'd rather worry them to death than answer their questions. My whole life I've been a Good Girl. I'm ready to be a little bad.

I don't know where I'm going. I fight to keep from turning down the road to Sunlake. No.

Clouds are gathering. We could use the rain. A torrent, a flood, something to push me off the road, carry me into the ocean, where I can slip beneath the waves. Just park and watch the fish swim by as I rot.

Have I eaten? What day is this?

I'm nearly out of gas. Maybe I should drive straight out of town, see how far it takes me, then get out and walk into the woods. There are places where you can walk for miles without seeing a road or another human being. Is this true or just my fervent wish?

Why do people need other people so much? Why can't we just do our work and go home? Why do we have to talk and touch and dream together?

This feels like something pretending to be my life.

How could things have gone this wrong so quickly? It was his choice; all he had to do was stay the course. He destroyed everything.

I'm driving too fast; does that matter? It's an act of will to keep Wilkie between the lines. But hasn't that been what I've always done up to now? Lived between the lines? What made me think I could go outside them? How could he have given me that kind of courage and then pulled it all away?

Is he thinking about me now?

I can taste tar blowing through the vents.

Vacation.

Just like Mom wanted, I'm suddenly ten years old again.

I can see the ocean.

We've driven a million miles to get here.

North Carolina, the Outer Banks National Seashore.

I'm walking down a sharply descending strip of sand; the surf comes in very rough here. A little ways out the bottom suddenly drops, becomes a long wedge of hard sand, a place where the edge of the continent is about to crack off. You can see it plainly when the sea pulls back between waves. This is where the surf strikes each time it falls, where the ocean sucks at every particle of sand, water, weed, makes them broil on top of this knife cut in the bottom.

I wade out to see what it's like. Suddenly I can't move my legs.

I see Mom and Dad a football pass away, but they might as well be on Mars. They can't reach me, can't even hear me because of the crashing surf.

The earth tumbles beneath my feet. I'm going under. God has just sat down in his bath. I'm rolling on the knife edge beneath the waves; there's nothing I can do about it. I'm going to be rolling on this underwater ridge forever. Until I'm beaten microscopic, become a part of the sea, scattered. Still, I fight it, clawing at the sand. It's scratching and tearing at me. Finally my lungs are bursting; I can't battle the pull anymore. I let go.

Suddenly I'm up in the light, flung far from shore.

They had to get me with a boat.

Blink.

Where am I?

Suddenly it's there again, not the ocean, but the road in front of me. I'm driving. I've traveled an unknown number of miles without seeing anything but memories. There's a billboard up ahead, huge and orange-yellow, with a line of painted green mountains in the background. The lettering is ominous, large, black:

SPRUNK REALTY
WHERE YOUR LAND-BUYING DREAMS COME TRUE!
SELLING RESIDENTIAL AND RURAL ACREAGE ACROSS NORTH
ALABAMA SINCE 1984

A leering face to one side of the billboard glares down at me as I pass by.

Alicia's father. Mr. Sprunk.

I remember that awful lizard face. From the wedding.

The road blurs; I'm weeping again.

This is the thing about life I've never really understood until now: we try so hard to control it, but bad things happen anyway. The only real control is an anti-control, a letting go. Like I did at the ocean when I was ten. That's what nature really wants.

Okay.

The steering wheel is loose in my hands.

I let it slurry back and forth, feeling Wilkie's tires shimmy on the pavement. A dull tingling starts at my temples. Spots are spreading across my eyes.

My hands leave the steering wheel.

I don't know if this is a conscious act.

There's a long moment when everything is perfection; Wilkie's alignment is Good and True. I run straight down the road, an electron in a particle accelerator.

Then.

Wilkie swerves, nearly jumps the median, recovers valiantly, slides across two lanes, heading for a group of corrugated buildings. Horns blare and rubber squeals.

Emily.

> *Good-by to the life I used to live,*
> *And the world I used to know;*
> *And kiss the hills for me, just once;*
> *Now I am ready to go!*

hearts on mars

A miracle.

That can only be what it is—instead of drifting into another car, nailing a telephone pole head-on, flinging us from an overpass, Wilkie has brought me here.

The car skids to a bouncing stop. Someone is still honking as they fly on down the road. Wilkie rocks on his ancient suspension; the engine cuts out and starts ticking. I close my eyes and lay my head on the steering wheel.

My heart is a hunk of Martian hematite, bloodless, frozen, pitted.

I nearly died. Nearly killed other people too. But somehow I've been saved.

After a time I lift my head and gradually my vision clears. I become aware I'm in a broad, empty parking lot surrounded by power poles with yellow guy wires. Nearby stands a group of low buildings. One has a sign in the window:

LAST CHANCE

That's all it says.

I'm not stupid enough to believe it's a message for me. It's some kind of sale that ran a very long time ago. But I'm certain about one thing:

I've entered a new country I never thought I would see. My second life.

Why here? Why now? There has to be a reason.

I think about this awhile. Crank Wilkie's ignition. Slowly pull out on the road heading back the way I came.

Looking for the address on the bottom of the billboard.

lizard killer

Get out.

My legs are shaking.

I haven't eaten since yesterday. The sun is blinding. Wilkie's hood is warm. I lean against it to try to clear the dizziness. My brain is coated with a fuzz; everything around me has a dreamlike quality. Maybe this is what an aneurysm feels like in the last microsecond before the blood vessel bursts.

Life number two.

I'm trying to figure out what I'm supposed to do with it.

Mom's cell phone buzzes in my pocket. I slowly punch in a trembly text message: *I'm okay home soon.*

Mr. Sprunk's office is last in a row of cookie-cutter brick cubes. Architectural style: Hand It Over. Plastic curtains are drawn across the big front window. Something tells me they are never opened. I walk toward them in a dream-fog, grip the handle as firmly as I can, step inside.

There is no bell. This does not feel like entering heaven. The interior is dark and smells of paper.

My eyes adjust. The paneling is thumbtacked with dozens of square topographic maps. Dad taught me how to read them when I was a kid. The swirling contour lines are hills, mountains, floodplains. Each map bears the name of a particular quadrangle of land: MOONTOWN, VALHERMOSA, RED BOILING SPRINGS.

Four leather chairs sit against the walls. I'm desperate to sit again, but I resist the urge. At the far end is a counter covered with office flotsam. A subdivision plat hangs above it: WALDEN PONDS. Photographs alongside the plat show tiny lakes molded around a golf course, sterile as new underwear. Not exactly Thoreau's *Life in the Woods*, I tell myself dully.

A partially opened door behind the counter leaks white-green fluorescent. Is anyone here?

Yes. Some large and energetic creature is rustling around in there.

I approach the sound carefully, conscious I'm making myself quiet. I peer through the gap in the door: a powerful back squeezed into a dark suit coat hunkers across my field of view.

If I slip out now, he'll never know I was here. I make myself wait, heart drumming.

The door suddenly opens all the way.

"Hey."

Mr. Sprunk comes in, rolling his massive shoulders. He's even bigger than I remembered. His brow is furrowed, making him look permanently suspicious. His upper lip juts out to meet the tip of his nose, reptilian.

"I didn't know anybody was out here," he says. "Can I help you?"

He's got a bad case of Elevator Eyes—they jump between my face and my barely existent boobs, settling somewhere in between. I realize I don't know what I'm going to say.

"Um. I need to speak to you, Mr. Sprunk."

He scowls curiously. "I'm really busy right at the moment, young lady. I'm on my way to a closing."

"A closing?"

"Could you come back another time?"

I think about it. Will there ever be another time like this?

"No, I don't think so."

He steps up to the counter as if he hasn't heard me, runs his thick fingers over a bristling pile of legal documents. For the first time I see it, the gun. It's a small pistol sitting on top of a black leather holster in the middle of all the paper. I don't know anything about guns. I wonder what it's doing there, what he could possibly use it for.

"I carry it for copperheads when I show land," Mr. Sprunk says, following my gaze. He straightens and his eyes dart to his watch. "Okay. You've got two minutes."

"I've got something to ask you."

"Well."

"It's about your daughter."

This gets his attention. The elevator goes back up. "Alicia? What about her?" He squints. "Do I know you?"

"No. I mean—I know your son-in-law, Mr. Mann." Matt the Jesus Phreak's definition of the word *know* rings in my ears.

"Mr. Mann. You mean Ricky?" The elevator drops a couple of floors.

"Yes."

"What do you want to know?"

"Um—how did they meet?"

"What?"

"Mr. Mann—Ricky and Alicia, how did they meet? How long have they known each other?"

"How old are you?"

I shift on my feet, uncomfortably aware of my sneakers. Mr. Sprunk stalks around to my side of the counter, moving with a dangerous muscularity. One of those men who can be accommodating only so long before his cerebral cortex starts to itch.

"Why are you asking me this?" he says.

"Do you know?" I say. "How they met? I need to know."

"Why don't you just ask Ricky?"

"I did. He won't tell me."

His face goes slack. "I think I'm beginning to get the picture. Look, I—"

"Please. This is really important to me."

"Why?"

"I can't tell you."

It feels strangely unfair to say the same thing Mr. Mann has been saying to me.

"Then I guess we're both out of luck, honey," Mr. Sprunk says. "Now I really do need to be going."

I stand my ground. "It's a simple question. Why is everybody so mysterious about it?"

"I'm sorry, but you'll have to excuse me, sweetie. Damn it."
He turns on his heel as if he's forgotten something in the back.

I'm going to do this. I am. "He's my teacher," I say. "I was
sleeping with him."

Mr. Sprunk stops, pulled up short. "Who?"

"Mr. Mann. I was sleeping with him when he married your
daughter."

Even in my dreamy state, my courage amazes me; I've somehow found it, inside, of all places, my fear. Mr. Sprunk makes a
kind of proto-laugh, bites it off. He turns his head slightly, blinking slowly, a crocodile considering its options.

"Why are you telling me this, darling?" He's using those
words, *honey*, *sweetie*, *darling*, like curses.

"I—I just thought you'd like to know."

"Bullshit. There's a reason for everything. You made this up;
you're trying to get something out of me, trying to get me to do
something for you."

Am I?

What do I want him to do, break Mr. Mann in half? Take his
body to Red Boiling Springs and throw it down a sinkhole?

The arrogance, both of ours, is breathtaking.

"You're one of those people." I hardly believe the audacity of
my own words. "Everything's about you, isn't it?"

I've never talked to a grown-up this way. I think he's getting
off on it. He licks the corner of his mouth, studying me more
closely, a loose kind of awareness dawning.

"Wait a minute. I thought I recognized you. You're that gal
who crashed the wedding, aren't you?"

I hover between the truth and a lie and decide on neither.

"Yeah. The one with the purple dress and the hat. That was

quite a package you gave my daughter." His teeth are clenched, but he's smiling. I realize this is his closest approximation for happiness: he's pleased with himself.

I ache to slap him. I do the next-best thing.

"So you don't care that I was sleeping with him? That he doesn't really love Alicia? That all the times he's with her, he's really thinking about me?"

Suddenly he's leaning into my face, crushing my wrist in his big hand.

He cares.

"Listen to me, girl." His pores are ugly and huge. His breath smells of coffee and hamburger onions. I feel faint again. "Don't you ever come around me or my family again. Do you hear me?"

I nod, glancing at the pistol on the counter. So close. This is how things happen, I realize. All you have to do is be willing to go just a little bit further than most people. And your life changes in a moment.

He gives my arm a final devastating pinch before letting it go.

"Now get out of my office."

He turns and goes into the back room, begins digging through a stack of papers.

Go.

I'm in the parking lot before I truly realize I've done it.

Slipped the copperhead pistol into the back of my jeans.

shovel of fire

Supper.

Chili cheese fries at the mall.

I throw them up ten minutes later.

All I can think about is Mr. Sprunk's pistol in Wilkie's glove box. How I've always hated guns. How I'm terrified of going back to my car.

"Oh, thank God, thank God," Mom says over and over when I call from the food court. I tell her I'm sorry. She pleads with me to come home. I promise.

I put the phone away. It immediately starts to buzz in my pants. I shut it off.

I limp from one end of the mall and back. My hip still hurts from falling off Mr. Mann's balcony. My mouth is sour. My fingers tingle as if they aren't getting enough blood. Calm down. Find a quiet place. The bookstore. But isn't there anyplace I can sit? It's criminal to have to stand and read.

Criminal.

Will he call Mr. Mann? Try to find out who I am? Send the police to my house?

God.

I squat cross-legged in the back corner with the picture books. This is the only reasonably private place in the store. I flip through *Mike Mulligan and His Steam Shovel*. I like these pictures, comfort food for the mind. There's Mike Mulligan, just as he always has been, sturdy, sure, competent. There's his steam shovel, Mary Anne, joyful in her anticipation of work. They're digging the same square hole they were digging when I was four. I like the color of the dirt as it flies out of the hole. It reminds me of clouds or the flanks of a friendly animal. I like the growing fury, Mary Anne's eyes, the hell-bent focus, her bucket mouth biting into the earth.

Now the page that always scared me—Mary Anne sitting in the basement, all those pipes driven into her side, her caterpillar tracks gone. All that power, energy, drive, stopped forever. They've made it where she can't run, can't dig, can only sit, her body pierced with ductwork, immobile.

A fire burning her insides up.

the parent particle

Home.

"Nine," Dad says when I come through the door.

Has Mr. Sprunk called? The police? This is what I've been dreading the most. Why I stayed away from the house as long as I could.

I try to gauge his face. His eyes are set, gray little circles, brows heavy. He seems more tired than usual. Here it comes—the shame, the great disappointment we've been building toward after so much promise. Ever since we started pulling away from each other after I got into high school. All ready to drop on my head.

"What can we do to help you?" he says.

I throw my arms around his neck and kiss his cheek and try not to cry. "You just did, Daddy. You just did."

Not bad for a man who can calculate the value of pi to more than fifty thousand decimal places.

Nothing.

For three days.

If Alicia's father were going to have me arrested because of the stolen pistol, he would have done it by now. Maybe it's not registered? Or is Mr. Mann lying for me? Or maybe Mr. Sprunk doesn't want to ask him who I am? Maybe he doesn't want there to be any contact between us, ever again.

All I know is, I've spent the last seventy-six hours in a heart-grinding terror. Every siren—

I'm desperately ready for a friend.

NAP.

That's what Schuyler calls them:

Nine's Access Procedures.

This means that before I can let you in to see all the strange, idiotic, important, ridiculous, scary, beautiful, sad, ecstatic stuff— before you can be my friend—you must pass a series of rigorous safety checks.

I don't know what they are.

I only know if they've been satisfied.

Schuyler gets a free pass. I've known him, trusted him since he used to throw himself out of the playground swings and was inexplicably terrified of ventriloquist dummies.

If Schuyler knew, he would say Mr. Mann is the supreme violation of NAP.

That I've handed my personal Rosetta Stone to a man who— what exactly has he done? What did he do? I don't know anymore. I don't know.

Help me.

This is eating me alive. I can't keep going this way. I can't eat, can't sleep; I'm barely able to function. I have to tell somebody. I have to tell Schuyler.

So why am I so scared?

I don't know how he'll react. He warned me. He tried to warn me again and again.

But do I want him to know he was so right?

To him it's just a stupid game, another crush to be stamped out, stomped on, chewed up. Horny Howard, part two.

But how can he ever know this: that Mr. Mann is life, breathing, love, wonder, joy, pain, rage, murder? How can he understand? And does Schuyler deserve to know this? Is he ready? Can he handle the truth?

Okay, what's the worst that could happen?

I will lose him too.

No. I can't believe that. I know him too well. He will be hurt, sure.

But why? What right does he have to be hurt? He didn't earn it; I did.

But best friends don't keep secrets from each other. Not secrets like this. What about that kind of hurt?

I hate this. I hate not knowing what to do. I hate arguing with myself. I hate being confused, stuck, scared, smashed.

Alone.

That's it, that's what I hate worst of all. Going through this alone. That's what I can't be anymore. Alone. Not one more day.

Tell him. Tell him now. Tell him before you explode.

"Schuyler."

He's sitting on the seat beside me in Wilkie Collins. The sky is
blue. The roads are clear. My eyes are itchy from crying.

"Are you okay?" he says.

"No."

"So are you finally ready to tell me? What's wrong? What is it?"

"It's too—I don't know."

"Too what?"

"Too big, too awful. I should have told you."

He raises one eyebrow, begins scratching an imaginary beard
like a half-assed Sigmund Freud. "Okay. Schpill, fräulein."

"Stop it. I can't tell you if you're going to act stupid like that.
It's too important."

"Sorry. So don't tell me if you think I'm like that."

"It's just—you know how you are."

"What. What are you talking about?"

See. He's hurt; I've hurt him already. But I have to keep
going.

"You know how you are—you'll say, *I told you so.* You'll say
you warned me. And you did, yeah, you did, over and over. And
you know what? It pisses me off. It really pisses me off like crazy.
Why do you always have to be right? Why do I always have to be
stupid and wrong and fall flat on my face?"

"Who says that? I never say that."

"Oh yes, you do. In so many ways—you just don't know it." I
feel fresh tears burning the corners of my eyes. "That's what
hurts. It makes me feel like I get punished for anything I do, anything I try that isn't what's expected of me. It's easy for you: you
never try anything, you always hold back."

"That's not true."

"It's true. You just don't know it. I'm the one who goes out and does things, who experiences things. You're the one who warns me about it, tells me things will fall apart or somebody's just after this or that, trying to hurt me."

He looks away. "I'm not stupid, Nine."

"I know you're not. Who said you are? That's the problem."

"This is all about him, isn't it?"

"Him?"

"Don't act like you don't know what I'm talking about. So why are you protecting him? What did he do, try to jump you? And you like the *Mustela nivalis* too much to turn him in?"

"Weasels! What? What are we talking about here? Weasels?"

"European common, to be exact."

"Weasels, Schuyler! That's what I mean! That's just what I mean. I'm too tired for this."

"Nope. You're stalling. Come on. Just tell me straight out. If you don't, I'll just have to guess."

"No."

"Then say it."

I'm quiet for half a mile, watching the road stretch, feeling my heart pound.

"Okay," he says. "Mr. Mann yodels show tunes outside your window each night."

"Shut up."

"He stole your favorite pink-striped undies from PE and has them hanging from his rearview mirror."

"Schuyler."

"You read each other moldy poetry every day after lunch to aid your digestion."

I elbow him in the mouth.

"God. God, Nine."

Out of the corner of my eye, I see him probing his lip with the tips of his fingers. We don't talk for a while.

"You really fell for him, didn't you?" Schuyler says finally.

"Shut up."

"Oh God. You did. You really did."

I'm having trouble seeing the road. I pull over into a parking lot, trying not to cry. I'm sick of crying. Across the way a fifty-foot red fabric worm with arms is shimmying with compressed air. The worm is holding a cell phone in one hand, a sign in the other:

TIME FOR A NEW PLAN?

I wail.

Schuyler leaves me alone, lets all of it pour out until at last I'm shaking with grief and rage and beating my hands on the steering wheel. He's afraid to touch me, but I can tell he wants to.

"Oh, come here." I put myself in his arms.

We hold for a long time; then I tell him everything. All of it. Right from the very start. Everything except the pistol.

The cell worm wiggles. Schuyler's ears steadily droop. Finally he shifts away from me on the seat.

"Enough. I don't want to hear any more about him. He's a bastard, and I don't want to hear any more. I hate him. I can't believe it, Nine."

"See why I didn't want to tell you?"

"I hate him."

"I knew you'd react this way."

"What am I supposed to say? The bastard. If I had any guts, I'd turn him in myself. No. I'd kick his balls up past his Adam's apple."

"But you won't. Because I don't want you to."

"No. I said if I had any guts. God."

"Stop saying that."

"I can't help it. God. God!" He's yelling out the window at the worm. I grab his arm, pull him back inside.

"Calm down."

He lies back against the seat, staring at the visor. "You know what I hate almost most of all?"

"What?"

"God, you're so much braver than me."

"I'm not brave. Believe me." I touch his hand. "You don't know how good it feels to finally tell someone."

Schuyler touches his face and frowns.

"I'm sorry about your lip," I say.

"You should have told me," he says.

"I know. I'm sorry."

"At least it's over now. Everything's over."

My throat tightens.

"What?" he says.

"It's over when I say it's over."

Schuyler's watching me. I have to find out now. Now that he has the power to stop me, to inject some sanity back into my life. Will he run to my parents? Try to keep me from my campaign against Mr. Mann? I'm holding my breath.

His ears go up. "Okay. So what do we do now? I've got ideas."

We.

For the first time in days, I smile.

tender earthquake

Bed.

Confessing to Schuyler helps, but I still can't sleep.

There is not a name for what I'm feeling. There is no description for it.

To call it *yearning* would be like calling the ocean *water*.

Whatever this thing is, it shoves you inside itself and you can't measure its boundaries, because they go too far and you don't have enough time. Or you move toward the boundaries and they move away.

There has been an earthquake in my life.

Catastrophic, civilization-ending. At least my tiny civilization of one. Followed by massive aftershocks. The fissure is still there, raw and crumbly.

No one can predict when the tremors will start again, least of all me. A thousand years from now? Tomorrow? Here?

for the dead

Graduation is a day.

That's all.

I'm not sure what I expected, but this Disneyland queue wasn't it. With a name like Livingston, I'm always in the forgotten middle of everything. Seven high schools attend baccalaureate together. In our gowns, the Civic Center is awash with a chemical warfare of color combinations. Here are the Burst Blood Vessels; over there, the Screaming Bile. I'm with the Neon Pumpkins.

For once, it's Dad who gets teary eyed. He doesn't remember the things you are supposed to remember; he remembers we were supposed to have a colony on Mars by the time I got this old. Terraforming other planets. Travel from New York to London in under fifteen minutes. What happened? He mourns the things people his age would have given to people my age by now.

Mom takes a hundred million pictures: Schuyler and me, arm in arm. Me accepting my ten-pound diploma, Zeb Greasy's football-sized handshake, strangers smiling, empty folding chairs. When Hub Christy lumbers across the stage, a Macedonian phalanx rises to its feet in the cheap seats and hyena calls:

"You made it!"

I'm the only one who doesn't throw her pasteboard hat.

My grandparents have all been dead for years. One of them lived until I was six and another until I was eight. They didn't last long enough for nicknames or savings bond graduation presents. I wonder what they would think of me now, the silent four of them. All I have of them is pictures. I know what they looked like when they were twenty. Or thirty-five—

Mr. Mann sits with the other teachers. I never see him look my way. His suit is black. His eyes are black. Alicia is nowhere to be found. Hiding in Sunlake, I suppose. Locking and relocking her sliding glass door.

They announce my scholarship.

I'm too ashamed to tell anybody I lost it. I never filled out the paperwork.

After.

So high school is gone.

We're sitting in Schuyler's bedroom, gowns crumpled on the floor. I've been here hundreds of times. There's a different feeling now. A sense of interests gone to clutter, a soul hovering between kid and man. Schuyler's embarrassed about it.

"Got to get rid of some of this junk," he says.

For as long as I can remember, this room has been a museum: heaps of dirty fossils like miniature grist wheels or emery grinders, Ping-Pong-ball solar systems, a starfish dangling on a string.

"You never get rid of anything," I say.

"That's not true."

"You know it is."

I flop back on his bed. Directly above me, thumbtacked to the ceiling, is a poster of M20, the Trifid Nebula, taken by the Hubble. I gave it to him. For the millionth time it reminds me of a backlit snail—if a snail were the Ultimate Ruler of the Universe and had posed for a Maxfield Parrish painting.

Schuyler flops on the bed next to me. This is the first time it feels odd. We're so close, our arm hairs are touching. His dark, mine tawny. All I can think about is—I look away at the bookshelf.

"You still have your grandma's Cenozoic wedding books about what it takes to make a good wife."

"A good beating," Schuyler says. An old joke between us that has lost its juice. He kicks a thin book with a socked toe. "You know everybody parks their trash in here. *Winning at Power Golf,*

for Hrothgar's sake." Schuyler's been reading *Beowulf* lately, figuring he can leapfrog freshman comp in college.

Is this what the future looks like? An embarrassed past?

"The future is nothing but a mythology," I say.

"Translation, please?"

"Can you really make a new life just by throwing out all the
junk from your old one?"

"If you throw him out on his ass."

"Quarter."

"*Ass* is no longer a cussword. I heard the president say it."

"Only one gluteus at a time, please. Try saying it in front of
my parents."

Schuyler laughs and props himself on his elbow. "Point
taken. Okay, at least you've got your sense of humor back. So,
on the subject of asses—what are we going to do about Mr. Dick
Waddius?"

"That's another quarter."

"*Dick*, as you know, is a diminutive form of *Richard*. And if
anybody ever needed to be made to feel diminutive, it's him. We
have to make a plan."

"Okay."

Schuyler's an INTP on the Myers-Briggs sorter. *Can become
very excited about theories and ideas,* his profile says. I'm an
INTJ. The difference between a P and a J? I want answers. I
like closure. I believe you take theories and ideas and make
them real.

I'm looking at an article tacked on his bulletin board. The
headline is blown up to max wattage:

TEENAGE GIRL'S X-RAY VISION BAFFLES SCIENTISTS

I know the first line by heart:

"Russian scientists are unable to disprove a teenage girl who claims she has x-ray vision and can see inside human bodies."

Schuyler has always said that's me, only I can do it with the human soul. Right now I'd do better with the spleen.

There's a knock at the door. Schuyler's mom. She's twenty years younger than my mom and beautiful, except for her protruding front teeth.

"Pick those up." She points at the gowns. "You'll want to save them forever."

"Most certainly, memsahib," Schuyler says in his best Hindustani. We're still on the bed, but miraculously the distance between us has instantly grown by the length of a cucumber.

Ms. Green slouches against the door. "So what do you two want?"

She's talking about the after-graduation dinner our folks have promised us.

What do we want?

"NPH," Schuyler says when his mom has gone.

He's christened a new acronym.

"NPH?"

"Nuclear Public Humiliation. That's the plan! That's your revenge. Only, now you've got me to help."

I'm unbending government paper clips, reshaping them into tiny zip guns, thinking, Is that what I'm after? Is it that mindless and simple? Or is it something much bigger and deeper?

"It's not about revenge," I decide. "It's about making sure he understands. Again and again. Until I know why."

"Why he did it?"

I nod, but this nod is a lie using body language.

No, I think. Not why he did it.

Why he ever stopped.

mouth work

Focus.

"First, we need some information," Schuyler says.

Now we're in my bedroom. We Google Mr. Mann on the net:

Accountants, a psychologist, somebody who knows what *Detection and Classification of Motion Boundaries* means, a college swimmer from West Virginia, a championship wrestler circa 1948.

"What the crap is a Bastyr homeopath?"

"Okay, maybe he doesn't exist after all," Schuyler says.

I slap him. But playfully.

"So let's try the Little Woman."

"*Little* is the operative term, all right."

A search on Alicia recedes in the opposite direction. Not one listing.

Schuyler leans back in my desk chair so far the casters squeak. "Maybe she's too young."

"Not funny."

"No, really."

"No, really, shut up about it."

"Okay. Well, anyhow, that's a bust. What next?"

Kitty Nation comes into the room and curls past my legs,

purring. "So we'll just have to stake out their place. Look for the best opportunity."

"*Naturellement*. But you promise, nothing too freaky till I get my sea legs under me?"

I touch my hip. It's still sore. "I know. I know. But it won't be quite as satisfying."

"Or dangerous. Or idiotic. I still can't believe you climbed up on his deck like that."

"You wouldn't understand."

"Try me."

"No."

"Come on. You wanted to catch them, didn't you? Catch them doing the nast—"

I stomp his toe and put a finger to my lips. "Shhh—!"

Mom pokes her head in the door.

"Children, could I get you something?"

"Something to drink, sure. Thanks." I wait until the door shuts. "Be careful!" I say when she's gone.

I get up to rest my eyes and stretch my legs. My room is just as bad as Schuyler's. Besides the trophies, everything I own is potential trash: jumbled books, old star charts, a Hitachi keyboard I've never used, a folk guitar missing two strings, my embarrassing watercolors Mom is so proud of. I did a couple from a book just to show I really was going to a class.

"So what was it like?" Schuyler says. He stands and arches his back, lacing his fingers behind him, his sternum pointing at me.

"What?"

"The whole thing. With Mr. Mann, you know."

"Keep your voice down! She may be old, but she's still got ears. I told you what it was like."

"I mean—"

"I know what you mean. You really think I'm going to tell you that?"

I turn away and stare out the window. Two rock maples are leaning toward each other, joining leafy hands, framing the view with a natural arch.

"You can skip the gory details," Schuyler says. "Just what was it like? Being with somebody like that. So much."

"I can't believe you're asking me this. I don't want to talk about it."

"Come on. Maybe it'll help."

"You're pissing me off, Schuyler."

"Seriously, it might."

"You don't want to help; you want to be entertained."

He frowns. "That's not fair. We used to talk about this stuff all the time."

"We did?" I force myself to remember. All those guy-girl trading-secrets-with-the-enemy chats seem like a hundred thousand years ago. "I don't care. I told you, I don't want to talk about it."

"Okay, just the first time," Schuyler says. "What was it like? Just tell me that. Was it like what we thought it would be like?"

Suddenly my temples are pounding. There's a red fury building behind my eyes. I sit on the edge of the bed clenching my jaw. I refuse to look at him. The carpet needs vacuuming.

"We were stupid," I say.

"How stupid?"

"Stupid. Just stupid."

"So educate me."

Educate me.

Teach.

The room fills up with red. I stand and walk to him mechanically. Drape my arms over his shoulders. Look into his eyes without seeing, without feeling.

"What?" he says.

I kiss Schuyler hard, grabbing his head, forcing my tongue between his lips. I crush my mouth to his, rocking my face almost violently from side to side. It's all I can do to keep from taking his lips in my teeth, biting hard, letting everything out I've been holding in. I want to make him scream, pour it all into him, make him burn in sweet pain, the kind of pain I've known.

He's trying to pull loose; I kiss him harder and harder.

Finally he rips his mouth away. I can taste copper on my tongue. Or maybe I just want to taste it.

Schuyler collapses into my chair. The lower half of his face is red and puffy. I can't identify his expression. I'm not thinking with my brain; I'm thinking with my skin, my bones, my hair. My face feels flat, detached, not a part of my body anymore. Reason lags behind emotion.

"Nine," Schuyler says. It's the most noxious thing he could think to say. The world's most evil, obscene number.

"Is that what you wanted?" I say.

Mom comes in.

"Children, I—"

The three of us look at each other in shock. A stranger stepping in at this moment would be hard pressed to decide which of us has been the most wronged.

I know.

the inertia tree

Leaves.

Here it is. My last tree fort.

There are no railings, no walls. It's high up here.

One Sunday a few years ago, Dad came out and built this platform in the crotch of this pecan tree. We used to build all sorts of things together: tree houses, play forts, a toolshed observatory with a roll-off roof. Things changed. This fort was his last attempt to jump the spark gap between father and daughter. I was nearly fifteen.

We still loved each other; that wasn't the problem. Somewhere along the way, we'd lost our point of contact, two astronauts whose inertia was carrying them apart.

I reach into space.

The rope in front of me is red and white. It was once a rope for towing water-skiers. This is my last swing, my last surviving piece of little kid backyard summers. I used it for a day, just to make him feel good. I was past that sort of thing, irretrievable.

This is where Schuyler finds me.

"Nine?"

His mouth is red. Something about the angle of the sunlight makes him look eyeless, a being from another world.

"Go away."

"Why? What just happened in there? That's the second time you—what did I do?"

"Nothing. It's not about you. Go away."

"No."

"Okay, you can sit there and count the grass."

He pleads with his hands. "Why are you so mad at me?"

I scoot to the edge, dangle my bare legs next to the ski rope. I loop the rope about my neck a couple of times. It would be easy to let myself slip off and fall into emptiness. And then—what beyond that? I uncoil it.

"I'm not mad at you. Not really. I can't explain it."

If I thought I could, here is how I would try:

With Mr. Mann, I was in a very big place. Always, every day. Now I'm in a very small place, even smaller than the place I used to be before he came along. I'm constricted and small, and I never want to do anything ever again outside this small place.

"Do you understand what I mean?" I say, as if I've been speaking out loud. Maybe I have.

"No," Schuyler says. "But I don't want to leave."

I shrug. "Then I guess you can come on up. I promise not to bite."

He touches his lip. "I'm not so sure about that."

He climbs the ladder and sits next to me. It's crowded up here. I can't look at him. I look at the head of a nail that is bleeding rust down the bark. Nobody has been up here in a long time.

"I don't want to talk about it," I say.

"I didn't say anything."

I want him to go. I want him to stay. I lean my head against his shoulder. He flinches. His shirt smells good, like a strong detergent, something clean. I need to feel that way again.

"Schuyler, tell me I'm not going crazy."

"You're not going crazy. You're already there."

"I'm not joking. Help me."

"Okay."

"Okay."

We squeeze hands. It's a bargain. I pull the rope through my fingers.

"You kids want your peach tea up there?"

Mom.

the cold number

Sunlake.

Another day.

We park farther back this time.

Schuyler's stuffing his mouth with Crackling Oat Bran from a baggie.

"Looks like you've come prepared for a siege," I say.

He frowns. "This is the first time my folks have ever gone on a vacation without me." His parents are spending the week in Destin, Florida.

"So throw a party. Blow the house up."

"Oh yeah. But really, it feels weird."

"Thanks for staying. I mean it. I don't know what I'd do without—ouch!"

He frogs my arm.

"You've only told me that a googolplex number of times. That's the number ten raised to the power googol, or the numeral 1 followed by 10^{100} zeros—"

"I know, I know. But I do."

"Anyhow, I owed you that."

"Agreed." I rub the muscle.

The day is overcast. We watch a braless sex pistol in frayed cutoffs sway to the Laundromat. A FedEx truck rumbles through. A guy with a cast on his arm gets in a Passat and speeds away. Every parking space has an oil stain the size of Nebraska. How is it possible this dreary place has become the emotional center of my universe?

"When he gets here, let's squirt mustard all over his hood," Schuyler says, gobbling some bran. "Country says mustard will take off the paint. We could write him a message. Something cool. A damning passage from Camus' *The Stranger*—"

"That sounds about like Country's speed. Besides, mustard only works if you leave it on for a couple of days."

"Oh. How do you know?"

"Don't ask. Remember, we're not here to wreak havoc. This is an exploratory missi—"

The door to number 220 swings open.

It's Alicia. I didn't think anybody was home. She's dressed in a baggy white outfit, frosty curls blown up on top and pinned at the ears. She scampers down the steps, keys twirling on a pinkie, and slides into a cream-colored Toyota. She backs out and comes our way.

We turn our heads, suddenly utterly fascinated by the Dumpsters. "What do we do?" Schuyler says.

"Follow her. Maybe she's going to meet him."

I wait a little while, then pull out, keeping two cars between us. Schuyler's beating his fingers against the dash. His jittery energy is making me nervous. "Does she know Wilkie?" he says worriedly.

"Possibly. But it probably helps that you're here." I glance at him and sigh disgustedly. "What are you so strung out about? You're no fun anymore."

"Neither is cell block D."

I shove his shoulder with my elbow. "Like you would know, Puff Dog."

Schuyler balances his baggie in the ashtray. "Hey, I can watch HBO with the best of them."

"Then just watch what I do and follow my lead."

He throws a European salute, the backs of his fingers against his brow. *"Oui, mon capitaine."*

"Wouldn't it be *ma?*"

"Je ne comprends pas."

"I'm a girl. *Savez-vous?* Or have you forgotten already?"

His ears droop; he stares straight ahead. He has to be thinking about the Kiss of Death in my room. We haven't talked about it much. Probably never will. Maybe it was so awful, he wants to forget.

We head southeast for several miles and exit the interstate. Alicia's in no hurry.

"She's even worse than your mom," Schuyler says.

"She's about to turn."

We pass a school yard infested with fourth graders.

"They must be on a different schedule here."

A few more miles and the neighborhoods are starting to change. Sprawling lawns, older homes. Architectural style: Re-elect Nixon. The children who climbed these trees are on low-carb diets by now.

I stay back as far as I can, but Alicia's driving so slowly now, I can literally follow without placing my foot on the gas. She has to wonder who we are, what we're doing.

"She must be looking for somebody," Schuyler says.

We pass a couple of elderly power walkers and a gray-haired lady snipping yellow roses with orange scissors. What would Mr. Mann be doing here?

Alicia suddenly parks in front of a white ranch-style house that has long black streaks of roof fungus weeping down its shingles. I keep going. In the rearview mirror I see her craning her neck as she gets out of the car.

"She's seen us," Schuyler says.

"I know. I'll circle."

I round the block and park a couple of houses over behind a museum-vintage station wagon.

"Wish we had binoculars."

Alicia has made it to the front door of the ranch house. She's on the porch, talking with an older woman. The woman is shaped like a barrel with pipe stem legs and hair dyed a color in the same zip code as ochre. She suddenly takes Alicia by the arms and hauls her inside.

"Her mom?" Schuyler says.

"I don't remember her from the wedding. Besides, I don't think Copperhead would live in a place like this with a wife like that."

"Copperhead?"

Whoops.

I glance involuntarily at the glove box, hoping Schuyler doesn't notice. I still haven't told him about the pistol. "Mr. Sprunk. Alicia's father. He reminds me of a snake."

"An occupational hazard."

We play the radio and wait, watching the house.

Schuyler chatters about Buffalo Bill on the History Channel.

"He called his rifle Lucretia Borgia. Dude killed sixty-nine buffaloes in a single day."

"Lucretia, indeed. The jackass."

The Crackling Oat Bran is gone. "Viagra," Schuyler says after
a while.

"Huh?"

"How long do we hang around waiting for the stiff?"

"Shut up. I don't think he's in there."

"So what are we doing here? Stakeouts are not particularly
exciting, are they, Herr Doktor?"

"Shhh. Something tells me this is important."

"You think maybe we could stop for onion rings at the—?"

The door opens.

Alicia comes out holding something small and rectangular. A
journal? Address book? She waves at the older woman and crosses
the lawn, never looking in our direction. Speeds away.

"Tallyho!" Schuyler says. "That's more like it—lay down some
rubber, Seabiscuit!"

"No."

"But she's getting away!"

I crank Wilkie's engine and pull in front of the ranch house
and get out. Schuyler scoots over and puts his head out the
window.

"Oh no. Come on, Nine. You mean I have to sit here while
you—?"

"Both of us. Come on."

bean genes

Ring the bell.

The house must be well insulated; there is no sense of anyone coming.

"Wait! What are we doing?"

"Like you said. Gathering information."

"But what are we going to say? We have to get our stories straight!"

I pinch Schuyler's arm. "Courage, Shadrach."

The weather stripping makes a sucking sound as Barrel Woman jerks it open. She looks older than Mom, but I suspect it's not the years, it's the mileage. Her sun-dried face cracks into a hundred pieces of one monster smile.

"Well, hell's bells! Must be last call for the Royal Order of the Water Buffaloes today." Her voice is raspy, eyes dinner plate blue, nose long and red at the tip. She's grinning delightedly as if she recognizes us. "Come on in; Ripper's tied in the basement. Mind the ceramic log."

We hesitate at the threshold. The blast of her personality is making my head swim. The house smells of stale cigarettes and coffee that hasn't been advertised nationwide since 1979. Somewhere a television is squawking piteously.

"Ripper?" Schuyler says.

The woman digs him in the ribs and winks at me. "This one's easy to tease, isn't he? Well, don't just stand there halfway in and halfway out."

She grabs our wrists, instantly affectionate, and pulls us in. Her fingers are thin and cold.

"Hello, I'm—we're, um—"

"I know, honey, you're selling something for your school, right? Sweet God, you're tall. Want to check me for fleas?" She offers the top of her thinning hair, explodes in coughy laughter.

"Well, yes," I say. "I mean, no! Um, we're selling magazines, but—"

"Just like Halloween," the woman says. "You kids know where all the old farts live. Okay, show me what you got. I'm a soft touch, goddammit. You just might hit me up for something."

"Really, ma'am, we're—"

"Ma'am's your mother. Call me Barb. You're lucky you didn't catch me bare assed. I was just about to jump in the shower." She tweaks Schuyler. "I'm just messing with you, honey. Today's not even wash day—Vince!" She tugs us along the hall and around a corner. "Look who's come to visit."

I don't like this room: circa *Brady Bunch*. The furniture is covered in smoky blue fabric, sandpaper #5 abrasive. The air conditioning is set to Thule, Greenland.

Vince is sitting in a recliner with duct tape on the arms. He has Miracle Grow eyebrows and a terminal case of White Man's Feet. He slowly looks up from the TV, antimatter to his wife's matter.

"'Lo," he says, and goes back to watching Melissa Gilbert murder a chicken.

Barb picks up something from an end table. She lights a cigarette and takes a punishing drag. Her words come out in little nicotine-flavored clouds.

"Don't mind him. Vince's like a big old wheel. Takes a lot to get him rolling, but lord, the momentum! Back in our navy days, we'd dance our legs off. The house was always full of people. There was this big Swede from Minnesota, a CPO named Werkhoven—"

I glance at Schuyler; he's screaming with his eyes.

"I'd throw together a pot of booze beans and dumplings— only use pintos!—with red wine. That was our first real house, Millington Naval Air Station in Memphis. Twenty minutes from where Elvis the Fat-Ass Pelvis crapped out."

Barb's voice is a comet orbiting our heads; it flies out to the aphelion of my consciousness. A question suddenly catches me like a piece of space stone in an interstellar vacuum.

"So?" she says.

"What?"

Barb cackles, lungs full of iron filings. "Keep up, honey, or I'll have to charge you time and a half. The magazines."

"Oh! Well. That's not really why we're here."

"Yeah?"

"We—um—we saw somebody we knew in the neighborhood and were wondering if she was a friend of yours? Alicia Sprunk."

Barb's face cracks again. "Alicia? Why, hell yes, she was just here! Too bad you missed her. Where'd you know her from?"

"Um—we don't really know her all that well. We know her husband."

"Ricky?"

I hate myself for smiling. "Yes. Ricky. Do you know him?"

"Hey, Vince!" Barb screams.

"Yup?"

"Do we know Ricky?"

"Huh?"

Barb sticks out her tongue in Vince's direction. "See what I mean? Retirement is hell. It's for the birds. My guy put in his thirty years; now he's got the personality of a Dutch oven. Don't do it!"

"About Ricky—have you known him long?"

"Well, I should guess so." She takes another choking drag. When the words come out, they're almost blue.

"He's my son."

peppercorn ice

Goose bumps.

Mrs. Mann lights a new cigarette from the corpse of the first. She's between us on the couch, a photo album spread open across her papery knees. We're looking at a naked baby lying on a fake Persian rug.

A naked baby who would one day grow up to make love to me.

"Those numb-nut navy doctors kept me flat on my back. Ricky went into fetal distress. Thought for a minute we might lose him. But I liked Millington well enough."

"So that's where he grew up?"

"Ricky grew up all over, sweetie. Tennessee, Texas, Virginia. A dyed-in-the-Woolite navy brat. Never kept the same friends one place to the next. Probably the reason he didn't like school so much. Sure wasn't lack of smarts."

She flips the page.

"Here's Ricky when he was six—look at the little shit! I made him that outfit from a Butterick pattern."

I swallow the image.

Straight black hair, thumbtack eyes, white chaps, a cowboy hat strung with red rawhide. He isn't smiling and holds his cap pistols slackly, as if bearing up under a tsunami of disappointment.

"What's he frowning about?" Schuyler says. I'd forgotten he was here.

"How should I know? Moody little bastard—one minute high as a 707, the next dragging rock-ass bottom." Inhale. Barb's setting the Land Speed Record for dragging a cigarette to the filter.

"It nearly killed Vince. Ricky hated Little League ball, would just as soon piss on a car as go near it with a wrench. Spent his days holed up in his room, reading. Half the time we thought he was deaf. Can you imagine?"

Yes. I can.

I rub my arms to restore the circulation. Is that my breath I see? It's so cold in here. More photos. Mr. Mann's childhood is surprisingly ordinary: wooden toys, bikes with rubber tassels, crooked teeth. Pajamas too small to keep his belly button covered. A Christmas tree strung with lights like banana peppers. Six Flags Over Texas. A dented trumpet. Schuyler has lapsed into a coma. I'm riveted.

"What about high school?"

Another album. At the third picture my heart jumps. I want to break furniture, scream until my throat bleeds, chew the carpet. Mr. Mann is skinny, a mass of dark hair, striped rugby shirt. My age! Those amazing eyes, but trapped in the body of a geeked-out loner, they're scary. He's hanging back from the crowd, uncomfortable. Looks like someone who could burn the school down on a bad day. So he had to grow into his beautifulness, his easier soul.

"Couldn't wait to move out," Barb says. "Had to go to college way the hell up north. Massa-*gesundheit*-what? That's what I said when he told me. Why so far? You tell me."

I'm too polite to tell you, I think. Because he had to get away. He was embarrassed, misunderstood. But it all makes me wonder—so the Boston accent is most likely affected, a camouflage. Just what else might not be real?

"What did he study?" I say.

"What else, artsy stuff. Thought he was a goddamn poet. The battles he had with his father! Join the navy, learn a trade. I had to laugh—Peter Pumpkin Eater couldn't even change a tire. No, he's going to be the next P. F. Eliot, Emily Frost, hell's bells. Where does the time go? Tell me, where?"

I hope I'm not jumping the gun, but I can't resist. "I've always wondered—how did they meet? Ricky and Alicia? How long have they known each other?"

Barb ponders. "Ricky could tell you better than me. The little shit barely calls! It was last fall, when he was still teaching at Duncan Hills. I think he met her over at the college. Him and that little gal were thick as thieves."

Vince shuffles through, heading down the hall. Metamucil must be kicking in.

"Naps," Barb says. "He takes a lot of naps. Doesn't sleep well at night. We tried those little Band-Aids you stick across your nose. No good. They have this spray for sleep apnea, three squirts in the back of the throat—"

"Were you at the wedding?"

Barb looks sour. "You were there? A little fruity for my taste, but whatever floats your boat. They had to throw it together pretty quick. I wanted to help, but no, His Lord and Master put the kibosh on that."

"Mr. Sprunk?"

"Ricky. Wouldn't let me in on one little detail! Why? Tell me and we'll both know. But you're right, I imagine Daddy Warbucks had something to do with it. Walden Ponds, my left titty. Don't get me wrong—Alicia's sweet as a little bug, but the rest of that bunch can kiss old Rosy, know what I mean?"

I reach behind her, pinch Schuyler awake.

"Hey!"

"You say the wedding was thrown together quickly?" I say. "Why?"

Barb taps an ash into her hand. "Oh, you know, it was one of those on-again, off-again deals. We thought they had split up for good in January. But I guess they were back to beating the sheets all spring."

She laughs. A nimbus of secondhand smoke forms around her head.

I exhale slowly.

All spring. Beating the sheets.

My mind is a nuclear flash fire. I'm irradiated by an image: Mr. Mann, Alicia, limbs entwined, moving, kissing, his bed still warmly rumpled from when I just left it.

"Nine?" Schuyler touches my arm, trying to pull me together. "So Alicia was just coming by for a visit?" he says to Barb, rescuing me from my speechlessness.

"Hell, no. They don't visit. They just show up when they need something."

"What was it?"

Barb stands and brushes ash from her blouse. "Come on, I'll show you."

I stand, do my best to follow, my exploded mind trailing behind me.

How could he?

How could I have been so stupid? So wrong?

Schuyler and Barb are waiting in a back bedroom. There's a

beat thrumming in my ears; for a moment I can't hear what she's saying. I look around, trying to orient myself.

The room is clean. Sewing table, guest bed, exercise bicycle. But something about this place feels skewed, out of square. My legs are leaden and my head is spinning. I'm feeling sick to my stomach. What's happening to me?

"Vince's been meaning to convert this to an aquarium room for umpteen years," Barb says. Her voice sounds very far away. She slides a closet open and I see magazines spilling over the shelf above the hangers. Barb steps on a footstool and fishes around in a box. My eyes have cleared, but I feel a strange terror over the way she's standing, as if she might lose her balance and topple over.

"Here you go."

She hands something down to me. My hands are trembling. I clutch it to keep from shaking too hard. It's a skinny chapbook: *One Million Secret Hills*. Poems by Richard A. Mann.

"Ricky won some big award a hundred years ago back in college," Barb says as I flip sightlessly through the pages. "Everybody gets their fifteen minutes, don't they? Where the hell are mine?" She brays laughter. "Anyway, he got me and Vince to pay to have four hundred of these printed up. Then doodle squat. Couldn't sell one damn copy."

I try to read one of the poems, but the type on the pages is blurring. My heart is fluttering out of control. Mr. Mann and Alicia—I need to get away.

"Keep it," Barb says. "We still have about three hundred and eighty-seven, if the mice and the silverfish haven't gotten to 'em yet."

"What does he want it for now?" Schuyler says.

"A special reading he's giving over at the college. At UTC."

"A reading?"

"Alicia says he's doing some kinda poetry show out there tomorrow night. They found out he lived in town, asked him to do it."

I can't think. Barb's face is beginning to blur. What is happening? Something is horribly wrong and somehow they can't see it.

"I've got to—I've got to go!" I say.

I can't tell if my words are audible. Schuyler isn't picking up the hint. Can't he hear me?

"Why didn't he come himself?" he says to Barb.

"Don't ask me. I wish we could be closer, but what can you do?"

What can you do.

The air in the room is closing around me. Why is it so cold? Everything's so cold! It's the Big Freeze, the time when everything stops moving. Heat death of the universe. Nothing in this house is important anymore, will ever be important ever again.

I'm going to die.

"I've got to go!" I say. I'm sure I'm almost shouting now.

"Wait! How about some lunch?" Barb says. "I've got some Polish sausage casserole left over from last night. I always make too much. Won't take two shakes to get it—"

"No, no!"

"No, thanks, that's okay," Schuyler says.

I'm almost pushing him down the hall toward the front door.

Time is hardening into something fragile, brittle. We've poked a hole in the sun; ice is starting to gather. I can't get outside fast enough. I feel the Snow Queen at my back. I'll freeze to death if I stay.

At the door Barb grabs my arm and presses something in my hand, a yellow index card. "Hold on! Here you go."

I stare, uncomprehending.

"Don't forget the peppercorns! They make all the difference. Ask Ricky."

A recipe for booze beans and dumplings.

escape velocity

Panic.

It's the worst kind of suction of all.

It comes from your center, makes a gravity well around your heart, pulls everything bad to you.

I slam into the car, fumble to get the door open. The instant I hear the ignition catch, I'm peeling out, bumping one tire up over the curb. I tear out of there, not even caring if Schuyler's got his door shut. I'm trying to achieve escape velocity.

For the first mile I leave the windows rolled up, holding June inside the car as long as I can.

"Wonder what temp she keeps her air on, freezer burn?" Schuyler says. His voice sounds odd, rushed. "Maybe old Vince is embalmed. He would fall to mush without it."

I hear him, but I'm not hearing him. I'm still measuring the distance between my heart and Mr. Mann's. He is my sun, and I'm moving farther and farther away. Crystals are forming in my blood.

Is this where you've left me, Richard? Is this what getting old is all about?

Is this what I have to look forward to? Barb's frozen world?

Desperately sucking the life out of people, even strangers, to get someone to listen to me, be with me?

Faster.

"You want to slow up a little, Nine?" Schuyler says. "Stopping would be even better. Did I mention my hunger? It's become apocalyptic."

I shiver, glancing at the recipe card poking out of Mr. Mann's chapbook. Schuyler pulls his seat belt tighter.

Faster, faster.

Wilkie's underinflated tires are shrieking as I move from lane to lane, dodging other cars.

"Okay, to keep from thinking about dying in a gasoline fire, let's recap," Schuyler says, voice tremulous. "Mr. Mann once owned a Sit 'n' Spin. His mother, subphylum *Party animalia antiquus*, likes booze in her beans. Booze in anything, probably. His father rents out his frontal lobe as a loofah sponge."

My heart is trip-hammering so bad, it's come loose in my chest. I keep waiting for it to reattach itself. I feel Schuyler's eyes on me. I press down on the gas pedal. Where am I running to?

"And how about Vince's bone structure?" Schuyler says, voice a pitch higher. "Definitely something supraorbital going on there. *Australopithecus afarensis*, my good doctor?"

I stare straight ahead, the lines on the road starting to blur.

"Okay. Not quite that remote," Schuyler says. "His knuckles were pretty clean. *Homo erectus?* But maybe without *erectus*'s stately charm. Say, *Australopithecus robustus?* Wait. I know what you're thinking, Dr. Leakey. There's not one thing robust about that man."

I feel him looking, looking.

"*Homo habilis*, then. That's my final offer."

We're roaring along. The other cars are falling away now. My face is locked. Schuyler leans over and speaks directly into my ear:

"Vince has three testicles. The one in the center is able to divine the future."

I laugh.

It bursts out of me like a jet of water under pressure. My laugh gets louder and louder. I laugh as if I might be cured or go insane.

"Hey, ease up a little," Schuyler says.

I pull over finally, nearly weeping with laughter. I collapse against his chest. I can't stop thinking about Vince, oracle-like on the toilet, communing with his loins.

I feel Schuyler tense—I'm scaring him.

"You okay, Nine?"

His chest is hard. I like touching it.

"You okay?" he says again.

The laughter is going down inside me; I'm deflating like bagpipes. This takes a long time. When it's over, I push him away more forcefully than I mean to. I swipe at the corners of my eyes. "I'm okay. I'm okay."

"What was that?" Schuyler says.

"I don't know. I feel like I could throw up. I think it must've been a panic attack. I felt like I was dying. God."

"You scared me."

"I'm sorry. Really. I'm sorry." We sit awhile, watch people trundling groceries to their cars. The world has snapped back to its regular shape. My hand brushes Mr. Mann's book. I suddenly remember—

"A reading!"

"What?"

"Barb—she said Mr. Mann is doing a reading at UTC. Some kind of poetry thing!"

"Yeah."

"Tomorrow night."

"That's what she said."

Schuyler starts to smile.

Perfect.

wet

_____

Home.

I smell the sauce the minute I come through the door. Mom senses something is up. She's making manicotti. .

"Your favorite, darling!"

She hasn't done this in months, maybe years. It's the fanciest thing she cooks. This is what she does when she doesn't know what else to do for me. Maybe someday I will get the connection, the motherly cause and effect.

"Let me help you," I say.

She pours out the egg batter into micro-thin shells. When they're done, we stuff them with ricotta, mozzarella, cottage cheese. Ladle sauce over the top and pop them in the oven. While we're waiting for the timer to ding, I give her an oregano peck on the cheek.

"You're sweet," I say. "I'm sorry about everything lately."

"I've just been so—" She dabs at her eyes with a pot holder and honks into a tissue. "Your father and I, we—"

"It's all right, Mom." I hug her narrow shoulders.

"Everything is all right. Please don't worry so much."

We watch TV. I feel as if I haven't eaten in a hundred years. When the manicotti is ready, I eat as though it's my last meal. Later my chest burns in the dark; I can't sleep, thinking about Mr. Mann.

Tomorrow night. The plan.

Mom hears me stumbling to the bathroom for an antacid and gives me some melatonin. "You father takes them," she says.

It's supposed to make me sleep naturally. The trouble is, I want to sleep unnaturally. I'm burning alive, thinking about my last time with Him.

Turn on the computer.

Kitty Nation curls around my feet. Niagara Falls at night could be anywhere. Newark, New Jersey. But I know they're still there, the couples, in their rooms, touching each other in the dark.

I close my eyes. Maybe they dress after making love. Get up while they're still liquid, flow down the halls that look the same at any hour of the day or night.

They stream outdoors past the sleepy clerk in the lobby. They're barefoot; the cement is cold leading to the falls. They hold hands. The closer they get, the louder the noise, a sound that makes them feel very small in the nighttime. They draw together in horrified fascination. A spray wets their faces. They're at the edge now, touching the cold aluminum railing. They can't see the spray, can only hear the thunder as the whole river throws itself over the abyss.

They jump.

Morning.

I'm still here.

But I wake up flat. Something has changed.

Something about meeting Mr. Mann's parents, seeing where he came from, his pain, his reality—everything is flat.

It's dead and flat.

The person I fell for, what part of him was ever real?

What if his whole life he has pretended to be someone else, whoever he needed to be? Maybe it's all a kind of survival mechanism. And the by-product of his survival is this: he makes you fall for him—that's how he survives it. How he survives life, love, anything. Maybe he's like that all the time, not just in class? It's just like he said—it's all an act.

That's his gift.

Was there ever really a chance for us?

What is down in the middle of him, his very center? Does he even have a center, or do you just cut away the layers, away, away, away, until you are left with nothing?

Every inch of Barb and Vince's cold, dead house—now it's tangled up with my thoughts of him. My memory of him, my image, my love—it's there, frozen in time with all the rest of it. There is no changing him now. No going back, ever again. It's flat.

I've lost.

The beautiful part of the love has leaked away—the part that mattered most. The only part that's left is the flip side, the animal side, the side that wants to gore and rut and bite.

Consume.

I jump out of bed and stare into my mirror—if I could just see his eyes right now, I would know if it's still there. I would know. But it's flat. A flatness spreading out before me so long and low and brutal, a flatness big enough to swallow years, lifetimes—I'll never be three dimensional again. He's stomped my whole universe, made me into a plane, a line.

A point.

I'm so tiny, I'm about to vanish. You can't atom smash me any smaller. There's nothing left. The part of me that was real, the God particle, is gone.

Did it ever exist at all?

No, there is no changing that now.

So there is no changing what I have to do, either. Somehow the flatness—it makes me stronger, more certain of my direction, sets my track. I turn away from the mirror. It's time to teach him. Teach him how you make something real.

looking for lincoln

The plan.

Time to execute it.

The Crackling Forest is different too. I can feel it.

The light? The wind in the leaves? How can spring not feel like spring?

But the weather is changing. A bank of black clouds is ripping the sky in half diagonally. We're racing into the black part without even moving. The Firestone Holy Tire Palace is silent, its bays closed and forbidding. A truck whistles by like an animal squealing for cover.

My mind is full.

Is this the last time? Is this where it all ends?

Can I do this?

Can I say goodbye?

I slither out of my bra, toss it in the trunk. Schuyler is waiting in Wilkie Collins. He has promised not to look. I wouldn't care if he did. Not today. Not ever again. I could give him that, at least. Before I go. What does it matter anymore?

I slip into his mother's things: an old emerald green pants suit that buttons aggressively snug up the center. What kind of material is this? It bunches and clings, feels like a cat's tongue slipping over my little boobs. I hope my nipples show. Mom would die. I haven't shaved my legs in days.

No deodorant.

Suede Birkenstock clogs, an olive beret. I mass my hair toward the front, covering as much of my face as possible. New shades; they look like round orange mirrors. Again I feel the confidence of anonymity descend upon me.

I'm a girl-woman in my mid- to late twenties. Occupation: Professional Student. Cocky in my element. An über-educated, hairy-pitted man hater. I change my own oil, dispose of it with respect for the environment, then charge back indoors to research my interminable doctoral thesis on George Eliot and Willa Cather. Title of? "The Burgeoning Feminist Imperative." A worm of sweat cools my temple. Come on, make me fierce in my rankness.

Something's missing.

I rummage in the trunk. The black bag is hot; some of the

makeup is running. But I don't need it anymore. Ah, there it is—I pull out a long red sash, symbol of the Anti-Sex League in George Orwell's *1984*. I cinch it like a tourniquet around my waist.

Ready.

"Fleetwood Lindley," Schuyler says when I get back in the car. His disguise is less elaborate: a slouch fishing hat swiped from my dad and rectangular Walgreen shades.

"Huh? Scoot over. Aren't you going to say anything about the way I look?"

"Fleetwood Lindley."

I'm starting to get pissed. I don't want to play this game right now. I'm nervous. I'm thinking about Mr. Mann at the podium in the lecture hall.

"Okay, you got me for a change," I say. "Who's that?"

Schuyler pulls down his shades, frowning. "I'm disappointed in you. Fleetwood Lindley was the last surviving person to ever see Abraham Lincoln. Well, his body, at least. In 1901 they exhumed Honest Abe to put him in a new tomb. Fleetwood's dad was in the honor guard. He hauled Fleetwood out of school to see them open the casket."

"Okay?"

"This is important! Fleetwood knew he was checking out something nobody would ever see again. Here's what he saw: Lincoln's face was covered with white chalk somebody had used to try to freshen the old boy up on the funeral train. His eyebrows were missing, but his beard was still there. You could definitely tell it was Lincoln. His chest was covered by a moldy flag—nothing but the stars were left. They put the top back on and Fleetwood got to help lower the casket into the new vault. He was thirteen. He had Lincoln nightmares for six months."

"And the reason you're telling me this is——?"

"To take my mind off the fact that you're wearing my mother's clothes."

"——!"

I make a sound that's not a word and kick his leg hard with the clogs.

We hurtle in reverse out of the Crackling Forest. "Did you bring your watch?" I say. "What time is it?"

"7:09."

"Dammit. The reading starts in six minutes. Is your watch fast?"

"It's synched with my XP. That's another quarter you owe me."

Buzz.

We rush down the interstate, pushing into the storm.

Schuyler navigates to the exit and the UTC campus looms. The grounds are a mix of stately older buildings and more recent disasters. The light is menacingly beautiful under the blackening sky. I wonder if this is how things look to a prisoner on his way to be hanged. Colors so full, everything sharply delineated, easy on the eyes.

Pure.

Only the important things are important now. The rest of it——

"Don't worry, we're almost there," Schuyler says, scattering my thoughts. "That way. Downhill from the science building."

"So you know where to go inside?"

"Yeah. I used to come here for meetings of the North Alabama Archaeological Society. I helped them with the slide shows."

"Doors?"

"Lots of them, all along the front."

"How many people?"

"You never know. The building holds at least three hundred. They wouldn't let us use it after our membership dropped below fifty. The national group disbanded our chapter."

"Aw."

"Rednecks apparently don't give a crap about Jewish necropoli—you just missed your turn."

"Shit!"

I hit the median hard, crank Wilkie's powerless steering around with the force of Starbuck driving home a harpoon. My shades bounce off; Schuyler slams against me. Wilkie waggles across the grass median. The horizon of low mountains dances, settles again, this time in the rearview mirror. Schuyler's face is the color of floured wax paper.

"We're going the right way now," I say.

chamber music

Heat lightning.

I feel it inside my head.

The squall line is closing in on the setting sun as we turn into the parking lot. The Chan Auditorium is low slung and white. Architectural style: DOD Blast Shelter. The lot is crammed with cars plastered with Piscean odes to kittens and anger-management bumper stickers:

I GO FROM ZERO TO BITCH IN 2.2 SECONDS

This is the place.

What I'm about to do is suddenly made excruciatingly real: Mr. Mann's Honda is parked up front.

If there was a time to stop this, it is over now. I'm definitely going through with it.

I reach in Wilkie's backseat and grab a composition notebook.

"You sure you want to do this?" Schuyler says. "It's insane, you know?"

You have no idea, I think.

I haven't told him. I'm not going to.

This is one time Schuyler doesn't need to know everything. Can't.

I lean over and give him a wet smack on the cheek. "Let's go."

We get out, shut the doors gently to keep them quiet, and head for the auditorium. A line of sweet alyssum points the way up the sidewalk like snow in the failing light. A thunderhead rumbles ominously to the west.

Six doors to choose from, one held ajar by a rubber wedge. I yank it open. From the interior comes a rush of compressed CO_2. A big crowd, perfect. I wait a moment, listening, not breathing, then step through.

Schuyler slips in behind me. We're at the top of a large bowl-shaped chamber fanned by rows of chairs with plastic backs. Six aisles going down to the stage bisect the ranks of messy heads. A few turn as we come in, sensitive eyes wary. My kind of crowd. Probably think Heisenberg is a high-end beer.

Schuyler taps my arm, frowning. "I don't like this, Nine. There are too many people. Let's get out of here."

I point an elbow into his stomach and try to smile. It's one of the hardest things I've ever done. "Buck up, Ozymandias. It'll be over soon."

"That's what scares me."

I sound much braver than I feel.

We separate. Schuyler stations himself in the back. I spot an aisle seat about midway down, just as if someone were saving it for me.

Where is he?

A group of professorly types is sitting at a table on the stage. Mr. Mann is not with them. I scan the rows of heads anxiously. The sunglasses make it harder to see, but I'm too scared to take them off. The wings at either end of the stage are lost in shadows. Maybe he's there.

My cold terror is expanding all my senses. My skin could be used to monitor barometric pressure. I catch a whiff of minerals on the air telling me the rain is almost here.

Wait.

A little guy gets up from the table, struts importantly to the podium; his hair reminds me of weedy grass in the wake of a passing train. He pokes the mike with a fingernail. The sound echoes behind me like a nightstick rapping the walls.

"As director of the College of Humanities," he begins, "I'm extraordinarily pleased and honored to be here."

Ten minutes later he's turned us all into unicelled creatures. Finally the first poet is introduced.

It's not Mr. Mann.

A fifty-ish woman with Salome veils and a Jenny Craig chassis approaches the podium. Her fingers are heavy with rings. From somewhere comes the scent of Herbal Essence and pot.

Salome begins in a quavering, artificial voice:

> *The stone jar of my*
> *Heart pours out*
> *Blood clotted with my*
> *Pain I shout at the nails in my*
> *Teeth scream as his dissonant*
> *Mouth weeps tears warm as*
> *Magnolia blossoms as he blasphemes my*
> *Womanly core*

Whew.

I glance at Schuyler. He's shifting in his seat like a man with a car battery hooked to his genitals. Lightning beats the air outside.

Where is he?

Maybe they're saving Mr. Mann for the big finish? I look back at the stage. Salome sways, cheeks flushed, anxiously post-coital.

Oh, she's done.

A smattering of polite applause ripples through the auditorium. "Tough house," somebody close to me says.

The director claps the side of the mike as Salome wafts to a seat. "Thank you, Halsey. Simply beautiful. Halsey Passwater-Rhodes, 'I Love My Love with a Bitch.'"

Where is he?

My skull is full of fire. I need to put it out.

We suffer through a succession of poets, each less healthy looking than the last. The topics of their poems run the gamut:

The asteroid belt as metaphor for HIV. Water rights in the Negev. Woman with older chickens. Weeping, fire, Nicaragua. Nintendo fetuses. I discover that good writing ability works in inverse proportion to the need to dress the part.

Someone behind me drops something. I turn, heart fluttering. Ah.

There he is, skulking in the back: Mr. Mann.

His presence paints the air around him: black pants, conservative tie, white shirt with tiny silver stripes. I remember the last time I saw him wear it.

I was kissing his belly.

Hate.

I can't stop it. It rushes into my fingers, pushes the fear out, makes my hands warm and tingly. I edge forward in my seat, gripping the composition book tightly. Soon. It will be over soon.

A poet with a scarf and Gandhi glasses is equating his girlfriend to Rwandan genocide. The director ushers him gently from the mike.

"And to conclude this evening's performances, I'd like to welcome a special guest. The featured poet of this year's UTC Fielding Poetry Series, *Voices from a Single Room.*"

His cue.

Mr. Mann begins making his way down the far side of the auditorium. The runty director goes on:

"His poem 'coming in from the garden like a surprised rain' won the American Academy of Arts and Letters Gold Medal for Excellence in 1990. Please join me in welcoming Richard Mann."

The applause is energetic this time, even a few Aerosmith whistles. I should be impressed.

Mr. Mann saunters to the podium and throws his head back, eyes burning around the room. He smiles appreciatively; this is his comfort zone. I realize he's playing Him again, the one who is in command, shows no fear.

For the first time I clearly see the symbiotic connection. How each personality fuels the other, giving you a tantalizing taste of both. The powerful and the vulnerable. The commanding and the artistic. The schemer and the dreamer. Until you're hooked, lost, gone.

Falling.

Now I feel only a heavy, numbing sadness, the flatness. The only thing it fuels is my fury.

Mr. Mann creases the chapbook open, raises it in his hand like a preacher holding a Bible, waits for the audience to settle. I chance a look at Schuyler; his seat is empty.

Here we go.

I'm blinking quickly; my heart rate zooms.

I close my eyes for an instant, pull everything into my center. The anger, my empathy, the pain, my fear. When I open my eyes again, invisible walls have risen on either side of my head. They give me a canyon of focus that closes everything else out, holds me on target.

Mr. Mann extends a single finger. He's Adam reaching to touch the hand of God. He begins in words clear and clean:

> *coming in from the garden like a surprised rain*
> *so firm and fleshed again the tomatoes*
> *he staked, the loosened furnace grate*
> *creaks one more goodbye*
> *to his shoes and lays him down to sleep his why*

I stand, screaming.

"Just one minute! Just one minute! I have something to say!"

I've dumped all the hate into my voice. It comes out a grinding squawk, a wire that projects to the farthest reaches of the auditorium. Mr. Mann stops and looks up, shocked. He sees me and drops his arm. I step into the aisle, conscious of Ms. Green's pants riding up my shins.

"Bastard!" I scream at him, pointing. I appeal to the audience, arms imploring, head swiveling. "This man is a bastard, a cheat, a liar! Bastard!"

Mr. Mann flushes; he shades his eyes to look at me.

"You thought you had destroyed me when you left my bed!" I yell. "But look what I have become! I stand here in the spirit of"—I consult Schuyler's notes—"Hipparchia! The world's first liberated woman! An Athenian Cynic and philosopher, wife of Crates, with whom she openly copulated in public!"

"What the f—!" a girl says nearby.

"Get her ass out of here!" another voice says, a guy this time.

Murmurs. Shouts. Gasps of incredulity. The little director comes forward uncertainly to the edge of the stage. "Excuse me, miss, but I'm sure this is not the forum—"

"Sit down!" I shriek.

I point at Mr. Mann.

"It's time to send a message to all men who think they can do with us as they please, come and go with impunity, defile the body of the Earth Mother!"

Mr. Mann turns to the director, covering the mike with his hand. Still everyone in the hall can hear him whisper, "Let me talk to her."

This is it.

He leaves the podium and hops down from the stage. He has to skirt the first row of chairs to get to my aisle. Closer, closer. My body aches to run to him. Away from him. Both.

"Listen!" I say.

The composition book is my lifeline.

Emily.

She makes my voice strong:

> *I wonder if it hurts to live,*
> *And if they have to try,*
> *And whether, could they choose between,*
> *They would not rather die.*

I reach into the large pocket of Ms. Green's pants suit, find the lump that is the pistol, take it out.

A moment of silent incomprehension.

The moment grows, stretches into history in both directions. Someone nearby gasps, says something I don't understand. There's a low-pitched grunt of animal terror.

People are screaming now, falling away from the middle of the room, scrambling over chairs, pressing toward the walls. Now there's nowhere else for them to go. I'm standing between them and the doors.

Mr. Mann stops coming up the aisle when he sees the pistol, face ashen.

"No! Don't do it! Think about this. What you're doing! Please!"

I bring the pistol level with his chest.

His arms are up, palms out, pleading.

Pull the trigger.

the color of love

Thunder.

The pistol pops in my hand once, twice, three times. It's louder than I expected. I can't miss at this range. Mr. Mann yelps and spins partway around. Large, wet splats of color appear on his shirt.

In the back, Schuyler slaps the light switches. The auditorium is plunged into gloom—the glass doors at the top let in some light from the parking lot, but my eyes are slow to adjust. A white flash of lightning suddenly marks the rectangles of the doors. I charge toward them up the aisle. Schuyler is already there, holding open the door. We hit the sidewalk and run for the streetlamps.

Raindrops spatter my back as I jump into Wilkie Collins. I sling Schuyler's paintball pistol on the floorboards in the back, gather my legs in. The key is hanging in the ignition; I twist it, the engine sputters.

"Come on, start, baby, start," I say, pumping the pedal.

"Nine! You didn't tell me. Why! Why didn't you tell me!" Schuyler still has the hat and sunglasses on.

"Come on, baby, come on."

"I can't believe you did that—I thought—we were just going to embarrass him. Oh God. We're in so much trouble. God."

He's pounding the dash, swearing, making choking sounds. Wilkie sputters and catches. Tires squealing, I bump over the corner of the curb on the way out.

I throw off the sunglasses and look over my shoulder as we fly past the student center. The last thing I see is Mr. Mann running up the sidewalk in the streetlamp, trampling the alyssum, his new shirt splattered blue.

and do it anyway

Getaway.

We race down the interstate, not speaking. Rain is flecking the windshield. I turn on the wipers, but there isn't enough water yet to keep them from making an awful rubbery dragging sound. I have to turn them off and on again and again to be able to see. Their rhythmic, pulling sound is huge and ominous by the time we get to the Firestone Holy Tire Palace.

In case we're being followed, I back Wilkie Collins deeper than usual into the Crackling Forest. The leaves all around the windows make me feel a little better. We've landed on a different planet, one that doesn't allow men and buildings and roads. One that's not so crazy.

As soon as I shut off the wipers, I realize Schuyler is making a noise. He throws the sunglasses and fishing hat down.

"Are you okay?" I say. The light is not very good here. I'm having trouble reading his face. I nudge him. "Huh?"

"Now I know what made me think about Fleetwood Lindley," he says gloomily.

I try to smile; it doesn't feel good. "But how could you know? You didn't know. So what are you saying—now I'm John Wilkes Booth?"

"I'm serious!" He almost yells the words. "I hate guns. I hate them! That was bad, Nine."

"I know it was, Schuyler. But I had to do it. I had to do something."

"Had to do what? Scare three hundred people to death? This was all about him. What did they do to you?"

"But couldn't you tell it was your CO_2 pistol? The one you used to shoot out my streetlamp. You left it over at my place, remember?"

"It looked real. I thought it was real! All those people! God, he thought it was real. I thought he was dead, Nine."

"That was the idea."

"Not mine. We were just going to embarrass him! You should've told me, given me a chance to—you dragged me into something—God, we are in so much trouble."

He puts his face in his hands, elbows on knees. Then he sits up suddenly, looking out the drizzly window.

"Do you think he's coming?"

"Not here. Probably he's at my house right now, talking to my parents."

"You're right. That's worse."

"But what have you got to worry about?"

"I was there. I helped you." Schuyler's speaking between his fingers.

"He doesn't have to know that. At least your folks are out of town."

I'm grabbing at his hands.

"Leave me alone!" he says, shoving me away. "What about the cops?"

"I don't know if what we did—if what I did—if it was illegal."

He lifts his head, starts pulling crazily at his hair. "These days? It's almost got to be. I know it's illegal to walk into a crowded theater and scream *fire*, and what we did was a lot worse than that!"

"It was a paintball gun, Schuyler. Not the real thing."

"Yeah, but all those people. They were scared out of their minds. It made me sick, Nine! I thought I was going to puke. The sounds they were making, watching them falling over the chairs. I've never seen people that scared. That was bad, Nine. It might've been funny in a movie, but that was bad. We shouldn't have done it. We're in so much trouble."

"You said that."

I feel the numbness, the battlefield exhilaration, starting to fade. I don't want to think about what comes next.

"I'm hot; this stuff is scratchy. I'm going to change."

I kick off the clogs and get out. The leaves are squishy and cold between my toes. Fat blots of slow rain patter around me. I hurry to get the black bag from the trunk.

Just as I get the top of the pants suit unbuttoned, I hear a terrible rattling sound crossing the interstate. It drives toward me, getting louder and louder until a wall of rain suddenly hammers the parking lot, water bouncing a foot in the air. The rain is coming down so hard it hurts. The whole world is stinging. I leap in the backseat, instantly drenched to the skin.

"Do you mind if I change in here?" I say to the back of Schuyler's head. He doesn't speak. "Just don't turn around; I'll tell you when you can look, okay?"

The ocean has been tipped over on our heads. The windshield smears, huge drops bursting against the glass. The floor of the Crackling Forest in the headlights jumps in dirty little fistfuls. A

current is already overrunning the storm drain and I can't see the
pavement anymore. There is a feeling of being trapped, attacked,
with nowhere to run.

I wriggle out of Ms. Green's pants suit—it's not easy, I'm too
long. After a lot of grunting and straining I'm down to my underwear. I wad up the steaming pants suit and sponge it against my
bare breasts, wishing I had a towel. Schuyler doesn't move. I
reach for my clothes from the bag and slip into them. That's when
I hear him crying.

"Oh, oh, come on," I say. "Come on, Schuyler."

I reach to touch his back. I feel his shoulders move under my
fingers. He's hot. A wave of affection rushes over me. I wrap my
arm around his neck, pull his head to my mouth. I kiss and pat his
wild hair, both of us making little noises.

"Come on, it'll be okay, really, Schuyler, it's okay, I promise,
come on."

My ear cups his neck. I hear a crunching swallow in his throat
as he fights to hold back a sob. "No," he says.

I keep kissing his head. This is something I've never felt
before, an overwhelming sense of protective love.

"No," he says again.

I lean over the seat and turn his head toward mine. Kiss his
cheekbones, his ear. He tries to pull away, but I scramble over the
seat. I take his head in my hands and kiss his hot, streaky face. I
kiss him again and again, gently working my way toward his
mouth. Gently, then more insistently. Finally I kiss him lightly on
the mouth; he pushes against me. But I'm gentle, gentle but insistent. He pushes.

I'm putting my hands on him, his chest, his shoulders, then
sliding them down to his waist. He keeps pushing, but not so

strong now. Lets me snuggle against him. My mouth brushes his lips. He doesn't push me away this time.

My arms go around him; his back is smoldering. He leans into me, I get his shirt out of his pants, pull it up, rub my hands across the bumpy hills of his spine, then around to the front, touch his lean stomach, his chest. There's only a little hair, right in the very center over his breastbone, with a silky line running down toward his navel. So different from Mr. Mann's chest. My breath is coming faster. I take Schuyler's hands and put them on me, hot on my shoulders through my T-shirt. My skin is tingling with the need to be caressed.

The fear, mine and his, it's feeding me.

It's pouring into my movements, becoming my need for him.

This is the other side of that moment we had in the snow. This is the side with the heat, the dirt, nothing pure, sparkly, or white, everything gone but flesh, his tongue in my mouth, teeth on my shoulders. But that's what he needs. And that's what I want from him.

That's it; I'm helping him. Just like Mr. Mann helped me. But I'm not helping Schuyler climb; I'm helping him down. He's been up there too high too long. It's made him afraid, being up there all by himself. It's freezing him. He needs to come down, get warm.

I move his hands down to my breasts, making him touch me through my shirt. Schuyler won't keep them there. I pull them down again, aching, aching. He keeps them there this time, but I need him to squeeze, make me realize the size of his own ache. I'm desperate for him to pull me to him, to need me just as much.

I'm fumbling at the snap on his shorts. Now. Now. This is everything; here is what is finally real, right here. Schuyler understands what I'm doing, but he doesn't understand—he takes my hands by the wrists, tries to push them away.

"No, no."

"Why, come on, why? Oh God, please, why, come on."

"I can't, no, Nine, I can't, I—"

I try closing his mouth with kisses; he can't hold my wrists and keep my lips away at the same time. I'm nearly weeping with the size of my ache. But he's twisting his head, jerking away from me.

"Please, please, let me do this."

"I can't! I'm not ready, I can't, it's too much—"

"Let me, please, let me do this for you—"

I have his shorts half undone, I'm pressing him back against the car door, overwhelmed with a hunger that is bigger than my will to stop it.

Schuyler yells, "I can't! No!"

"Why, Schuyler, why?"

"You'll—you'll—!"

"What? What is it?"

"You'll hate me!"

"I won't!"

"You'll hate me just like you hate him!"

sting

Stop.

I fall back, shuddering. Suddenly conscious of how far it's gone, how much I've done. I cross my arms, hugging them to my chest, digging my fingernails into my skin in rage, in shame.

Is this true? Is that what I'm doing? Turning Schuyler into someone else I can hate?

He's sitting up now, away from me, hands fumbling at his shorts. I wish I could see his face better. I don't know what to say. There is nothing I can say.

Neither of us speaks. I crank the engine. The headlights are defined by hurtling slashes. I'm almost afraid to drive, but we can't stay here; the parking lot is filling with runoff.

I dare to glance at Schuyler. He's staring straight ahead, lips tight.

"Why would I ever hate you?" I say. "Why?"

He shakes his head violently, throwing off flecks of shine.

"Please, Schuyler. I'm so sorry. Please forgive me. Can you? Can you forgive me?"

"What do you want from me?"

"I don't know, I don't know!"

"Do you know—?" He stops.

"What?"

"Do you know how important you are to me?"

"I—"

"Did you know that? Did you know how tough this has been? For me? I know you just want to be friends. I've always known it. So I did anything I could just to be around you."

"Hey, I'm—"

"But I won't take it like this. It can't be like this. You're just trying to make me into him. You don't really feel that way for me."

"Schuyler."

"Two years ago you kissed me—it meant everything to me and not a damn thing to you. It was just fun for you."

"That's not true!"

"Just something new to try. Maybe it wasn't even fun, I don't know."

"No. No, really—"

"And then the other day in your room—I think you would've killed me if you could have when you kissed me. It's something I've always wanted, but all you wanted was to get back at him through me."

"I'm sorry, Sky, I'm sorry." I haven't called him *Sky* since the seventh grade. He doesn't like it.

We listen to the rain.

"I don't know," I say. "I—I guess I was afraid of losing you. I didn't want to lose you," I say.

"Lose me! How could you lose me?"

"As a friend, I was afraid it would mess everything up."

"So what has changed?"

"Everything! Everything has changed." I start to cry. The tears are warm on my face, but I'm so cold. Schuyler puts his hands out to me. I don't know if he wants to hold me or push me away. We touch each other's fingers, trying to find a comfortable middle place.

"I'm sorry," he says. "I'm sorry about what he did to you. It's going to be okay, really."

I'm not sure of this at all. I brush my eyes and take his face in my hands. "I'm sorry too. I shouldn't have gotten you into this. I'll tell them the truth, it was all my idea, I made you do it."

"That's not true. Don't lie for me. I wanted to help. I was right there too."

I take his hands. "Okay. Then we'll go through this together. Together. Whatever happens."

I lean over and kiss him lightly on the cheek. He lets me.

We're heading home.

Whose home, I'm not sure.

I try to talk Schuyler into letting me drop him off; he won't.

"I'm here," he says. "I'm always here."

"Okay."

Rain is beating the road ahead of me. I can barely see; we're crawling along. Here and there cars have pulled over to the shoulder, emergency lights flashing.

"Damn," Schuyler says.

"Quarter." I sniff.

"Not funny. Be careful."

I watch the flashing cars go by. "I'm taking it easy. If I keep going this slow, nothing can happen, right?"

"I don't like this."

All I can see on the windshield are fat circles expanding and vanishing, replaced by new ones faster than I can think.

"I should have replaced these wipers." They sure aren't squeaking now.

"I don't think anything could help in a rain like this."

The sky is utterly black. A lightning bolt shivers in the air between two shoals of thunderheads, stitching them together, hanging in the air for an unnaturally long time.

We drive forever. It's hard to find my street. My heart is in my throat as I pull alongside the driveway. Nothing there but Dad's pickup and Mom's Bug. No cops, no green Honda. Are they already in bed? I should've called. Mom's cell is standing in the ashtray, the ringer turned off. What did they do to deserve a daughter like me?

"I don't want to go home," I say.

"What do you want to do? What can we do?"

"I can still drop you off. Tell him nobody else was with me."

"No. I'm sure he saw us together."

"I bet he wouldn't recognize you. You want me to drop you at home? Come on."

"No."

"It figures," I say.

"What?"

"That it would end like this, one big messed-up downer. I was feeling so good back at the Chan Auditorium."

"Be honest."

"Okay. I was scared to pieces. But so what? We pulled it off, didn't we? Perfect. Now the rain, the dark—it makes everything bad, doesn't it?"

"That's because everything *is* bad."

"I don't know. Maybe he won't do anything."

"Oh, sure. You're going to stop, right? You want to stop?"

I swipe wet hair from my face as I think about it. "As Country would say, hell, no. But it's over. It's got to be."

He squeezes my arm. "Let's run away."

"Oh, come on, Schuyler."

"Really. How much gas do you have?"

A truck suddenly lumbers across our field of view. Its glistening blue panels could be the hull of a freighter. I'm going so slow, there's no possibility of a collision; still, it's like a wall appearing from nowhere. When it's gone, when we're breathing easier again, I check the gas gauge.

"Quarter of a tank. You're not serious."

A lock of Schuyler's hair has slipped down over his eyes. He pushes it back. "Who says?"

"Where would we go?"

"I hear Madagascar is charming this time of year. The children eat hissing cockroaches for treats."

"Not funny."

"I don't feel funny. In fact, I've never felt less funny in my whole life."

"I feel flat. I feel like a flatworm must feel."

Schuyler scratches at his hair. "*Arthurdendyus triangulatus* or *Artioposthia triangulata?*" he says gloomily.

"Aren't those the same thing?"

"I don't know. The ones from New Zealand. That project we did."

I'm becoming hypnotized by the wipers. I'm hunched over the wheel, my chest almost against Wilkie's horn. There is hardly any traffic now, but this is worse—there are no brake lights to follow. We're in a submarine.

"Talk, just keep talking," I say.

"About anything?"

"I'm a flatworm," I say. "I have two simple ganglia instead of a brain. You can cut me into segments; I'll grow new copies of myself. I'm parasitic. That's all I can think about. Attaching myself to another person and living off him."

"Mr. Mann?"

I can't think of how to respond. I'm too busy listening to my mind.

"The male flatworm has a copulatory center in his last abdominal segment. Remember? But there is an inhibitory center in the ganglion that holds the copulatory center in check. It's simple. You don't need a female flatworm to make him want to screw. You can cut off his head with a razor blade. Once he loses his head, the copulatory center is released. Mechanics."

"So you think all men are like that? Mechanical? Is that what you think about me?"

I wait to answer and then don't answer. I ask a question instead:

"Do you want to live forever?"

Schuyler thinks in watery shadows. "Maybe we will," he says. "Maybe science—"

"I think we already do." I'm clutching the steering wheel very hard, face straight ahead, hands pale. "Not in the body, but in the germ plasm."

"George Wald," Schuyler says. "I knew this flatworm jazz was going somewhere familiar. His writings. *The Origin of Death*—"

"Every creature alive today is part of an unbroken line of life stretching back to the first primitive organism to appear on the planet three billion years ago. That's what he said. That's immortality. All the immortality we can hope for."

My voice is getting higher, hands gripping more tightly. Go on.

"All that time, our germ plasm has been living the life of single-celled creatures, reproducing by simple division. All that time, that germ plasm has been making bodies and throwing them away when they die. What was it Wald said? *If the germ plasm wants to swim in the ocean, it makes itself a fish; if the germ plasm wants to fly in the air, it makes itself a bird. If it wants to go to Harvard, it makes itself a man.* Something like that."

"Nine."

"So what are we here for, Schuyler? Just to make sure the line of life isn't broken?"

"Nine."

"Is that all we are? Tiny little chunks of one big, unbroken life? So do we really matter at all as ourselves?"

"Nine!"

He's grabbing at the wheel.

"What?"

"Car!"

It's coming straight at us, headlights jiggling in the lines of rain. The two of us wrestle Wilkie Collins to the side and the green car passes.

Green.

I see the color in the moment when the car slides past in the reflection of our headlights. The rain has washed away the world of shapes, identifications, but the green smear is still visible. Then it's gone.

Green.

"It's him," I say.

growing season

Schuyler flinches beside me.

"Who? Mr. Mann? How do you know?"

"Come on!"

I can't make the turn here; there's a median, but I can't see it. It would be too easy to drive off the road. A little farther I find a break in the grass defined by the flow of water rushing through the gap. There must be six inches of rain pouring across the road in this place. I swing Wilkie around like a boat. "There!"

I've made a 180; the green car is not very far in front of us.

I can see Mr. Mann's brake lights, that's all: two receding red eyes. No other car is visible. It's only possible to move at about ten miles an hour, especially in the low spots. The road is filling with water. I can't see the wake we're making, but I hear it rubbing aggressively at the bottom of the doors. I've never driven in water like this.

"What are you going to do?" Schuyler says.

"Follow him."

"But it's a flash flood! Don't you see that water? Come on, Nine. Enough! Let it go for tonight. Pull over onto some high ground."

"No. I've got to see."

"See what?"

"Where's he going! My house? Sunlake?"

"What does it matter? I don't like this. Please leave him alone. It only matters if he's bringing the cops, and nobody else was with him."

"It matters."

Schuyler settles back into the seat, resigned to whatever I'm going to do. "You're obsessed," he says quietly. With the rain, I don't hear him; he has to repeat the words.

"Yeah, I guess I am," I say.

"You even admit it!"

"Sure, I do. Except you're wrong. I'm focused. There's a

difference. That's what I do, Schuyler. I focus. I don't know any other way to do it. There!"

This is a very weird chase. It's majestic. Slow. We're close now, a couple of car lengths behind. Enough for my headlights to wash over his trunk. But I'm only aware of a metallic green rectangle and the silver line of bumper floating away from me.

We're coming to a place with large blocks of watery, cube-shaped lights. An intersection. It must be. But where?

I can see the stoplight now. It's hanging at a forty-five-degree angle in the wind. Mr. Mann and I move so slowly, the light changes from green to red to green again by the time we get there. I'm in danger of losing him if he makes it through the light first.

"He's turning," Schuyler says.

"Where?"

"I can't see. But his blinker's on. Turning left."

One of the bright cubes of light is shaping itself into a Texaco station.

"Sunlake! This must be Zeirdt Road."

"So he's going home."

"Yeah!"

I put my blinker on ridiculously and sidle over to where I think the turn lane might be. It's impossible to tell, there's so much water.

"So you know where's he's going," Schuyler says. "Maybe it's okay. Let's go home."

"No."

The turn is stately and harrowing—the intersection is a double trough crossing four lanes of traffic. In the troughs the rushing water must be more than a foot deep.

"Don't!" Schuyler says.

Wilkie shudders and balks, splattering the windows with spray. Mr. Mann is out of the deep place first and gains some distance. The other part of the road must be higher, up in the dry. I'm back to following the red eyes, but at least I can tell where the road is again.

"If I can trust him," I say.

"What?"

But I can't speak.

Something white is blooming on either side of Mr. Mann's car. From here it's impossible to tell what the blooming things are. They blossom and fall away, blossom and fall away again, like white smoke from the NASA test stands when they fire the shuttle engines. There's something frightening about them.

Just as suddenly, the white things stop, fall away one last time. I don't see them anymore. Mr. Mann is pulling away again, the red eyes getting smaller. I put on a spurt of speed.

"Wait. No," Schuyler says. "Stop."

I see what he must have seen. The red eyes are swinging in a smeary arc; they disappear after a quarter turn, are replaced by twin white eyes.

He's turning around.

"Stop!" Schuyler says. "Turn around, now!"

"He's coming!" Coming straight at us

The whole landscape is jiggling and dark. I have no streetlights here to gauge the boundaries of the road. I can only assume he's staying on his side. I steer away from the center for what I think is the width of one car.

"Stop!"

"I won't hit him, Schuyler. Besides, we're going so slow, it wouldn't be much of a crash. Want to play chicken?"

"Not the car, the—there!"

He's terrified. Not warning me about Mr. Mann; he's warning me about the white things. I intuit the word before he can actually speak it:

Water.

That's what the white things were. Water so deep it was raging over Mr. Mann's door panels. We must be coming alongside the swamp. The swamp behind Sunlake. The swamp that winds between the cypress trees. This part of the road is completely flooded. How deep, I don't know.

We hit the flooded part with a smashing roar.

Water fountains around us like foam hitting the prow of a ship. The water is jetting so high, I can only see white out the windshield.

Schuyler makes a noise; I don't know what to do. Some knowledge surfaces inside me. My father's half-remembered words, something about the points getting wet in the engine. You can't stop or you might never start again. You'll be trapped in the flood. I plow ahead.

All my attention is on getting us through the water. I lose sight of Mr. Mann's headlights. I'm forcing the car forward on pure telepathy now.

"Nine!"

I see the headlights again. Moving inexorably, suddenly much closer. I fight the wheel hard to the right and there's a feeling of leaving the earth, a craft flying with no night instruments.

The swamp.

We've left the road.

The twin fans of illumination from the headlights rear up, then land on a broad, swirling surface. The weight of what is happening, the horror of it, settles on me in an instant with the intensity of a dream.

In the middle of the air, in the microsecond of the car's crashing, I again see the truth: There is no control. It's a myth. Whatever happens, happens.

Wilkie's hood enters the flood first. Water explodes over our bouncing roof, drowns the world. Wilkie rebounds for a moment, lights jerking crazily. I see the shiny wet branches of trees. Our heads hit the ceiling with a sound of tearing fabric.

We're falling now.

There is no sense of a bottom, only a bouncing motion, then a settling.

How deep is the water here?

Moments.

I've had them before like this.

Falling from a tree and catching myself. Losing traction on a hill and finding a root to hold. Sliding down a roof until my toes catch in the rain gutters.

None of those moments ever lasted as long as this. Time is broken into slices so small, they are tiny beyond measure. I have plenty of time to understand that the Last Bad Thing has come; my life is over. But a decision confronts me:

Give myself over completely or fight?

But fighting is silly, stupid, impossible. We're still moving forward. There's a great shuddering slam of metal against something immovable. My forehead smacks Wilkie's steering column. My eyes flash with lights. I don't know what's happening to Schuyler. One of us screams in pain. Maybe both.

We've struck something. One of the trees?

I feel blood oozing down my forehead. Everything is as dark as anything can ever be. Wilkie's lights are gone; we're sliding down the base of the tree into deep water.

neural meat

Where am I?

Floating here.

All these things in my mind I can't turn off. There's a time coming that's very close, a time when my head shuts off for good. But in the meantime I still know a few things.

I know the average human brain weighs three pounds.

It takes up 2 percent of the body's weight but uses 20 percent of the blood and 20 percent of the oxygen.

It's made up of 100 billion neurons. It has 111,000 miles of myelinated nerve fibers, enough to get you nearly halfway to the moon.

But none of this is any good to me now.

I'm winking out.

Operating on my ancient reptilian brain stem.

Wood.

Dark.

Wet.

Cold.

Die.

the language of leaving

Light.

I can see again. I can't see anything, but I can see.

Something has shivered my mind awake. I sit up and shout at Schuyler, but I'm not speaking English. I'm not even speaking Indo-European. This language is even older, much more primitive. It's a language spoken on the slopes of erupting volcanoes or while sliding into a black crevasse on a glacier. Everyone understands it, or will.

Schuyler doesn't reply.

The car. We're still in the car. I have a sense of Wilkie listing, a buoyancy that is false and won't last. In the dark I work at the driver's side door and get it open. Freezing water floods in.

My own language comes back to me. I'm yelling at Schuyler to come and kicking away from the car. The darkness is pitted with smears of light, squarish shapes, windows of the apartments around the lake.

Now I'm swimming in reedy water, my legs banging submerged objects. I can't tell how deep the water is. It's pushing too hard against my legs to let them touch bottom. Suddenly I'm floating in a cone of light; I see the tree where Wilkie is lodged.

The current shoves me against it. I angle my body, grapple with my arms. My legs swing free in the current. I see a dark figure inside Wilkie through the spattered windshield. It isn't moving.

"Schuyler! Schuyler!"

Anything else I could scream never makes it to my mouth.

"Schuyler!"

I scream his name over and over as Wilkie's hood takes on water. I try to bring my hand around to grab the metal grill, but the current is too strong. Every time I start to pull loose and grab the hood, the floodwater threatens to rip me away from my hold on the tree and carry me somewhere deeper. The car sinks. I get my feet braced against the roots and push.

Still Schuyler isn't moving. I can't tell how high the water is in Wilkie's front seat. It's too hard to see with the contrast between the darkness of the water and the brightness of the car lights shining on us.

Car lights.

Someone else is here.

It's the other car, still on the road, its lights barely above the flood, but it isn't sinking. It's angled, pointing at me.

"Help us!" I scream.

I've got to make an effort, even if it means getting swept away in the torrent pouring into the lake.

I get my fingers into Wilkie's grill and pull hard, letting go of the tree. I'm snapped straight out, but my fingers hold, even as the skin begins to tear.

The slanting hood is underwater. I have two hands on it now, can feel the grill.

It's all I can do to hold on. I can't pull myself closer to Schuyler. The car continues to sink. I realize it's not sinking in water, but mud.

I scream at Schuyler to come out. The dark shape doesn't move. Maybe the crash did something to his head. Maybe he's— don't say it. Don't even think it.

The water is freezing. I find the roots again with my sneakers and push hard, propelling myself against the current. My right hand cups the front quarter panel near the tire. I pull; my strength fails me. Pull again, pushing with my feet, and get both hands on the jagged edge of the wheel well underwater.

I scissor my arms and try to stand; my body snaps out horizontally again. I fight to get my shoes back on the roots. Wilkie is lower; the water is covering his hood all the way to the windshield now. Still the shape inside hasn't moved.

Blood comes into my eyes mixing with the rain. I can barely see. Slowly I draw myself to the wheel well and edge my way toward the door.

It's no good.

I'm not strong enough. Schuyler's going to die here. In this swamp. Choking on mud.

And it's my fault.

come back for me

"Hey."

That's all he says.

I'm not sure it's a voice until his hand is on my arm.

The voice is connected to a strength that pulls me forward until I can grasp the edge of the open car door.

Mr. Mann.

"Help! Help us!"

His hair is plastered against his face and across the bridge of his nose. He has a nylon rope knotted around his waist that leads back to his car, where the headlights are shining over the racing water.

We work together to pull Schuyler out. Mr. Mann's arm is around my waist. This means nothing as I slide into Wilkie and tug at Schuyler's belt. Nothing but life, safety, the future. I can't tell if Schuyler's breathing; he's cold, heavy, and logy. I can barely move him in the frigid water, but he comes slowly to us.

I'm cupping his jaw with my hand, keeping it above the flood. The closer I get him to the door, the more I can see. His temple is gashed and blood is flowing into his ear, blood that looks black in the reflection from the headlights.

I get him to the door, dragging him under his arms. Mr. Mann has hold of him now, letting me go and wrapping an arm around Schuyler's waist. He hauls against the force of the water with one hand on the rope, dragging Schuyler along.

"I'll come back for you," Mr. Mann says.

He does.

I don't remember how we wrestled Schuyler onto the backseat of Mr. Mann's car. Maybe we pulled him through the window. I don't remember the ride to the hospital.

I remember this: Mr. Mann's arm around me. Our bodies joined against the surging flood, holding each other, the cord around us tightening and loosening until we are back on solid ground again.

mountains of time

The Door.

To keep from thinking about it, I focus on seven words:

"Don't worry, he's going to be fine."

Those are the words I have to hear.

One word for each day they say it took to create the earth.

Though I know it really took billions of years and swirling dark matter and hydrogen snow.

But we are waiting God days in the emergency room of this hospital. God hours and God minutes. Whole epochs pass.

Think of anything but Schuyler back there behind the Door.

Focus. Observe.

The people shift and change like Geologic Events.

Here's a man, head slumping. His chin slouches into his chest like a tired mountain range. A woman lying on her side is covered in fault lines. Someone she loves dearly is behind the Door. She's a continent trying to keep itself from tearing itself apart. A couple of kids run back and forth like rivers.

Where is Mr. Mann?

I know he came in with me. We sat side by side at the desk, getting Schuyler registered. I remember him leaning against the wall. Surely he hasn't left me. Again.

My raw fingers ache. The TV high in the corner makes me need to vomit. No sound, just a series of jeering, flashing heads. I sit with my back to it. If this is going to last an Age, I want to feel it.

My forehead is bandaged, but not many people are bleeding tonight. I don't know what's wrong with them as they come in. These are sleepy emergencies.

Seven words.

"Don't worry, he's going to be fine."

I'm wrapped in a blanket. The Door never opens out. People go in but never come back again. The woman at the counter is so drowsy, her face is three inches from the computer monitor.

The Door keeps inhaling people.

I was born in this room, on these plastic chairs. I've lived here all my life. This is my school, my neighborhood, my street. Outside, I see cars flowing by. They are not lodged in this iceberg of time.

I haven't prayed since the sixth grade. I'm praying hard now. Praying for myself as much as Schuyler.

But how do you talk to God? Sometimes I can't think of him as anything but a Size.

How can I pray? Especially when I've done something like this? It's too much to ask. Please just be good to Schuyler or the whole world is over. I've been stupid and pissed everything away.

The Door opens.

The doctor is pinching his eyes as he crosses the room. Triangular patches of bare scalp range deep into his hair. How does he know to come to me? Oh no.

He unscrews his face and exhales a long time, arms crossed.

"Are you Carolina?"

"Yes, please, is he okay, please tell me, is Schuyler okay?"

"Don't worry, he's going to be fine."

Seven words.

I lose focus in all the crying and the relief and the wave of injured love that comes over me.

I grab the doctor—he's shorter than me—and squeeze the life out of him. When I let him go, he tells me things I can barely stand to hear.

Concussion, broken wrist, ten stitches on the side of Schuyler's sweet head. He's staying overnight. The hospital has contacted his parents in Destin.

I can imagine them furiously stuffing clothes in bags, trip cut short, hair exploded by sleep, trying to find a place with gas in the middle of lower Alabama on the drive back. I can imagine what they're saying about me. What they think.

I haven't called Mom and Dad. I don't think I will. They go to bed so early these days. They're sleeping. Let them sleep through it. Let them have one more night of relative peace before they see just how changed I've become.

Is it possible to be driven home, crawl into my sheets, just wake up tomorrow? When will they notice Wilkie is gone? My bandaged fingers? The butterfly tape on my forehead? The doctor is about to leave.

"Can I see him?"

arm crazy

Inside.

Schuyler looks better than I expect, but it doesn't help.

I touch his bent hair and stroke his temple. I'm trying to find places that don't hurt and places that can still feel good.

"Sky, I'm so sorry," I say.

He looks at me, doesn't say anything.

"I nearly got you killed."

He raises his arm to indicate something; it's somehow been transmogrified into a telephone pole. He puts it back down.

"You're the shittiest driver I've ever seen," he says. "Excuse my Middle English."

"Quarter."

We laugh a little and it might be okay. I hope it's okay. I can't lose him.

"I'm stupid," I say.

His ears go up and he shifts a little onto his side, where he can see me better. "That's one thing you never will be. Mentally unbalanced, maybe."

"Stupid."

"Okay, yeah. But everybody is sometimes."

"Not you. Not much. Does it hurt much?"

"No."

"Don't lie."

"Okay. It hurts."

A nurse comes in and does things with his arm. She says there are people outside I need to talk to. Police.

A look passes between us. Okay. Just get through it.

"Come back?" Schuyler says.

"Sure. I'll sneak you something in."

The police are here for the report.

There are two of them. Their uniforms are tight and harshly creased; their pants float above their shoes. They move slowly. One is large, with a shaved head. The other is not so large, with a shaved head. Both carry receipt books: whatever I say, my words will bleed through from white to pink to blue to yellow to green.

Which is the customer copy? I've paid enough.

I'm ready to tell them anything. They might as well know it

all. Stalking Mr. Mann, the poetry reading, the crash. What good is anything I have ever done if I can't tell it now? They're ready, pens poised.

"It's all my fault," Mr. Mann says.

raining words

He's there.

Standing across the room behind me. For how long? He comes to where I'm sitting. He's wet and wrinkly, still wearing the clothes he wore at the Chan Auditorium. The paint is gone, washed away by the rain and flood. His left sleeve is soaked with Schuyler's blood.

"Everything was my fault," he says again.

He talks to the policemen. Says nothing about the poetry reading, nothing about us following him. He says it was his fault we ran off the road, an accident in the rain.

They believe him so easily. Why do older people seem more honest, dependable? But it's true. People think lies are like the food pyramid or Maslow's Hierarchy of Needs, broad at the base. What does a ninety-year-old have to fib about?

The policemen hand us our receipts, tell us where we can go to pick up copies for the insurance. Do I have a ride home? Mr. Mann says I do. They leave.

I sit across from him, trying to decide what I feel. Forget it. I'm too relieved, too tired.

"You okay?" Mr. Mann says.

I nod.

"Sure?"

Nod again. "So I'm not in trouble? You don't want me arrested? What about the people at the auditorium?"

"I told them I'd never seen you before in my life. They figured you must be a nut, somebody off the net with a cross to burn."

He laughs.

It's the most horrible laugh I've ever heard.

He's looking at me, but I've never felt so far away from anyone in my life. I'm standing on Titan, my feet wreathed in methane. He's still laughing.

"What?" I say.

He stops laughing, comes back from somewhere far away. "Something I've just realized," he says.

"What?"

"The mystery. There had to be a mystery. Something you could investigate, study. Figure out. I just realized what it is."

"What?"

"It's me."

adoring machine

I stare.

Mr. Mann is speaking softly. I ask him to repeat what he said.

"The mystery is me."

"I don't understand."

He pins me to the spot with his eyes. "That's one of the things I love about you, Carolina. You figure things out. You find the answers. I love how sure you can be. You want so badly to understand, don't you?"

He slumps in a chair with his chin in his hands, lets out a great shuddery exhalation. I sit across from him. I want to touch him, crush his head in my arms, but I can't. My legs won't let me. He lifts his face.

"I'm sorry to disappoint you. This is not that kind of mystery. Not the kind with answers. There is no figuring it out. There is no understanding. You want me to explain something I haven't been able to explain to myself."

"What?"

"Somewhere along the way I think maybe I stopped."

"Stopped?"

"Something happened. Or maybe something didn't happen that was supposed to happen. Something important. Anyway, somehow I got stuck. High school, junior high. Who knows?"

I nod as if agreeing. "So now you're going to tell me your parents are all to blame for your arrested adolescence? Poor little misunderstood Ricky. All that moving around. So many schools, lost friends, sensitive little writer soul. Isn't that convenient."

"No. I blame myself. I don't know why it happened, just that it's something inside me. Something I never knew how to fix. Not that I didn't try."

He rubs his face with his hands and keeps going.

"I tried so many times to break out of it, to grow, move on. But no matter what I did, it was always a disaster with somebody my own age. I was too messed up inside."

"Okay."

"So I kept trying to rescue myself, turn things around. But the rescue attempt always failed. I never could follow through. I was stuck."

"So what changed? You don't love Alicia."

He sits up. "Oh, but I do. That's one of the things you don't understand. I was utterly undeserving when she came along. There was no reason to ever believe in me. My track record was too awful. She loved the shit out of me anyway."

"Maybe she was too young to know any better."

I watch his face, but nothing changes. "It's not what you're thinking. She wasn't a student of mine. I met her when she was already halfway through college."

I know, I want to say. *I just wanted to know for sure, wanted to hear you say it.*

"So what happened? Why'd you ever break up, then?"

"I was in my old cycle. It was great for a while, then when things got serious, I got spooked. I used her father as an excuse. He's never liked me all that much. Really I was just running away again because things had gotten too close. Just like I always did. And then I found you."

"Victim number what—five? Six? More?"

Now his face definitely changes—goes slack, weary, sad. "It wasn't like that. It really wasn't. You were so different. And even then, I still fought against it."

I give him a look.

"You're right," he says. "Not very hard, but I did. But you were everything I ever wanted. For the first time I believed it would be okay—I could just give in to what I wanted, finally. You were perfect. You were so young, but you were different. You were smart enough, mature enough to handle it. You were so focused, knew what you wanted. Nothing was going to stop you. But you were still growing, too. Maybe I wanted to see how you did it. Maybe I thought we could grow together. Maybe you could teach me."

"That's bullshit. Psychological bullshit."

"You're right. It's bullshit. But that's what I'm good at. Making people believe in bullshit. Things I can't even believe in myself." He covers his eyes.

"If you expect me to feel sorry for you, Richard, I don't. I never will. Save it for *Oprah*. Better yet, *Jerry Springer*."

His jaw goes hard. He takes his hand away and looks at me again. "I'm not asking you to feel sorry for me. I'm telling you the truth. You more than anyone else."

I try to run my fingers through my matted hair and fail. "Wow. I'm a lucky girl. Top of the heap in your stable of wannabes. How's that poem of Emily's go? *Success is counted sweetest by those who ne'er succeed—*"

He winces. "I meant what I said. Everything."

"I know. But I'm tired of talking about you."

I stand, look around. The walls, the chairs welded in rows. Anywhere but Mr. Mann. Something about the light in this room is green. I'm in a space station. Everyone else has been killed by an alien virus.

"I don't like hospitals," I say after a while, still not looking at him.

"Who does?"

"Why can't they just heal people outdoors?"

He shrugs, thinking I expect an answer. And I do. Just not the one he wants to offer.

"It's better if you're close to nature," I say. "I don't like buildings either. I especially don't like cars. Not anymore."

"Anything man-made?"

"Right. Man-made. Anything made by man. Look at what they do."

I'm not looking, but I can hear the anguished smile in his voice.

"What do they do?" he says.

"They make things and make people want them. Then they keep them away from you or tear you to pieces. That's what men do. That's what—"

"She's pregnant, Nine," he says.

closing doors

"Alicia. She's pregnant."

The words are a needle. My lungs are deflating like pricked balloons.

Pregnant?

I can't wrap my thoughts around the word, now that it's something real, not just a weapon. Pregnant. That explains the flouncy clothes, the swollen ankles, the way she always seems to have a glow. He goes on.

"She came and told me. That's what it was. I had to make a decision quick. Her father expected us to get married, had already been pushing her, arranging things. But she left the choice up to me. It was the hardest decision I've ever had to make. I knew it—"

I start to say something, end up only making a sound.

"I knew it would kill you," he says. "I knew it would kill us both. But for once in my idiotic, selfish life I decided to do the right thing. For once I stopped trying to rescue myself and thought about somebody else for a change. And guess what? Somebody else did the rescuing for me."

We look at each other. An ambulance screams up outside. Two paramedics hustle a gurney through the glass doors, bumping the handles. It's an old woman with her hair bundled in pink curlers. She's clutching her robe around her shins and speaking. I can't make out the words.

A tightness comes across my chest.

"Were you—with her and me? At the same time?"

"No," he says. "It happened when I was just getting to know you. I was desperately lonely. Stupid. I told her not to, but she came to see me one last time."

I watch them shove the gurney through the Door. I'm trying to find the hate I've been carrying inside, see if I can piece it back together. Maybe it's behind the Door. On the other side. I can't get to it anymore.

I find his eyes. "So why didn't you just tell me?"

He spreads his hands, palms up, moves them, trying to speak. I'm reminded of Boris Karloff in the old classic version of *Frankenstein*. Imploring his creator for food, light.

Love.

"There's no easy answer," he says finally. "At first I think it was mostly shame."

"Shame?"

"Yeah." Mr. Mann looks at the floor. "Shit, this is hard. It's just—you meant so much to me, Carolina. I was finally over a really bad time in my life. I wanted to be good for you. I thought I was. I thought we were good for each other."

"Okay."

"But when I found out about Alicia—I told myself, *enough*. It stops here. Everything. Even if it meant I had to sacrifice you. Then when I saw the shock on your face, the hate—I couldn't stomach myself. Couldn't stomach you knowing why I did it. Maybe I was scared to death of making it any worse. I'm not as strong as you are."

He looks at his palm, starts rubbing at the crease of his lifeline with his thumb as if he could wash it away.

"You said at first it was shame," I say.

"Yes. In the beginning."

"But what about after that? What stopped you from telling me?"

He stops rubbing his palm and lets his hands drop to his side. He doesn't seem to know what to say.

"You're so intense about everything, Nine. I've never known anyone as intense as you. I thought maybe someday I could tell you. But after what you did at the wedding, my apartment—I was afraid if I told you, you might go a little crazy on me."

We look at each other.

My bandaged head. Schuyler's blood on Mr. Mann's sleeve.

"Crazy," I say.

He laughs.

I laugh too. Now we're laughing together. But it's a good laugh this time. Cleansing. It takes a while to settle down again. Little bursts keep popping out like sneezes.

I'm cold. I pull the thin blanket around my shoulders. We don't talk for a long time. I think about Alicia, the baby. In the middle of the silence, I realize I'm still falling, but maybe not so fast this time. It's a controlled descent. The shields are holding. I think I'm going to be able to land. There's a chance I can fly again.

"So. What does this mean?" I say finally. "We have to be friends?"

His face goes slack again. He breathes out. "Probably not. I don't think we can. Not after what you've—not after what we've done to each other."

Silence.

"I forgot to thank you," I say.

"For what?"

"For saving Schuyler's life. Saving mine."

He looks down at his shoes. They're muddy. His cuffs are starting to dry.

"You want a Coke?" he says.

I shake my head.

"Let me teach you something," he says.

I give him a hard look.

"No, I'm sorry. Something I found out about hospitals. Did you know if you want a Pepsi, you have to go to a different floor?"

"No."

"It's true. This floor has nothing but Coke machines. If you want a Pepsi, you have to go one floor up. Coke and Pepsi alternate."

My head is throbbing. I don't say anything.

"I think I'll get one," he says. "It's been a long day."

He stands and heads to the elevator.

"What if I want a Dr. Pepper?" I call after him.

He stops and looks at me.

"I don't know, Carolina," he says. "I don't know what you do if you want a Dr. Pepper. But I'll see what I can do."

He goes away getting smaller and smaller. The elevator opens for him. Closes.

Something has closed inside me. It will always be there, but it's closed.

water days

Months.

Today I'm thinking about differences.

Wilkie Collins doesn't feel so much different. His handling is a little more sluggish, if that's possible. He still screeches and farts teal smoke. But his upholstery is new. Dad is a genius and an angel. I'm glad he didn't look in the glove box.

Today I take Mr. Sprunk's copperhead pistol out. I hold it by the tip of the handle between thumb and forefinger, a venomous creature. A swamp is a good place for a gun. It sinks in the mud with barely a bubble. I'm sure Mr. Sprunk has found another. For all those snakes out there in the world.

Mr. Mann's chapbook is still lying on the floorboards, a wrinkly mess. I let it dry to read it; I'm surprised his poetry doesn't do much for me. It feels complex, distant, not like Emily's at all. Maybe he was trying too hard. I remind myself that he was very young when he wrote it.

Maybe that's what being young is, pushing too hard.

Back home I open my book of Emily's poems. I've read this one many times before. It means much more to me now.

> *THAT I did always love,*
> *I bring thee proof:*
> *That till I loved*
> *I did not live enough.*

x-ray heart

The mall.

Another May.

I'm with Mom and Schuyler.

She's let her hair grow out straight again. It's brittle and mousy silver. Cleopatra with an AARP card instead of an asp. I like it.

We've been to Dillard's and the Gap; she's loaded me down with clothes, some I even like. I smile and let her take her time. She's taken her time with me, hasn't she?

"What, sweetheart?" Mom says.

"Nothing. Just thinking out loud."

Schuyler's ears go up. "I've got my license," he says.

"No!" Mom says.

"Yep. Guess I'm just tired of being a freshman, Miz Livingston."

"Well, good for you, honey! I know your parents are proud."

I bump into him on purpose when Mom is out of earshot. "Why didn't you tell me? I would have come with you."

"And hexed me all over again?"

"—!"

"I'm kidding, Nine."

"So what's college got to do with it? Being a freshman?"

"Not just college. Everything. I guess I just want to be able to do things. Older things."

I smile into his frown. "Are you getting tired of me?"

"No! No, not at all. You know that. It's just. You know."

"Sure. You just want to grow a little. Let your hair down." I brush my fingers through his springy mop. "If you can."

"Cut it out."

We're passing through the food court on our way to Sears. Everything smells of chicken. Spring sunlight is flooding the atrium through the skylights.

I'm thinking about Mars, how it's gone away now. But Dad is helping me build a new telescope, a twelve-inch Dobsonian reflector. I'm tired of refractors, trying to see surface details. I want to go deeper. I want to gather more light.

We're cutting through a crowd of snacking shoppers when a raspy voice cuts into me.

"Well, cut off my legs and call me Shorty."

Barb.

I gawk. She's here with Vince. Mr. Mann. Alicia.

She rushes over and takes my arm, gives it a good wringing, then pulls me close for a hug that smells of Kools and peppermints.

I haven't seen Mr. Mann in nearly a year. He looks fit; his hair is long again. If he held his head just right, he could touch his tongue to the locks.

He's pushing a stroller.

"Hi," I say. Nobody knows I'm saying it only to him. The moment feels like raising a flag that has no colors.

"Hello, Carolina," Mr. Mann says.

Barb makes introductions all around. I do the same for Mom and Schuyler, minus Barb's delighted braying. The baby thankfully gives us a focal point in the center of the awkwardness to park our attention.

"My goodness, how sweet!" Mom says. "And so big!"

A girl. I can't help but look in the stroller. She's plump. Her eyes are cobalt blue. On top of her head is a shiny half-pipe of hair, translucent as a fingernail. She smiles and coos. She doesn't look like either one of them.

My eyes flick at Mr. Mann, hoping my expression passes for a coded message: *Don't worry. Everything's okay.* He's poker-faced, stoic. Alicia's face is even harder to read.

"So, you're still nursing?" Mom says. "The first year is the most important. What did you name her?"

"Emily," Alicia says. Mr. Mann glances at me, mouth closed, the muscles of his jaw working.

"Emily. Lovely. What a lovely name. You don't hear old-fashioned names like that much anymore."

"No. You don't."

So this little girl is the big, nasty secret. I'm surprised at how I feel toward her. I'm interested, an observer. But that's all. There is no more. I don't ache to take her in my arms, make her my own. Somehow she has nothing to do with me—and it hits me: of course she doesn't. She isn't mine. There is no connection there at all.

I meet his eyes again. There's a piece of all this, everything that has happened, all that we felt between us, that will always be there. But more than that—there's something settled there now. Something settled and good. I couldn't call it happiness. Maybe he just seems content. Yeah, that's it. Content.

He'd better be.

Like that, it's over.

We're moving away again. Mr. Mann is joining a swirl of shoppers lining up for teriyaki.

Will he look back?

I have to think about each step that carries me away from him. Don't look. I won't let myself look. I feel him pulling at my back. But it's not so bad. Less of the fever, more of the dream.

He's gone.

A woman in front of Sears is waving a pen, trying to get my attention. She wants to sign me up for a credit card.

"What? Oh. No, thank you. No."

Why didn't she approach Mom? How old do I look, anyhow? We walk past a rack of purple shoes.

"Isn't this fun, darling?" Mom says.

I smile. "I'd rather be bitten by rat fleas infected with bubonic plague," I whisper to Schuyler.

"*Xenopsylla cheopis* and *Yersinia pestis*," he says.

"Smart-ass." I put my hand on his shoulder. It doesn't feel quite so bony anymore. "One of these days you're going to figure out it's okay not to know something. It can even be a good thing."

Schuyler frowns. "That's a quarter."

Today, for the first time ever, I put one in his hand.